TRUTH OR DARE

Visit us at www.boldstrokesbooks.com

TRUTH OR DARE

Amanda
Happy Pride!.
C. Spencer

by

C. Spencer

2018

ISBN 13: 978-1-63555-148-8

This Trade Paperback Original Is Published By
Bold Strokes Books, Inc.
P.O. Box 249
Valley Falls, NY 12185

First Edition: March 2018

CREDITS
Editor: Ruth Sternglantz
Production Design: Stacia Seaman
Cover Design by Tammy Seidick

Acknowledgments

I began writing fiction assuming not a soul would read it. In fact, I'm not sure if I wanted anyone to. I just hoped to tell a story about a bunch of friends I wished I had topped with romance and regrets and that good kind of angst that comes along for the ride. And that story somehow made it to you. The fact that you chose to pick up this book means more than you'll ever know.

The truth is, though, this book represents the culmination of talent, hard work, and advice offered by so many amazing people. First, I am exceedingly grateful for Ruth Sternglantz, an editor extraordinaire, for all of the time, brilliance, and creativity she put into this. Her ideas were essential to making *Truth or Dare* extra better in every single way. I'm also grateful for established authors for welcoming me, along with Bold Strokes Books and the entire team for saying *yes* and offering this amazing venue specifically for LGBT publication. And I owe a huge debt of gratitude to my daughter, who cannot read this but offered so much encouragement—not to mention tips on how to use a mobile phone since I don't own one.

A special debt of gratitude goes to my wife for reading and suggesting and (even) disagreeing—and always saying *yes, you can* if I dare say *I can't*. I love you.

To all of life's perfectly imperfect mishaps.

THURSDAY

CHAPTER ONE: JESSIE

Catholic girls are easy to pin. They're either buttoned to the chin (translation: don't bother) or they have a regular booty call programmed into their phones and visit confessional to repent every Sunday, religiously. I prefer the latter.

That's what brought me to this campus. Her building's just ahead past another group of stressed-out undergraduates lugging North Face backpacks and travel mugs. The snow has just started to come down, and it's crunching with each step I take. It's a decent beat given I'm still humming that tune I heard two days ago and wishing I could replace it with something better.

The main doors ask for a badge after hours, but they're unlocked now. I pass the elevator and take the wide stairs, which impress me with their marble, exiting into a hall that echoes. Door after door touts a new name, each engraved in brown plastic and ending in PhD. I'm surprised I fit in. I expected this place to be all corduroy; it's not.

I hear her in someone's office and they're talking about a mass spectrometer. I go unnoticed and wait outside, wandering. Across the hall is a lecture, and it's brash like a loudspeaker.

The airs of academia: that idealism and disappointment.

As soon as her conversation enters the doorway and hallway, I get that lingering look. It means *I'm glad to see you.* It means *I'll be right with you.* She looks amazing. Her hair's inelegant at the collarbone, and freckles flush that nude complexion left over from her stay in Barcelona. I'm picturing her in a bikini under a beach umbrella, feet tucked in heated sand. It's a nice fantasy right now in twenty-eight degree weather.

As I admire her small build, we share too many distracted glances. Finally I catch their good-byes and I can't help but notice how soft her tone is when she greets me. "Jessie Miles." It's not the same as the voice I heard a minute ago. "Your hair."

"I know. It's a mess," I tell her. "It's really starting to come down out there."

She takes me down a hall with walls covered in posters and ads for graduate programs. She's walking like we don't know each other. Eventually we reach her name plaque. She keys the door, and I follow her in. She shuts it.

Inside shades are wide open letting overcast shine its way through. Snow tries to cloak her mountain view.

"Early day?" I want to know. With every other school in town canceled, I'm surprised higher education isn't as well.

She tugs the cord on a green lamp. That unusable desk squeezes into a corner.

"Class is canceled tomorrow. It screws up my entire lab schedule." It's more than uptight—she's bordering on irate. "I'll get my things."

The office has no floor space. It's clean but paper littered with books and binders towering above us. I'm thinking it beats her bedroom with that crucifix staring down over the door frame.

She does this thing where she stands on tiptoe to reach for something. I'm watching the muscles in her calves flex. It's up there with that librarian…When was that? She's kind of a contradiction like that, which is what I get into. I push into her, and she sinks down into my arms. Determination's written all over her face.

"Why do you do this to me?" I ask. She's just giving me this look of indifference. But this kiss is shameless, which is why I'm beginning to imagine that taste between her legs. I'd rather be there. That's where my hand goes.

"You're hot, you know that?"

And this look is why she's naturally mistaken for pious, haughty. It doesn't matter to me. In fact, I'm pretty sure it's why I'm drawn to her. Besides, her touch is quite the opposite. It's more timid, sensual. I don't have to understand her, do I?

She's exhaling thick and heavy between my lips as we make our way to that door and I back her up against it. I slide my hand up her blouse.

"I'll get fired," I hear.

"The perks of tenure," I mumble. I love when she feigns virtue. She seems torn or trapped but more overindulgent than anything else. She tends to do everything in excess. Drinking. Learning. This. That's how she's always been with me.

When I hike her skirt, she's not resisting anymore.

"I don't quite have tenure yet," she tries to say.

The hem of this blouse untucks too easily and the arch of her back makes everything that much more accessible. I'm pinching around her back and thinking, Who wears this to work? It's sheer, this mesh, and I let it fall aside and off her shoulder.

And I'm tracing tan lines.

The next time I kiss her, it's weaker but feverish. I move past the hem of her skirt and glide a palm under and behind elastic. She's too driven without me, too pent up, and I'm thinking it's been far too long (at least that's how she feels) when I slip two fingers inside her. She's slick.

It's always that first moan, isn't it, when she gets what she wants. It's merciless. It's the loudest one. Someone's going to hear in the hallway, but she's forgotten already.

Instead she glides against my fingers—rigid, unyielding, oblivious. I like when she gets like this, warm and throbbing, legs parted, swelling and tightening around my knuckles. I'm using hips to push my fingers deeper. When I look over again, her cheeks are flushed, and I watch as she fades into soft, to serene, and then to absolutely uninhibited. Her breath like steam on my cheek and I need more and so does she. I want trembling. Shuddering. Disheveled. I want painfully spent and hunched over. Clinging to me. I want to bolster her up so she doesn't fall down. And I'm thinking about that small desk over there, but the wall's fine once I can get this off her.

By the time I head out, before I even hit the lot, I get a text. Make that two. I file both under *maybe next month if I'm lucky.* Because it's five at night and I need a bite before heading home. My cooking skills are, to put it mildly, sub-amateur. That's not to say I'm amateur everywhere. Trust me on that. It's just that food prep was never a zone I could master. I do appreciate good food, though. Home cooked, take-out, gourmet, grill. I'm not all that discriminating. As long as it's a meal that someone else has prepared.

In fact, I have this nostalgic peculiarity about me. I recall people by the way they cook, what they cook, why they cook, how they cook. Sometimes I remember the food and not her name.

Take Elaine for instance. We lasted a pretty long time—four weeks. Elaine was a bona fide vegetarian, which conjures images of tofu to some. But she never used tofu. Ever. Despised people who automatically assumed she ate tofu just because she was vegetarian, so she stopped talking about it altogether. If you ask me, she was a culinary artist, her spices and sauces. She made a mad black-bean burger with sweet potato fries and, once in a while, I'm tempted to ring her up just for one of those meals. At least my stomach is. Her current girlfriend might not appreciate that. For anyone to convert a meat lover like myself into a proud bean-burger eater is extraordinary. She did that.

That breakup was tough. I mean, it was cruel enough losing the conversations, the Friday nights, and the sex. But I also lost her cuisine, and no two women cook quite alike.

And who doesn't like watching a woman cook? The flex of her forearm as that blade comes down. When the back of her wrist brushes her forehead because every fingertip is covered and untouchable. How feminine her fingers look when they pinch.

I met Sophia before I broke up with Elaine. Full disclosure, they did overlap a few days. But my short-lived romance with Sophia was bound to end if only for the fact that I could not eat the sheer quantity of food she served. Her enchiladas, though, with hot Spanish rice and her red sauce. Mercy. I don't know if anyone, even Sophia, could've maintained that body eating like that for the long term.

Lynn didn't cook. Not at all. Since I didn't cook either, we survived for two full weeks on deli sandwiches with a wide assortment of cheeses and crackers, fruits and berries, nuts and breads. I'm keen on those fresh bakery rolls and baguettes. Ciabatta. Cheese breads. With Lynn, I learned to appreciate the nutritional benefits of the almond and the vast diversity of apples—from Gala to Empire. I heard she married a chef. Hats off to her.

I met Ella shortly after that split. She runs the bakery downtown, with partial credit to yours truly, and she's in happily married bliss. Even with too many years' distance, I'm still not ready to resurface her. After Ella, I didn't get too serious with anyone—not that I was alone, mind you.

Then came Alicia, my last girlfriend. She made me lose interest in nourishment altogether, of the food variety at least. Take the time she greeted me in nothing more than her twenty-four-year-old splendor topped with a strappy tank top and loose-fitting boxer shorts embellished in teeny tiny red hearts. She fed me Swiss chocolate that evening, served the sweetest red wine, and the rest of that night could have gone down in history.

And that it did. I called it quits two weeks ago. I'm not sure if that's registered with her yet, given her text bombs today, but it will.

Tonight, without a personal chef, I'm fending for myself. And I've decided to grab a quick bite out before the worst of this snowstorm hits and I'm holed up in my tiny studio, all by my lonesome. I know, woe is me.

To this end, I spot the perfect parking spot right up front at Hops Brewery and walk in, helmet in hand. I sit at one of those two-seater wooden tables. It's packed wall-to-wall with regulars as well as plenty of unfamiliars.

This place is low lit and appealing, brightened by mini lamps and a few open laptops. The kind of lighting you pray for at two a.m. after a few pints too many. Bookshelves are filled with creased paperbacks that attract the geeked-up literary crowd from nearby colleges. A sunken section in the rear seats the see-and-be-seens in firm leather chairs where they sip cappuccino or tea or one of Hops' infamous custom ales.

The wall beside my table is a floor-to-ceiling chalkboard with a menu written out by hand. All of that dusty script spans the entire length of the room, from the front windows to the bar in the far rear. A bar that's always crammed, even on a slow night like this.

I rest my boots on the opposite chair. And I already know what I want.

After a glance at a new text that rattles my phone, I slip it back on the table without a response. It's just Alicia. Again.

Hadley creaks the floor as she ambles over, Chapstick lipped, recently cropped Bobby Brady hair, black-rimmed glasses, cute plaid skirt, and a powder blue oxford shirt buttoned conservatively.

"Back again?"

"I know. This is getting to be a bad habit. You look pretty thin staffed tonight. Why are you out here?"

This is the only friendship I haven't ruined by taking things too far.

"I'm down three servers. Of course it was three of my best. They couldn't make it, so here I am. On the floor."

And that prudence has earned me the ultimate best friend. I'm talking decades long. She and I go way back. We're like glue.

"Could be worse. Job security."

"I know. I'm off in a few hours," she tells me. "The usual?"

"Yeah."

"Stay for dessert. Look at you. You're too skinny."

"Hey, hey—I'm working out."

"Yeah, yeah—you're working out."

"It's stress."

"Can you give me some?"

"Some what," I ask, admittedly flirtatiously.

"Some of your appetite-sucking stress."

"You don't need it."

She rolls her eyes, changing the subject. "Looks awful out there."

She's chewing cinnamon gum. I can actually smell it over the aroma of grilled burgers.

"That would be why I'm in here."

And she's not-so-subtly eyeing my dripping boots and the sopped jeans I've propped on a chair. I take the hint, settling my feet on the floor.

Then she asks, "Think I'll get home?"

"So far, so good. I made it. On my bike at that."

"Why on earth are you still riding that thing?"

"My truck's on its last leg. Not much good that'll do me."

"Take it in."

"Dude," I say. "We don't all make what you make." Over my water glass, my gaze trails a twosome.

"How's Alicia?"

"Fine."

"She stopped by the other night. I guess you had a late shift or something?"

"I did."

"Is that who's texting you?"

"Possibly."

Hadley flattens a palm softly on the table and whispers, "You know? You're way too good for her." Her voice is high, unassuming. I lift my shoulders.

"I swear I just don't trust her."

If you only knew the half of it, I think.

The lady at the next table raises a finger, catching Hadley's eye. "Shouldn't be long," she tells me. It's not until she darts away that I realize I was distracting her from a busy shift, which is a tad embarrassing. After her quiet exchange a seat over, I watch those hips curve around the bar to enter my order.

Let me pause right here to say that the bar is wicked. Like the kind you'd find at some gilded hotel or something—carved wood and glass shelving. I'd probably eat here just for the atmosphere.

There's a takeout counter near the bar where a fidgety girl waits to pay and pick up, dark somber hair covering her eyes. She's hard to miss, like some eighties British transplant. A little Echo & The Bunnymen. A little Dr. Martens. She sports nothing now, though she can't be older than twenty.

I drop my head to thumb through messages, not because I want to but because I have to. Her last one reads, *Miss you.* That just angers me. Until I catch one from my professor earlier today.

A happy couple pushes in making a loud ruckus. They bring another gush of cold air in along with them, both hunched in laughter and slightly out of breath. I watch as one takes the other's coat and hangs it. Then she pulls her own down over her wrist. They share a kiss. How cute is that?

It's not. So I go back to my phone, which I've hidden under the table rim, shifting to an incoming text. *I need 2 C U.* Guess who?

"Veggie burger and sweet potato fries with a side of mayo," Hadley announces, startling me for a second. I set my phone down, covering the screen. Okay, that looks suspicious but it's not meant to be. She'll just lecture me. She sets a tall glass of water in front of me and picks up the empty one. The water-stained coaster makes me smile. Keep Calm and Move On. How utterly appropriate.

Then Hadley puts a hand on mine for what seems an eternity. She's worried about me, I can tell. It's a pleasant thought, I confess, but I'll be damned if I look up. I feel more than a little wobbly after this fallout, and my heart thumps. I pretend not to notice, like it's nothing.

I use the other hand to grab my napkin, glancing over at her gold ring. And I'm torn. Just when I'm ready to look up, she makes the decision for me, slipping her hand away.

"Just give me a shout if you need anything else."

I grab a fry, eating quickly. I've got to get home before the roads get too slick. I overhear my pal striking up a conversation at another table beside mine. I listen for a while, then I block it out.

It's dark out, but the mere speed of headlights on the other side of that window tells me traffic has already slowed to a snail's pace. You know, blizzards are about the only time people drive reasonably well. For that reason, I wish storms like this would travel through these parts more often.

I scroll social media as I eat. #Snowmageddon. The general consensus: Bring it. That said, the governor has declared a state of emergency and a driving ban after midnight.

When I finish, I leave cash on the table to cover my bill plus some, make my way through a party of four, and use my body weight to shove open the heavy door. The wind cuts. It's dropped at least ten degrees.

I use my glove to brush powder off my seat, swing a leg over, strap my helmet on. Then I weave my way into northbound traffic.

Handling a bike in the snow and slush is a feat. I focus on balance and swerve around patches left by tires and plows, taking it easy on the blacktop and keeping to the main drag where cars have already trod a pretty smooth path. My apartment's right downtown, but five minutes from here in good weather.

I creep past the few remaining parked cars along the curb. Shopkeepers are flipping door signs from *Open* to *Closed*. Pedestrians are using mittens and hats to block wind. Two dash to their car, one in a long black coat, another wrapped to the nose in a rust-colored scarf. Holiday lights blink from trees, flashing across patches of salt-thawed pavement.

I make a spontaneous loop on a road that slants down past Ella's bakery. You know, just to check up on it. It's off the main drag but still humming with pedestrians. This town's relatively safe, and you can walk pretty much anywhere even at night and not be afraid in the least. I pull a stop. It looks like she closed early, which is expected. I hope she made it home okay, at least before it got too bad out here.

The town's installed a system of small blue lights that flash when there's a parking ban. One casts a reflection on the front window signaling the impending storm, and snow continues to spit in my face. I'm not sure why I drive past here anymore. I guess it's just an old habit I really need to break.

Home is just around the bend. When I pull in, I take my usual spot in the lot right next to my door. Beside me is a half-full bike rack and a handicapped parking sign. As I cut the engine, my phone rattles in my coat pocket. Again. I roll my eyes and tap the screen mechanically, not really wanting to answer.

But it's not what I expect. It's a text from Hadley, which hits my pulse first—then my brain.

car wont start want company?

❖

I'm sunk in my chair watching television when I hear the feeblest knock on my door, happy that all of my appendages are thawed after kicking it weekend-style for two straight hours.

I almost hate to admit it but I'm psyched to see Hadley again. I mean, who wants to be company-less during a snowstorm? Not I. I just hope that hike wasn't too painful. In any case, I do have extra blankets—and the heat's cranked up to seventy-four.

Half self-conscious, half fidgety, I check my hair in the mirror. Then I get the door. The girl's red faced and drenched. Frost coats her specs to the point of opacity. Ice is caked on her hat and it's thick on her scarf. And that's when guilt hits me. I should've insisted, demanded she accept a ride. What does this girl have against my bike?

The least I can offer is an arm around those shoulders, which she gets. I shut the door.

"You poor thing!" I snicker, hiding behind my hand. "You should've let me pick you up."

"I'm not riding on that thing," begins her monologue. "I'm so afraid they're going to tow my car." She sinks in that chair, unlacing her boots, her thoughts. I stay where I am, just listening. "It's totally insane, I mean, I can't believe it didn't start. I just thought, why me, why now? Nobody made it in. And all night, why is everyone so angry all the time? I did my best and got atrocious tips. I'm just glad I don't do this thing full-time—you know what I mean, serving."

She slides one boot off. Her specs frost up again. She pinches the joints, lowering the frame to her skirt and clearing the glass before moving to the next heel.

"I tip well."

With a shrug, I make my way to the kitchen.

"You do, Jess." She's behind me, following.

"Let's see what I've got that'll warm you up. Cocoa, coffee"—I shove things around for a better view—"and chai. What do you say?"

"Aren't you the hostess?" She grins all smart-ass like, now close enough that I can take in her faded perfume. "Tea's delicious. Thank you for this."

I center that teakettle on a burner. She makes her way to the window. Though I wouldn't call it a view per se, it is pretty as a postcard right about now, icicles yanking at gutters. Trees weeping, limbs drowning—even the stern and stubborn of them. She unwraps and unwinds and continues to liquefy.

"I'm getting your floor all wet. Towels still over here?"

"Hall closet," I say.

And the kettle's already shrieking at me. I drizzle it (steaming) into two huge mugs over bobbing bags. I've tied the strings around their handles. Then a spiral of spice: cinnamon, fennel, nutmeg, clove. I set them on the kitchen table and pull up a chair, hers first. I motion with the milk.

"I'm okay, I mean, just this way is fine." She holds the mug with two hands, partially hidden behind it. I settle in my seat, and our eyes lock for a passing moment.

"Is it all right," I ask.

"What, the tea? I mean, sure. Why do you ask?"

"No reason."

She sounds drowsy.

"So maybe we can pick up where we left off? You know, I mean, what gives?"

I knew she wouldn't let me off easy, but still. Why does she have to harp until she gets every last detail? I slouch. "Things just suck."

"Care to elaborate?"

"Not really." I wink.

"I don't mean to pry, but...you two split up, didn't you?"

"It's complicated." I try to brush off the questions with a hasty blow on my mug.

"Isn't it always. But I'm usually the first to hear when things go south. It bugs me when you wall up like this."

None of my friends like Alicia. That should've tipped me off. "I don't want to talk about it."

She peers over her mug as if to ask, *What for?*

I trace the seams between boards on the table. "She stepped out on me."

"You *are* joking."

"She stepped out on me," I repeat, frustrated. "A week ago. But, get this, that's not even the best part."

She sits closed off yet open at the same time.

"She slept with a guy." I chuckle.

Then I get those eyes. That inquisitive stare. Deep. Sensitive. This girl could get secrets out of a CIA agent. She can get anything out of me.

"Dude, you told me so—go ahead and say it. The girl's straight and I'm her big experiment."

Aside from a hum of acknowledgment, she's hush.

My knuckles crush my mouth. I glance outside. "She doesn't even know what she wants—and the lies. Christ, the lies. This, though…" I start to recall a conversation I actually had with Alicia. "Fuck—it's nauseating."

"She's foolish."

"Whatever, it's for the best. That's behind me."

"So," she starts in. "You back to playing the field?"

"I'm back to playing nothing."

Now I'll get the lecture ending with, *Oh come now.*

"I'm done."

"You'll have three girls lined up before next weekend. You always do. I'm sure they're texting you already. Word gets out, you know. You're a catch, Jessie Miles."

My eyebrows jump. She's hit last name status. "We all have our sins. But, no." Because I'm not even going to mention my professor earlier. She'd flip her shit.

Then she continues, "Exactly why I'm glad we never went there.

I don't like Alicia or what she did, but I tip my hat to the girls in your rearview mirror."

"Why?"

"Because I want to be here. Not back with them in your history book."

"You sound like you're trying to convince yourself." I mess her hair. "You look kind of..." I grunt. "Out-of-the-shower hot like that, but here, I'll get you a blanket. At this rate, you'll never dry."

In the closet, a few blankets tumble down on me. When I get back, she's at the window again admiring the snowscape. Her mug's still frosting her specs. I flip the kitchen light off to watch as the storm takes over. Then I wrap a tartan blanket across her shoulders, leaning against the window myself until I zone out.

I feel eyes on me when she says, "It's pretty awesome, wouldn't you say?"

"That it is."

"Have I ever told you my blizzard story?"

She's the best person to be around when I need to get out of my head. She talks and talks about anything and everything.

"No, spill."

"Well, you were all into...Who? I can't keep track. I was with April, so this was before the ceremony and we wanted to do something different for the New Year. Just the two of us. No ball drop, no Lang Syne. I booked a couple nights at this really, really sweet bed-and-breakfast." And then she turns. "Is it okay to talk about her, you know, like this?"

"Of course. Why not?"

"I don't miss her or anything. Just for the record. I want to remember the positive, don't you think?"

I nod.

"So we had three nights on the slopes. Night boarding under the stars. It's incredible. You've never really lived until you've night boarded in Stowe."

I'm thinking I have to do this one day.

Then she says, "Maybe you and I could do that. You know, one day."

We've got a lengthy bucket list by now, and it keeps getting longer.

The French Riviera and Notre Dame and Versailles, that's hers. Vatican City, that's hers as well. I only seem to remember hers.

"Not there, though. Somewhere better," she says. "I'll take you somewhere way nicer."

"I'll hold you to that."

That's a pretty nice smile I get.

"So, you know me, I made reservations months and months ahead of time. Still, you never really know. Sometimes we don't get a flake by then." She takes a drink, speaking as she swallows. "Next thing you know, this fantastic storm rolls in. You must remember. You got it down here. So like this."

"Yeah, yeah, I was house-sitting for you, right? That morning, damn, I wasn't feeling too hot."

Her expression is more than mildly critical.

"Somebody made martinis, strong ones. I can't remember who."

"I bet."

"Dude, it was New Year's. Sorry, go ahead."

"Okay so we couldn't leave. Nobody could. The innkeepers just let us all stay two more nights. That probably happens a lot up there, right? But, anyway, we had nothing to do. So we all hung out in this common room—me and April with four other couples. Playing board games. Charades."

"You rock at charades."

"I kind of do. So there we were, a room full of strangers stuck at this inn. And you'd think we'd all go mad. But we didn't. It was really cool. We just talked and listened and talked. And some of the stuff that came out...You look at folks every day and you never really know what they've gone through or what they're thinking. Who they are. You're too busy living. Why does it take some sort of disaster to slow us down like that—to look at each other?" She won't turn away. She wants an answer. "I mean really look at each other."

I think about that for a millisecond, grateful she's here for me tonight. She eventually turns back to the window. "I hear you," I say. Her cup's empty. I'm about to take it and mine back to the kitchen when I hear a knock. She looks to me like I should know who this is.

"Maybe a neighbor needs help," I say. "I don't know." We don't get it right away, like maybe it was the wind or something.

Then comes another but, this time, a heck of a lot brasher. I sense her next to me as I make my way to the door.

"Who is it?" I want to know.

"It's me." The voice is muffled, but I recognize it along with Alicia's distorted features peering through the peephole. Shit.

I unlatch the bolt, and Hadley ducks to the dining room. I hang my head out the narrow opening. "What are you doing here?"

"I was worried. I kept texting. Did you get them?"

"A few."

"Why didn't you respond?"

I think that answer is obvious. Still, I'm struck because, mercy, why does she have to have the most erotic voice ever, and I'm hearing it again, which is so different than a cold text on a screen. It drives me sort of…I don't know, and she knows that. Smooth. Southern. As if she just lit her cigarette afterward.

"I've been busy," I lie.

"With what?"

"With work."

"I haven't seen you."

"I'm on mornings."

"I didn't wake you, did I?"

Snow blows in through the door. She's shivering.

"What's with the questions?" Post-breakup conversations are so much easier by text.

"It's just that—it was dark. Your lights are out. Can I come in?" She's reaching for my fingers, which are curled around the door. But her face hardens when dishes drop in the sink.

"I kind of, well…" Before I can think, my coat's on and I'm heading out in unlaced boots.

"That was quick."

"What are you talking about?" I figure whispering will shroud this drama from the neighbors. "Can you please keep it down?"

"Who is she?"

"You stepped out on me. Not vice versa. You're not in a good position to be asking these questions."

"You don't even understand." Why is she touching my cheek? Maybe I'm just reading into this. "Jess…I miss this." I'm listening until it dawns on me that her words are slick as can be. "How do I say I'm sorry? I know I've said this ad nauseam. I wish you could physically feel this remorse." She wets her lips, guiding my bare hand behind her coat. "I can't breathe without you." Nor can I, but I'm not about to bend.

"Why are you doing this?" I ask.

"Why are you? Why can't you believe me? That wasn't me—it wasn't."

I hurt. And I'm starting to buckle, which is why I'm getting pissed. "Here you go. You fuck someone and regret it. There's your closure." I'm about ready to lose it. "Head home. Get somewhere safe."

Still her eyes won't let go and they're welling up. "I didn't mean it."

"I know. What's done is done." I'm relieved to sound semiconvincing, yet admittedly, I'm losing courage. "That sort of thing, it can't be undone. You do know that, right?"

And while we stop speaking in words, we're still having a conversation. She's saying, *Remember?* I button her coat, and I am remembering. I purse my lips, searching for that anger. She's saying, *Let me in.* And I want her just the same. Her hair glides between my knuckles. I'm saying, *No, I can't.* Her chin falls. We find our voices again.

"Why'd you go home with him?" And there's that sting in my eye. "You didn't think that would hurt me?"

"I can't say what I was thinking. I was—"

"No, wait, I don't want to know."

"But—"

"I really, really don't want to know." Her cheeks look raw. Her eyes glisten. I wipe her tears off with one singular index finger. And I enjoy it. I like seeing her this way. I want to hurt her more. I want to dig into my arsenal of *don't go there*s. But I'm frightened by that side of me—the side that wants to break her down to the ground until she grovels.

So I just say, "It's freezing," and find that my tone is alas indifferent. "You'd better get off the streets before you can't. Isn't this your shift? What time is it?"

She says nothing. I walk her toward the parking lot. We pause. She kisses my cheek. It's a good-bye; it feels it. Then she turns, walking into the storm. And she gets smaller and more hidden in the darkness. It feels colder. My rage whips away in a gush. I feel deserted.

I don't go in right off. Instead, I watch as she makes that curve and vanishes, hair tangled in a twirl of flakes.

When I do make my way back, I'm greeted at the door. It's a long, needy hug.

"Are you okay?"

"I'm fine," I lie as I step out of my boots.

"I made you another cup of tea, chamomile. Here, have my blanket." And she drapes it over my shoulder the way I did for her before. Her eyes are prying again. They're asking questions, but they don't push. We settle into the couch, and I scoot down to rest my head on her shoulder. She knows what just happened, and she'll be the first to hear when I need to talk. But that won't be tonight. Right now, we can just enjoy this silent cup of tea together.

I can't place this. "Jessie. Jessie."

Huh?

"Jessie, the power's out. The whole place is pitch."

I bolt up, still in bed and still in a fog. "Huh? Are you serious?"

"Not really. I needed an excuse to slide into bed with you," Hadley says. "Of course I'm serious." But there's a lag between her words hitting my ear and the time it takes to actually register with my brain.

I get out of bed—a warm bed, a comfortable bed—and I dog-ear the flannel behind me. A rush of cold jets up my pants and straight down my neck. Damn, I think. I was actually having a pretty good dream there. Can't I just go back into that?

But I'm wide awake the second I flip a switch up, as in *on*, and nothing happens. I've lived here for eight years, and I've never, ever lost power. I'm not even the least bit prepared for this.

I stretch my hands out sightless, finding that familiar door frame and then the front room. It never dawned on me how much light shines in from outside—until it's gone. I see Hadley's silhouette against the window burritoed in a thick blanket she pulled from her makeshift bed on the couch, which is unmade. I make my way over.

"The refrigerator stopped humming," she says, brushing the hair off her forehead. "That's what woke me. It doesn't look like anyone else is up."

"What should we do?" I ask dumbfounded.

"Don't look at me."

Then a memory hits, one of those déjà vu things. "Remember way back when—"

"When you tripped the power off and freaked out because you thought you broke the house?"

"Yeah!" I chuckle. "You were over at my parents' house—just like this—"

"We had the whole humungous house to ourselves. They went away, right?"

"That was awesome," I say with a nudge.

"No kidding."

This was the era of slick new technology called CDs that played Dave Matthews and Nirvana. It's when plastic handle bags at the grocery store were new and novel and not yet the environmental disaster they are today. Movies were just beginning to be affordable for purchase on VHS, so everyone wanted a home movie library, including me. And computers were at someone else's house. Not your own. And we all wore bobs.

"You built a bonfire," she says with a far-off look.

"I did." I'm a lumberjack, what can I say? Just hand me an ax and call me Paul Bunyan. I did wear flannel, and I do remember feeling rather rugged and scout-like when that flame sparked, even though that bonfire was a hibachi with grates removed. Hardly rugged. She didn't have to know that I had absolutely no confidence in myself up until the moment that orange flame lit. In reality, I went through two packs of matches as she wandered the yard gathering bits of sticks that had fallen from trees.

I wink at her rather smugly. "You were impressed." Her cheeks flush. I love toying with her.

"What, with your culinary finesse? We ate s'mores for dinner."

"We did. And you loved them, don't lie. All chocolaty and marshmallow gooey."

"I was sixteen."

"Was it really that long ago?"

"We were really young."

"I was still a virgin."

She laughs through her nose. "That can't be right. I didn't even know you when you were five."

"Shut. Up."

"That was the best night, ever," she says with a shoulder bump.

"What, losing power...breaking the house?"

"No, we sat up in front of that bonfire and played truth or dare."

I chuckle. "Yeah, the dangers of truth or dare."

"Come on. I told you too much that night. And that rainbow sunset. Remember?" I do remember that sunset. Fiery red melting orange, dissolving teal, smudging indigo. The air was wet, the kind that curls your hair. "All those fireflies. You got that humungous bedspread out and we found the Big Dipper, the Little Dipper." A smile curls up her cheeks as I duck under our blanket. "You know," she says, "if I could point to one moment when our friendship began, it was that night."

"You could say that." I'm not sure what came into me that night. As I recall, I think I tried to make a move on her. You know how it is when you're a teenager. Parents being gone is the best thing ever. Add an illicit sleepover with a hot girl and you're golden. And truth or dare got a lot out of her. One, that she liked girls, and two, she was sort of into me. *Sort of*, she told me with air quotes.

"And even when crazy bad shit happens in our lives, we still pull each other through. To this day. That's kind of cool."

I can see my pajama top peeking out from under the blanket along with a wee bit of cleavage. Hadley's blessed in that department. I am not. Her wet clothes are hanging in my shower, and I'm pretty sure they'll stay damp without that heat going. Whatever. She'll look way sexy in my clothes tomorrow. With her bedhead right now, she kind of looks like we just did the deed. I raise my eyebrows at the thought.

"What?"

"Nothing," I lie. "Listen, we can't just sit in the dark. It'll get colder. I can actually see my breath. We need to call someone. See what's up."

She shuffles to find her phone.

That's when I catch a flashlight moving around from room to room in the apartment across the way. Then one flashlight splits into two. And those beams bobble their way window to window. It's pretty hilarious.

The snow's still intense. There were benches, but now those are buried, and taking a wild guess, I'd say we have about two feet.

"What's this, you rearranged?" Hadley asks, breaking me out of my drowsy voyeurism. "Where's the phone book?" When I turn, she's carrying her phone like our own flashlight.

"In the kitchen drawer." I hobble toward it. Under a box of envelopes, some click pens, a random loose cap, my wallet, and car keys, I find that thick bound yellow book. Do people use these, still? I use Google. I drop it on the counter with a thump and start flipping thin sheets of newsprint. Meanwhile she's sparking her lighter inside a few pillar candles and carries one over to help me read, careful not to drain her phone battery.

"Don't tip it. The wax'll spill."

She leans in and I'm reminded again of how busty this girl is, pressed against my arm. For a second, I forget it's Hadley and get a little worked up.

"*Rhe...Ts...W*. Here's *W*, and here's the number." She recites the digits, sliding a perfectly manicured nail down this shadowed page to bolded letters. I listen as her phone beeps with every number. A ring. "Outage," she says, rolling her eyes. "Report an outage."

I get a fake smile before she presses that tiny receiver against my ear.

"Why me?" I protest.

"It's your apartment."

I have no time to think before hearing the dreaded recording.

She's still pressed against me, and it takes more than a little effort just to focus on what the heck I'm supposed to do. I click through a string of options, choosing two then four then finally reporting the outage.

When I end the call, Hadley's stare is more than a little nervous. "This night can't get any weirder. First my car. Then your ex. Now this."

"Alicia showing up. Yeah." I laugh. "I'm glad you were here."

"Why?"

"Why? Isn't that obvious?"

She shakes her head.

"For starters, you're an excuse to come back in." I tip my eyebrow. "Plus you're my rock. You know that."

"Aw, Jess. Look at you. You're getting all sappy on me."

"Sap I'm not. I just…I appreciate you, that's all. You know."

We share a long comfortable pause, frozen with the same corny grins. Then she lets her head tip back as if unsure of her next move, which is when it dawns on me that it's kind of hot, her head tilted back like that. So when she's not looking, I find my eyes dawdling down to her shirt again and I linger a little too long. That's when I sort of forget where I am and zone out.

When I look back up, she's looking right at me. Which is why I dart my eyes away so quickly, but not before a dash of apprehension settles in the pit of my stomach.

It's too dark, I tell myself. She didn't see.

"On the topic of Alicia, can I just say I don't care who did what to whom. Do what's right for you. But…" She pauses.

I motion her to continue.

"Well, do you realize that something sabotages every relationship you ever have, and it always happens when you give a shit about them? The only exception being Ella."

If words could physically pierce my heart, the last one did. Don't even go there.

"And now with Alicia. Something's seriously messed up with that. I love you. But."

"So this is my fault?"

"I feel bad for her."

"Why would you say that?"

"She wants you back."

"She can't have me back."

Her eyes roll.

"Why would you want me with her?"

"I'm not saying you should go back to her," she tells me.

"Then what are you saying?"

"I'm just wondering."

"What?"

"I don't know. Like, if you're afraid of commitment or something."

"No," I answer. She gives me her don't-mess-with-me face. "No, I'm not afraid of commitment."

"And—"

"And what?"

"If you're over Ella."

"Whoa, where'd that come from?"

"I don't know. Are you?"

"Of course I am."

"Sometimes I wonder."

Why is she so angry all of a sudden? I'm not quite following. This is a topic we don't speak of. What could've come of Ella and me had I not—okay, had I not been such a commitment-phobe. Full disclosure, maybe I used to be. Maybe I fucked up there. Maybe if I hadn't, this might be our anniversary.

Do I care that she's celebrating her anniversary this weekend? No. Ella's an old habit. We've changed. That simply will never be again, even if we both wanted it. Which we don't.

I walk over to my couch and her bed of blankets topped with two pillows. I'm not going to spend the evening fighting with my best friend. That's for sure. Besides we're stuck together all night, like it or not. So we might as well get along.

I sit smack dab in the middle of her makeshift bed, kick my heels up (stocking-footed), and pat the couch beside me. "C'mon," I say, gesturing her over. "Let's make up."

She makes her way to my couch. "I guess the only way we're going to stay warm is bundling up," she says as if surrendering. Then she binds herself using two hands to secure the top of that blanket. When she does, I think back at being caught peering down her shirt and have to wonder if she's doing this deliberately to block my inappropriate view. Once she sits next to me, I prop my arm around her and yank her stubborn self to my chest. And here come those nerves again.

"Gimme some of that, stingy," I tell her with a tug. She breaks out of burrito mode and offers me a wee corner, which I graciously accept. She's never been the generous type, so I take what I can get. When I do, she reclines against me. I inhale and it's my shampoo. In the silence, a muffled whop of snow hits the ground.

I sit in this, the here and now, the faraway look in her eyes, the sleepy sultriness of her voice. But with some angst. With her body pressed against mine, I try to recall a time in my life when I've ever felt this much love unconditionally toward another human being, and I can't.

I hear her swallow. The building settles, and more snow crashes to the ground. Soon the moment passes and my drowsiness takes over. My body begins to collapse.

"Look. We can't sleep here," I say. "We can share my bed. But don't get any ideas."

"Keep flattering yourself." Her hand rests on my knee.

At the count of three, we rise in unison, huddled and waddling clumsily to the bed giggling as if we were still sixteen.

I'm feeling more than a little something here. I don't think she actually thinks of me that way—at least not since that fated bonfire a good twenty years ago.

In bed, I'm tempted to reach over to her side and see where my hand might land. On a hip? Down the slope of her waist? Damn, I want to touch her skin, her lips, those curves that fill out my pajama top better than I ever could. If I did, though, then what?

"Are you awake?" That voice of hers jars me, and I drown in shame as if she heard my thoughts.

"Yeah. I can't sleep. It's too quiet." A sleepy stillness envelopes us.

"Me either." It's an unnatural silence. "I was just thinking. And… well. I wanted to say thank you."

"Thank you? For what?" I ask.

"For always being here for me, like even now when my car breaks down. I don't know what I'd do without you. Thanks for letting me crash here."

I roll over, but her back's to me. Then I put my hand on her shoulder. In my world, she's here for me tonight. She's always here for me.

And I tell her just that. "I'm the basket case. You're doing me a favor."

"Whatever, Jess."

Weak willed, I push my luck and scoot in, pressing up tight against those curves of hers and reaching my arm around the nook of her waist. She doesn't even flinch. Instead, she takes my hand in hers on the other side. I don't think I've ever actually held her hand. I feel her from my chest to my hips and knees, making it excruciating to resist going farther. Molding against her, I effectively eradicate any chance of falling asleep. But I won't push it. I need to work through this, whatever it is.

"You're such a tease," she tells me.

If she only knew. "Right now, you're the only heater I've got. So don't go getting any ideas." I grin at my little white lie.

Then I hear, "Love you, babe."

"Love you, too," I say. "Sweet dreams."

CHAPTER TWO: ELLA AND SAM

Sam

This weekend was supposed to be epic. Like the first time I, along with hundreds of other bare-legged women, saw Melissa Ferrick play at Boston Pride. Or that time Ella stopped at that red, got out, and kissed me through the car window—right in the middle of that intersection.

I need that kind of epic.

Ella planned a modest celebration with a few of our good friends. A nice dinner. A couple glasses of cabernet sauvignon. And the kind of hilarity that only happens among those treasured few. Your confidants. Your compadres.

But things don't always happen as planned.

Which would be why I'm here at Whole Foods, wheeling past beat-up wooden crates filled with locally grown organic produce.

Because tonight marks the arrival of our first snowstorm of the season. And it's not just any old blizzard. It's a nor'easter that has kept our meteorologists teenage-girl giddy for at least a week now. And this right here would be the closest grocer I could duck into on my way home from work.

I do enjoy blizzards. I mean, they're par for the course for anyone who chooses to live in New England. But the unfortunate aspect of this particular storm is that it just so happens to collide into our five-year wedding anniversary.

So instead of relishing in romance this snowy anniversary eve, which is what we should be doing, it's been a mad dash, with lines backed up at every gas station, convenience store, and liquor store in town. Folks are scooping up potato chips and brownie mix and dog kibble so even their Jack Russell terrier has a full belly should we actually get snowed in for days on end, which is what they're predicting.

It'll be epic all right. Just not the kind I'd imagined.

Which brings me to where I stand right now, staring at the bulk bins under warm ambient lighting, immersed in the scents of spices and whole bean coffees on a day that repels and bonds total strangers who cross paths as they struggle to choose between dried mangos or apple rings.

I guess you could say that I fall hook, line, and sinker for all of that hype because I, too, am filling up this miniature cart with enough food to feed our family of two for weeks. Because that crushing snow could bury us. Or we could lose power. It has been known to occur. And if nothing catastrophic happens, no harm's done.

Besides, I figure as much as this storm would like to crush my weekend, as much as everything would, I still have tonight. And I've made some plans in that regard as well, plans that involve this little bottle of bubbly right here. So the sooner I get home, the better off I'll be.

Which is why I push forward, determined. Solid 72 percent dark chocolate because, after this week, I deserve it. Smoked whitefish salad to help her recall that summer sunshine. And then I catch baby blue scrubs peeking out from under an unbuttoned navy pea coat with that silver woven basket dangling across a forearm. Of course Alicia has to be here. Just look at her, mindlessly thumbing her phone. I'm just thankful she's preoccupied, for now at least, and didn't see my eye roll.

One day, just once before I leave this planet, I'd like to grocery shop without running into someone I know. This is why I buy tampons elsewhere. Not that it would matter if Alicia knew we bought tampons. She probably does as well.

And the closer I get, the clearer I see her more disheveled than usual appearance. In fact, she looks downright sleep deprived and dejected, the poor thing, and that alone tugs at my heart.

I cut off a cart inadvertently as I toss a polite greeting her way, but her eyes don't break from that gadget. So I follow up with a clumsy elbow nudge followed by a "Hey," which she notices, happy-exhausted and impishly cordial, turning to me with a swing of thick hair that billows from under that dark hat.

And she starts the conversation, slipping her phone in her coat pocket. "You're storm-shopping, too, I see."

"That I am."

"I'm just picking up essentials before heading in," she tells me.

I scan the contents of her basket. A bundle of kale. A box of frozen shrimp. A bag of trail mix. Cotton balls? "That moment you realize a storm's heading in and your nail polish is chipped?"

"Looks to me like you're living on champagne and chocolate. That lucky girl. Where are the flowers?"

"Oh shit! Thank you!"

She has a vulnerable smile. "Anytime."

"So they're forecasting, what, a foot? More?" I ask.

"And hospitals never close," she tells me. "So a lot of accidents and highly pissed-off people."

"I don't know how you do it," I say, parking my cart along the refrigerated wall of milk, goat and cow, non-fat and whole, strawberry, lactose free. I shiver, resting a forearm on the cart's handle.

"You get used to it," I hear as I dodge wheels and arms. "I love going in, gets me away from myself, you know. I'd rather listen to their gripes than think about my own."

Her eyes are pink, but even that can't diminish those goddess-like features. Not just the angle of her eyes but fingers that go on and on. Unapproachable if I didn't know her already. Alicia's one of the lucky few who've made out in the gene pool. Albeit not as lucky as my own wife, who I'd love to get home to. But I digress.

I hear her ask, "Still meeting up Sunday?"

"Of course," I say. "We're expecting you two."

She reminds me of a curious child the way she cocks her head, peering at other shoppers as if to stall. Which makes me want to say something, but I don't. I just watch her eyes think. Her hair and those fingers. The way these jewelry lights drop shadows across the angles of her face. She's lovely, even with worried eyes.

And that's when I hear the sound of rejection as leisurely as thick amber honey down a dipper. "I don't know." I can't figure out if I'm disappointed or relieved. I won't miss Jessie. Still it's not like we have an abundance of replacement friends. "I don't know. I'm still trying to figure it all out. Maybe I can ask you something?" Then she wants to know if I've heard from her girlfriend.

"Ella has in the past few days. Today, no." But since she won't look at me, I can't exactly read her. "Why?"

"I've texted a few times. She was upset and, you know, feeling like…Look, you never know how someone's going to react. At some point in our lives, we just get ourselves into situations." She chuckles, nervously. "She was upset. Upset with me. And she just isn't responding anymore."

"Jessie—upset?"

"Yes," I hear.

She tucks her chin. Even as I rest my palm on her shoulder, she won't look up. Most people would, look up that is. And I have an inkling I'm thinking what she's thinking and she's thinking what I'm thinking, so I attempt to console. "Alicia—"

"No, don't make me out to be the victim here. I'm not."

"I find that hard to believe."

"Well, believe it."

This is the beginning of another end. And how am I supposed to gently inform this girl that she needs to move on, that Jessie's not the one? I can't. Besides, I resent being put in this position in the first place.

"Excuse me, ma'am." I'm blocking the aisle. "Can I just grab a carton of—"

"Hey, yeah, yeah," I say. "Sorry about that."

I don't even know if I want to get involved in this. Do I have a choice at this point? As we make our way toward the yogurt, I utter under my breath, "Can I ask—"

"It's complicated."

She starts to read a label on some strawberry lactose-free yogurt tub. Then she puts three in her basket.

"It's Jessie, you know? She can be…she's stubborn." Her eyes search mine for answers.

"I wouldn't know."

"Maybe if I corner her. I could do that, swing by her place later."

"You could do that." My voice sounds compassionate enough, but I follow with a shrug and half smile just in case she needs some added reassurance. I do get the start of a smile back. "But, listen, stay off the roads if it gets worse out, okay? Promise me that."

She all but assures me, though not verbally, and I'm relieved to say our good-byes and carry on, soon putting their problems on the shelf and redirecting my thoughts back to my life, my wife, my weekend. And I seize the last two remaining jugs of water.

My cart fills up with rosemary crackers then breakfast bars, a pint of my wife's favorite ice cream. And, yes, a bouquet of flowers. I pass the meat counter, now swarming with a flurry of folks shouting at two white-coated staffers who slice and wrap and price-up packs of free-range chicken and grass-fed ground beef.

And in time I find myself staring blankly at floor-to-ceiling shelves of olive oil pretending to read a label. Gravity drains me. What is it with this week? I catch a gentleman peering, well-dressed, his glasses all but dangling off the tip of his nose. Everything about him screams Ivy League education. I nod and smile as I roll past empty-handed.

And I head to the checkout counter, where the guy just ahead refuses to place a bar behind his stuff.

I can hear the chill whistle past the automatic doors. Carts clank over rugs and crash into neat rows. I catch Alicia pushing on out and into it, waving before parted doors seal her exit. I take in the fragrance of patchouli and ready-made café meals.

And I wait, eavesdropping on small talk and glancing outside occasionally at the drifting flurries that circle the lot. My items beep, hit the second belt, and one by one I place each packed bag into my cart.

Four bags and nearly two hundred and fifty dollars later, I, too, shove off into bitter whipping wind. Behind me, thin lines form a trail through the parking lot already layered in slush. It takes some muscle to ram the cart toward the car. But I need to get home to Ella. She should be home by now. And when I take too long, she freaks out.

❖

Ella

Sam should be home with the groceries by now. She wanted to pick up a dozen eggs, a loaf of sourdough bread, fettuccini, and whatever else she needs for the next few days. Shouldn't be much.

She left work early to beat the storm, but now I question whether she should've done so and if it might've been safer just to order a pizza for takeout instead. That is, if our favorite pizzeria's open, which is doubtful.

I tie my boots and realize that this house is finally starting to feel like us. Even that eau-de-previous-home-owner is dissipating thanks to the earthy scent of woodstove. It gives off the fragrance of warmth and home-sweet-home this frigid evening.

In fact, it almost pains me to head out into the great outdoors to lug yet another batch of wood from the barn. The snow's drifting slowly but steadily, and a scattering of imprints follow along my path.

I push back a craggy branch heavy with snow and scratching the barn walls. Between that and this hissing wind, it sounds downright eerie, which makes me a little reluctant to be alone out here. Or maybe I'm just being ridiculous.

There's a hint of crisp and thick smoke in the air as strong as an old man's pipe. It takes me back to the day I met Sam, before I had my act together. When I was stuck in white-collar quicksand and weighted down with a useless degree and constantly complaining. When I was with Jessie, or sort of. *Go back to school, Red. Hang a shingle. You'll make a killing.* Jessie, the eye candy relationship that always sours.

But she has a way of wearing you down, which is why I packed my bags and headed for Vermont. In a few short years, I'd have my degree in baking and pastry arts.

As far as trusting that our relationship would survive the distance, call me naïve but I did. That's how love is. At least, that's what chick flicks told me, and I believed them. I wanted that crazy reunion on the train platform like every other girl.

And in the interim, just for a few short years, Jessie and I would be apart physically and our phones would have to replace our hands, our entire relationship. I thought it'd be fun, and so did she.

Jessie: *Why don't you tell me a hypothetical?*

Me: *What'd you have in mind?*

It was interesting at first. I played along.

Jessie: *Hypothetically, let's say, I'm a student and walk into class on the first day.*

Me: *You in a culinary class?*

She and I both cracked up.

Jessie: *Humor me.*

Me: *Well that would make it awfully hard to focus. We may need to practice after class.*

Jessie: *We could arrange that.*

I was seeing a new side of her. I don't know why, but it felt bolder to talk about what we'd do than actually do it.

When are you free?

How about evenings? Could you make that?

For you.

And it was always some sort of story we'd narrate. Sometimes she'd start. Sometimes I would.

Being all alone with you in that empty class like that. I'm warning you: I'll have...thoughts.

Like?

I'm imagining there's some sort of countertop in the room.

Uh-huh.

And I'll want to give you hands-on tutoring. Maybe stand behind you and dip a spoon in some pastry concoction you made, and I'll hold it out for a taste.

It was hard not to laugh sometimes.

Needs a bit more...honey.

And that's pretty much how it always went. I worshipped her and what she did to me.

I'll need to try too...and I'm not a fan of spoons myself. Maybe we could be a bit more, I don't know, creative?

I worshipped her, all right. I needed her. Until she dumped me. And then I wished I'd never met her.

I worked crappy catering jobs on the weekend—mostly weddings—to pay the bills. And one day that autumn, there was this reception on the lake. A small wedding cruise. There were a few email exchanges with the coordinator, but we had not met face-to-face. I arrived early at the dock and sat on a bench, mustering up the mental fortitude to smile all evening though my heart was crushed to bits. The other side of the lake burst with maple leaves in peak oranges and rusty reds and yellows dancing in the breeze atop white birch bark. And there was a crispness in the air.

The same hint of burning that's in the air right now, as I crash an armful of logs down heavy onto a steel rack in our three-season porch. The screen slams behind me. Under my sole, a nick in the white floor paint. Through the window, a cardinal's taking shelter in a pine tree tugged by snow and cones.

But there was no snow that day—just smoky air. The wedding

party drove up, chauffeured in a string of Bentleys, all sparkling and freshly washed. The final one rolled up wrapped in streamers and shadowed by a cameraman. I glanced over, more focused on work than anything, and that's when I saw that smile emerge. That perfect fauxhawk. There was a veil alongside and a billowing dress gushing for the photographer who crawled on his knees to get the shot.

I was in a trance. She was the event coordinator extraordinaire. Do this. Put that there. My cheeks grew warm as I connected this face with our emails. So self-assured. Centering vases. Counting silverware. One would think she was a professional wedding planner. But she was just the groom's sister.

And she had it together. I did not. I was still devastated.

As the sun set, and as I paused to marvel at so many reflective colors floating on the lake, a voice called my name with an uptick of curiosity. "Ella? We're going to put that right over here." She put her palm on my shoulder, and my heart fluttered.

In fact, it made me so nervous that I nearly dropped the second layer of cake—a masterpiece that took hours to mix and bake and frost.

"Let me show you the cake table." She grinned.

Sure, I thought, please show me whatever. And my name just rolled off her tongue as if we'd known each other already, her voice low enough to command respect but softened with a tone of indisputable femininity. "That looks perfect," she said forefinger to lip, backing up to scrutinize placement. I inhaled deeply, enjoying the air dense with the scent of October.

As she drew closer to me, though, it was *her* fragrance that drew me in.

"The cake looks amazing. And based on what my brother says about your pastries, I'm sure it tastes even better than it looks." She winked at me and then lowered her head to comb her fingers through that thick hair of hers. I mirrored her smile as water crashed against the side of the boat and a fine mist cascaded over the railing.

And after that extremely fleeting moment we had, I lost her to a restless florist carrying armfuls of burlap-wrapped flowers. *Where do you need these, honey?*

From what my brother tells me, I thought. What else did she know about me? What did I tell him? I tried to recall everything.

As the night progressed, the volume rose. I served, still giddy from our encounter. "Lemon pavlova?" Is she single? "Cake pop?"

The sky quite literally glowed that night as it shone down on the water, decorating waves in an enchanting shade of blue. The sun set without a fuss, and the flashlight of a moon beamed curiously from behind crinkled branches along the horizon. It hung low that night, but vivid.

Later, I caught her leaning against the railing looking down at the lake now sparkling like liquid glitter. She was far from that gregarious woman I met earlier. She was spent. I stood back watching for a while and basking in the scenery—and her silhouetted strength. There was a muted calm on deck paired with the sound of crashing waves. I wanted to curl my arms around her. Take care of her. I feared someone would whisk her away again, or worse that I might look like a stalker. So I broke the ice, asking but more joking, "Cake pop?"

She turned to my voice. "I'd love one." Her eyes sparkled when she smiled.

"You must be exhausted."

"Am I! My feet are throbbing. Can you believe that? I don't think I've spent a full six hours straight on my feet in decades. But it's worth it, you know, to see his face in there."

"It's…amazing. Very well planned."

"I tell you. My now sister-in-law in there, she insisted on having her reception at a facility. That's so cold, don't you think? You know, those banquet halls at hotels and conference centers? But I kept harping. Invite just a few of your closest and dearest friends and go all out on the little things. The cars, the flowers…and you. Catering. Something really nice. Not a large sterile hall with metal folding chairs and colored paper taped across tables. She ultimately, thankfully, gave in, and I'm glad she did. This turned out great. I mean, she's got to be the most romantically challenged woman I've ever met," she tells me, taking a bite out of her cake pop. "And my brother's no Romeo. They're made for each other. But this turned out great." I felt a breeze hit my hair. "Seriously?"

"What?" I asked.

"This," she said, pointing to a half-eaten piece of frosted cake on a stick.

"Shut up. It's cake batter and some sugar." Then I immediately regretted my modesty. *Put on your sales hat, Ella.*

"Yes, really. Where'd you learn to make these? Bake these, I should say. You should sell these." And we both laughed, her out of exhaustion. Me from flattery. "Oh, wait, you are. Selling them, that is."

"I am." I slid both hands in my back pockets, noticing her eyes drop to my chest.

"I could eat these all day, but then I'd have to up my gym time."

"I don't think that's an issue for you."

"You don't think?"

"No." I smiled.

"Do you do a lot of these events?"

"It's pretty crazy right now. I mean, it's the best season to be in Vermont, October. Everyone's tying the knot. I had a wedding earlier today and one yesterday."

"Working all weekend? Your, um, your significant other must really miss you." She was trying to toss that one out rather innocently, raising an eyebrow in an oh-so-sexy way.

"No significant other."

"Ah, that's good—right?"

She seemed to be happy with my answer, even through her obligatory frown. I was smitten, enchanted. And our conversation went on, flowing as comfortably as if we were lifelong friends. *You don't say!* Yet the newness kept sneaking up on me, the flutters and the oops-why'd-I-say-that. Eventually she was whisked away again by a silver-haired woman. *Samantha, where should we be putting these?* Samantha, I thought. So Sam is Samantha. I went back to serving and smiling and enjoying the bells of bubbling champagne flutes as they toasted.

Sam's speech came third, scribbled on a slip of paper that she pulled from a pocket. She slowly unfolded each crease, clearing her throat to speak, which sounded loud in the microphone. Her hands were strong, which I've always found incredibly sexy.

I took in everything about her. The tilt of her head, the way her mouth curved up in a crooked smirk. Her hair, I thought, was a few shades lighter than dishwater blond. When she turned to the side, I noticed her profile, her chin and the curvature of her nose and the flip of her hair over her forehead. I noticed the creases around her eyes, but only when she laughed. Until her brother lifted a knuckle to wipe a tear, and fizzy flutes were raised again above a sea of heads in unison. The speech was over, and I was back to work.

Two hours later, the boat docked back at shore. When the horn blew, passengers filed down the ramp, arm in arm, coats bundled over silk gowns. I tore down the banquet and packed up my truck, setting the last tray down, closing the rear, and flipping the latch. As I turned, she was leaning against a parking meter watching me. There were those nerves again.

"Hey, there," I said.

"Hey," she replied, dragging the word out into a low crackle at the end.

"Last one here?"

"Apparently." She looked coyly around at the dark, empty parking lot. "You were a hit. I wanted to thank you."

"Whatever."

"I have the final payment here for you, too. The last envelope in my stack," she said fishing through a manila folder.

"Oh, I can invoice."

But she shook her head and wrinkled her brow in disapproval.

"I know I'm going on and you must think I'm a complete idiot. But I've never tasted anything so…debaucherous. You've got me hooked."

"I don't have you hooked." I felt my cheeks go red. "The buttercream has you hooked."

She winked at me again, and for a moment there, I thought she might be flirting with me. And that's about when my imagination took over and I hardly heard her next ramble.

"Well, you made this event a work of art, exquisite, and I'm indebted. I was doubting myself this morning, not too sure if this would all come together. But it fell into place. And, well, you really—not to be corny—topped the cake. Man, I was guilt-ridden just watching people bite in. It had to have taken hours—the details, the dots and bows, really impressive. Just so—you're a class act. Do you know how many times," continued her ramble, "I've tried to make a cake? Each was an epic fail, and I'm referring to boxed SuperMoist Betty Crocker." She took a few steps closer. "Just add some water, oil, and eggs, they tell you. One, two, three. I followed every step, mixed that batter, popped it in, and down she sank. The sides are black, and the frosting melts because I have no patience whatsoever when it comes to waiting for something I want." She lifted her eyes to me almost bashfully.

"Don't knock yourself. It's taken a lot of years and practice, believe me. I can create something in my mind and find a way to make that edible." I caught myself talking with my hands. "Let it cool first." My eyes dipped and lingered a little too long on her lips as she took slow steps closer.

"Yeah, that's what I'm told." She stopped advancing when she was close enough to kiss me, and it was as if I jumped on a roller coaster that never stopped dipping. "I can cook, you know," she said, finally. "Pretty good actually. I just don't bake."

That's, I think, when I saw that signature smirk for the first time along with that singular eyebrow raise, an expression I've grown all too familiar with. By that point, I could see dimples in her cheeks that I hadn't noticed in the distance, and I was reminded again of her scent.

Then, taking her voice down another notch, "Thanks for everything tonight."

I wanted to stand there with her under the lantern in that waterfront lot until the sun rose, even in its clumsiness and unease. But she was wrapping it up.

She kicked her toe gently into the pavement and thrust a rock into the grass. It tick-tick-ticked its way in the distance. Then I watched as she peered from under her eyelashes, seeming to hold something back. I mirrored her smile for the thousandth time until she looked away, shaking her head side to side. "Drive home safely," she told me, handing me a sealed envelope with the check.

"You, too," I said, brushing windblown hair off my face. Still, her body language didn't tell me good-bye. She stood her ground, unyielding. Then came my obligatory sales pitch. "And if you know anyone planning an event," I told her, "here's a few of my business cards." Okay, it was half sales pitch, half here's my number.

She looked at my cards under the streetlamp, running her thumb over the embossed letters. "You bet I will."

I didn't open that envelope until the next day when I discovered, clipped to a check, a small slip of paper that read: *I'd love to see you again. Call me?* It had her number.

❖

I crash down my last armful of logs, spattering wood chips and dirt on the floor beneath. Then I yank my boots off and set them on the rubber mat, hanging my coat on a wall hook. Around is the sound of absolute silence for a fleeting moment followed by, "Babe, are you going to come get these from me?"

"You're home...thank God, I was getting worried about you out there."

"It's nasty. The roads are awful. Our street hasn't been plowed at all, but the main routes are touch and go." She stands on the rug next to two floppy fabric grocery bags. "Here, can you put these away for me," she says, lifting and handing them to me. "I'll go get the others from the car."

"How much more did you get?"

"It's snowpocalypse, babe. We need to be prepared."

❖

Sam

I'd like to tell her how much this weekend means to me. But I don't. I just give her a cocked smile over this candle, twirl my fork, and take another coil of this amazing fettuccini because we don't say those things. Not with words, anyway.

We used to tell each other lots of corny things, mushy things—most of which makes me wish she had dementia. Things that were highly embarrassing. Why do I know this? I held on to those emails, for whatever reason I don't know. Maybe I wanted to reminisce one day when we were gray haired, but they just make me wish I hadn't tried so hard. Once in a blue moon an email pops up in my search and I reread it and have to wonder. Things between us are so natural now in comparison.

Except compliments. Those aren't at all natural. I thought that, when you married, the walls came down. It's the opposite. A few weeks back, Ella was talking and I was listening and I interrupted and told her that I loved her lips because I always have but I've never actually told her so. How her bottom lip is so much fuller than her top. The way it tilts as if she's always telling me *whatever* (even when she takes a bite of fettuccini like that). But she looked at me like I said something amusing or insincere and changed the subject. I know she appreciates it. But my compliments don't hold weight anymore, not like they used to. Maybe I just suck at timing.

In our normal weekly routine, we don't eat in the dining room like this. It's too formal and constraining and uncomfortable. We don't use these fabric napkins, either. We use brown recycled napkins that we toss away. We eat in front of the television watching David Muir. But we try to do this dining room thing on special occasions. Or, I should say, she tries.

She made dinner tonight. She unpacked the table runner and her inherited china, lit these (inappropriately) scented candles, used the pewter vase as a centerpiece. I just got the fire going.

She's not talkative tonight. I'm used to her constant chatter about work. The only time she doesn't talk my ear off is when she's ready for bed or on that iPad or when we're in the car and have her music up really loud. I should pop the champagne. That'll get her talking.

That car outside has been spinning its wheels for a while now. Maybe I should go take a look. Which reminds me, I need to take our car in for an oil change next week. And, while I'm at it, they can check that noise it's making. It's probably just a belt, but it could be something really bad, and then what? It's not like we can afford a major car repair right now.

"Where are you going?" she wants to know.

"What's that noise?"

"It's just a neighbor," she tells me. "They're probably stuck."

"Obviously. Don't you think we should help?"

"They'll knock if they need help. The light's on."

I suppose she's right.

"Pour me a glass?"

"That was my plan," I say.

I use the same champagne flutes I bought for our engagement. Now they're engraved with our wedding date. I set them on the counter.

The cork always startles me when it pops, even though I'm the one twisting. She's taking another spin of pasta. I pour one, then the other. I put a glass in front of her. And that's when the lights dim. They dim and brighten and dim again. We both look up, but they don't come back on. I ask if she paid the electric bill this month, joking. Then I tell her, nonverbally, that it's nothing. But her face is already drained. Without the lights, the woodstove casts a strange shadow-light on the table.

I take my seat again and put my napkin back on my lap. I take a piece of bread from the center of the table. When I look up again, I catch those eyelashes of hers over that pewter flute.

That's when the lights come back on for good.

❖

Ella

I wasn't always like this, I swear. I remember when I could let anything roll off my back. A deadline from my boss late Friday afternoon. That zigzagging line out the post office. Even a snarky service rep.

Except when it came to my sister. She always knew how to push my buttons. Still does, which is why I haven't spoken to her in a good year. I'm still waiting for her apology. That aside, I've never been panic-stricken in catastrophes like this. You should see me at work.

But at home, forget it.

I blame my better half for existing in a perpetual state of Zen. Someone needs to worry around here. So now the unexpected makes me ballistic. I go passive-aggressive, you know like those bickering couples who cloak jabs with a wink. *Must you wear that? You didn't really just do that?* I'm like that now, blurting stuff out I instantly regret. One minor irritation easily morphs into rage in a matter of seconds, and we play out our Ricky and Lucy moments. Maybe this is menopause. She's always the bigger one, and that only worsens matters.

Take this background music. She put it on. And it's a great song, so I get on my groove. The champagne helps. Admittedly though, I'm the worst dancer even if I'm drunk (more so if I'm drunk, which I'm not at the moment) and when I attempt to tap my foot or swivel my hips, it looks about as natural as blown-up, lit-up plastic snowmen do in the middle of actual snow. And she makes me stiffer when she looks at me like that. It's put me in a mood.

I'm relieved when she makes her way over to the window to look out instead of at me.

"It's really coming down," she says in a highly inappropriate tone that reeks of juvenile excitement. When I flip on the outside light, the flakes look more like winged bugs swarming.

"Lovely," I say, half in wonder, half in dread. But the power could go out again at any minute. So I tip the last drop of champagne. It's warmed me sufficiently. "Did we finish that entire bottle?"

"I think we did, babe." When exactly did nine o'clock become our staying up late, our big deal? Then I hear, "I forgot to mention." Her voice follows me into the kitchen to the dishwasher. "You'll never guess who I ran into." I raise a brow, never a fan of prolonged drama. Which is why she takes no time to tell me. "Alicia."

I think I just felt my eyes roll.

Then she starts talking about trouble in paradise. And this news stirs up a mixed bag of emotions. I'm apprehensive. I'm satisfied. I'm elated. I'm intrigued. I'm bitter. I'm neutral. I'm ashamed. I'm thankful. I'm troubled. It's not that I liked Alicia. But Jessie was actually giddy over someone.

As opposed to spilling too much of this response, which champagne tends to make me do, I resolve that there are some things best left unsaid if you expect to stay happily ever after for any length of time. So I tell her, simply, "I never liked her."

"I know you didn't."

"But I thought she'd last longer. I really did." Like maybe two months instead of two weeks. Why'd she even introduce us?

"Does anybody last with Jessie? Think about that for a moment." She's less than amused, offering me that I-wish-Jessie-didn't-exist look.

I head back to the window, where the porch light's still on. And that's when things get quiet. Her: likely excited about roughing it tonight, snowmageddon style. Me: dreading tomorrow. The cold, the shoveling. It's going to take up most of our day. So much for time off. That snowblower's sounding mighty appealing about now, even if we'd need a home loan to buy it. Maybe I can palm shoveling off on her and do something useful inside—like nothing.

Eventually she gives me one of those shoulder nudges. "Suppose we should hit the hay. We'll need sleep if we're shoveling out tomorrow. I'll go get the dishes and add a few logs. Go take your face off."

But she's still mad at work on those dishes when I wrap and tuck my towel into my chest. I brush my teeth. I floss. I comb my hair. I skip the moisturizer. And when I open the door, it's not the most pleasant temp on the other side and I'm chilled in places I didn't even know existed. But I reach into the dresser, finding a little bit of nothing. Slip it up my hips and across my torso.

And that's going just fine when I hear, "Let me help you with that, babe."

"It's freezing," I tell her rather matter-of-factly.

"And you're still damp."

"Slightly."

"Don't walk around with your hair wet like that."

But it's not my hair that's an issue; it's my clothing—or lack thereof. I don't know what I was thinking wearing next to nothing so I could seduce my wife tonight. Flannel would be more appropriate and just as effective. So I reach for my robe.

"You don't honestly think I'll let you cover up." She wraps my towel behind her neck and flings my robe to the floor before I can tuck in. The folds of her shirt and the thickness of her jeans rub against me. I can't really form a proper response.

"Stay damp," she tells me. And I feel a tickle up my sides. "Just... like...this."

CHAPTER THREE: BRIE AND RYAN

Brie

Crap. Did I seriously just spill coffee down the front of me? Why do they always fill these cups so full? Even when you ask for half an inch on top, they never leave room for cream. The barista, though, what she lacks in latte-making skill she more than makes up for in personality. She's a doll, which is why I never mention it.

Besides, I usually see her at the table flipping textbooks. She reminds me a bit of myself not that long ago, and I'm always cognizant to leave a good tip in the jar just because. If anything, I know what that's like.

I press the lid hard, slip on a cardboard sleeve, and grab a handful of napkins to clean up. At least it landed on my thigh, and this dark denim will camouflage. Stains only make jeans better. At least that's my philosophy. I'm just grateful it didn't hit this expensive shirt, which would've been destroyed. Maybe it's a sign that I've had enough. Caffeine, that is. After all, I'm starting to feel jittery from the pots of Sumatra I've consumed. Okay, slight exaggeration. But my stomach doesn't feel so hot. Besides, it's nearly dinnertime. At this rate, I'll be up all night. Oy.

Ryan thinks I drink too much of it. "So what," I tell her. It's my vice. We all have one. Food, alcohol, exercise. Or for her, sex. At least mine happens to make me highly productive. Hers, on the other hand, obliterates all productivity. She'll keep you up all night, and that is not the slightest exaggeration.

She says, "It's an Italian thing." Maybe so, but you can get too much of any good thing, doll. I don't know how she functions without a wink of rest. I can't stay awake until three a.m. five nights a week and still perform on any job.

Instead of barking at me over coffee, she should be grateful I get as much done during the day as I do. Before I joined the ranks of the unemployed, I would've given anything to come home after a crazy-long day to a clean house and hot supper. And that she will tonight. I spent a good four hours today just cleaning her house spotless before heading downtown to this home-away-from-home caffeine sanctuary to search jobs, send résumés, and clear my own head.

It's not even the drinks that I come here for. It's the slice of privacy. I can tie my hair back, plug my laptop in, reflect on life, and escape Ryan's confining walls. It makes me feel like a reasonably industrious citizen again. With an emphasis on *reasonably*. I'm still unemployed.

I'm lucky, too, that this window seat is nearly always open. It has the best view of downtown. From my vantage point, I can see everything that happens out there. And while I can't easily see the café door, I sure can't miss that cowbell just above or the boots pounding on the mat as people dislodge all those salt rocks.

Last summer, just outside, they lined the walk with two-seater tables shaded with seaside umbrellas. Still, I prefer working behind the cloak of windowpane. Less sun. Fewer bugs. Air-conditioning.

I click on a potential job opportunity, though well below me, for a paralegal (that's how desperate I am right now) when an email alert glides across from my Notification Center: *While your background and experience are noteworthy, at this time, we are pursuing other candidates who more closely match our needs for this position.*

What a great way to end my day. My week. Ugh. I'm turned down—even before an interview—for a legal secretary post. So much for that little *Esq.* tacked at the end of my name. Just this past week, I widened my search radius far beyond a realistic commute. I applied for smaller firms and one solo practice with not one iota of upward mobility. I've delved so far below my credentials that my pride may never recover. But, alas, I do have that tiny weekly unemployment check to get me by, right?

Let's just file this rejection letter and call it a week. An unproductive week, at that, with only three not-so-perfectly matched résumés en route. En route, that is, to law firms in Maine up by Mom and Dad. Not here. Maybe moving down here for a chance of a lifetime job in a gay mecca wasn't such a great idea after all. Maybe I wasn't meant to move on. Maybe I'm meant to stay a Portland girl forever.

As soon as my finger brushes the power button, one more notice settles on my screen. A state of emergency has been declared. Shelter in place. Yes, it's definitely time to head home. Pronto.

On the drive home, I try to get a handle on it all. *Try* is the key word here, because I feel like an absolute failure.

I pass the sign that reads *Bridges Freeze Before Road*.

Just past, at the end of this winding road, is that dagger-pointed intersection. My wipers struggle to lift their weight, and I can hear their motor over my music.

Speed Limit 30, another sign warns just before I reach the building. Snow's building up on wooden shutters and window boxes that are impeccably decorated along the first, second, and third floors. Evergreen. Red berries.

There's no oncoming traffic. There's no traffic at all. It's desolate.

I turn into the parking lot, shut off my engine, and open my compact—bringing it to steering-wheel height. I sponge powdered foundation across my forehead and then coconut lip balm. Clouds are making it murky and difficult to see. It's getting so dark. I think I look all right even with brown coffee stains down the front of my jeans.

A deep inhale. An even longer exhale. I need a job, I think, as my truck beeps and the door locks. When I step inside, it's another season altogether. It's stuffy. Condensation drips down their windows. Good music plays overhead but not obnoxiously.

The woman in back has a tank top on and khaki shorts. She's muscular. She's always making dough.

The counter girl greets me by name as I slide two fingers behind and pull up my wallet. "Should be two. Large," I tell her. I unfold two twenties. She does this thing where she glances up at me sideways while putting my bills in the register. It's cheeky. She has brown eyes. She's bronzed still from summer, which seems oddly out of place. Her hair's wavy and uncombed. Natural colored. No gray. She's not wearing a bra but young enough to get away with it. I reciprocate her smile thinking she's too hippie for me. And short. I'm okay with short if it's not hippie short.

She does this all the time, eyes me. She doesn't look away, either, as if she's worried I didn't catch on yet. As if she needs to be more obvious. It makes me more than mildly uncomfortable especially when I bring Ryan.

Like when we stopped in after painting her bedrooms and were encrusted in white, wearing matching baseball caps. She'd waited for Ryan to get sidetracked and then settled on me even though that meant ignoring other paying customers.

Do I look that unhappy? I'm just hungry. Like those nights work ran late, when we drove in after three long days on the Cape, when it was too hot to cook, when we just wanted pizza. I don't come in for her. I'm not into her. I swear I must give off some sort of vibe, the unemployed girl needing rescue vibe. Even still, she's just not my type.

That dough girl out back, though.

A man and woman walk in just as the cardboard lid closes on my order. Counter girl walks it over to me on the bench where I'm sitting. She even goes so far as to open the door for me. So dough girl takes the register instead.

Figures. It's not like I could have brought that doll up front. Whenever I pay, she's always busy spinning dough.

❖

Ryan

Old Man Winter blows through every year like clockwork. At first, it's charming. Who can resist the romantic lure of snowmen, thick soles and swagger, snowboarding? November lets off a chill that's easily tamed by a warm fire and a beau tucked alongside you. Even December's freeze is tempered by holidays and harmony.

Come January, though, with ice on sidewalks and plows and stripping wind, the season sort of loses its cool. In February even the rugged outdoors-women, the ice climbers, not even they can muster up enough enthusiasm for the monotony of single digits. But that's still a ways off.

Here it is just early December, and cabin fever is already settling in, which is especially harsh for those of us who spend our nights in bed with a woman whose heart was raked away with the pile of leaves last month.

As I stand in my bedroom dripping after a shower, I hear Chris Pureka's "Cynical" accompanied by Brie, my emotionally distant girlfriend. Her harmony is more than slightly off-key. I cross the room to roll down the shade, peering out at miles and miles of bleak and lonely landscape. I know that the only life out there is an occasional bird nested in straw and huddling against tonight's blizzard.

This house was built by hand in 1856. She sits on a scenic hill overlooking land that more recently grew tobacco, or so I'm told. Right now, my acreage abuts an organic farm, which abuts an even bigger farm. And it goes on like that for miles.

She has her original windows, her cracked plaster walls, her tall ceilings, and her wide knotty floors that whine when they're stepped on in that certain way. For the most part, I've adapted to walking around the touchiest of boards if only to avert the racket. Given most of her doors don't even shut, you could call her an open book. I daydream about the stories caked beneath layers of thick paint, some of which we've applied ourselves. Some are our stories.

While seclusion was initially what attracted me to this place, it's now become my nemesis. Brie moved in with her good job, her bed table clutter, her loans, her sunrise yoga ritual, and a roomful of IKEA furnishings, most of which were purchased during college and all of which are in a style not quite my own. She could fit everything she had in her truck and a single hitched U-Haul—some tattered CDs, a couple bottles of expensive perfume, two vintage suitcases, jewelry— all packed neatly in clear plastic bins. She hung a closet full of pantsuits and white shirts, each custom tailored. She brought the basic kitchen appliances like the toaster and the coffeepot, duplicating my own. We didn't keep hers. She also brought typical lesbian baggage.

But it's this house that seduced her, not me. Brie is exquisite, breathtaking. But I think everyone needs at least one relationship that pushes beyond her boundaries. Gets her out of her safe and secure zone. She was that for me. Is still that for me. And up until two weeks ago, even with the job loss, things were okay between us.

I give my hair another scruff with the towel, pull my pj's out of the dresser, and yank a hoodie over my head.

Her vocals escalate in volume until she's in the hall, in the bedroom with me, and then standing immediately behind me. As the song fades into the next, she plops herself on my bed, reclining on her side braced by one single elbow with hair draping down her shoulder. She's somewhat lanky yet delicate, ethereal. Of Swedish descent.

"We're getting buried," she says with a sigh.

"And don't you love storms?" I know she doesn't. I don't expect an answer.

"Have you taken a look outside?"

"Cozy, eh?"

"No, doll." She rubs one nail against the other. "I thought it was less...flannel here. More Kennedy and Cape Cod. So much for sophistication."

"The house looks great," I tell her, changing the subject. I mimic her posture (but not her pinched fingers), holding my towel in a tight wad against my chest.

She keeps her attention on the bedcovers, avoiding my questioning eyes.

Nearly a year together and we've already settled into LBD. But that might be her lack of gainful employment, I rationalize. It would put a damper on anyone's temperament, including my own. After all, I haven't been without a job since the age of eighteen.

Regardless, I did hope to coax her into some sort of fun tonight. The long weekend together could rekindle whatever spark we had left. I tell her again how great the house looks, how she looks. She continues to flick her nails, and I put my hand over hers as if to say *stop*. To give her no choice but to look at me. I'm unsuccessful.

I lift her chin and roll closer. I want so desperately to feel a connection. Physically, at least. My body aches for her. Yet every two steps I advance, she retreats three until she's on her back. I roll on top of her, looking down. She likes when I take control. She enjoys being submissive, I tell myself. But I can see her hollow eyes now. She slows down, and I catch up with her. My lips and hands try to draw her out of her thoughts. To consume her and please her, and even the slightest moan is enough of an impetus to stay on course.

Ultimately, though, I surrender. Her body isn't responding to me. Instead, she squeezes me with her thighs and shoves against my shoulders, not allowing me to touch where I want to.

"What's wrong?"

"Did I tell you I got another rejection today?"

"No. I'm sorry."

"And it's snowing again and it's cold and everything's just going to shut down."

She's dodging my eyes more than usual.

"Back home…" she starts. There's that faraway look again.

"I know, I know, in your perfect utopia."

"Gee, thanks."

"I'm joshing with you." Though I do tire of her harping so often about this *home* I've never seen. "Take a joke, already."

"Seriously?" she asks. "You really don't have a clue how hard it is for me to fit in to your world, do you?"

"Where's this coming from?"

"This," she tells me, arms outspread. "It's yours. The house and everything in it. Your friends. Their loyalties. Why can't you have one speck of empathy for what I've gone through over the past year? What I'm going through?"

"I am empathetic." I curl my shoulders forward to loosen them. "Stop worrying."

"Stop worrying," she says under her breath.

"You'll find a job."

In truth, I rather enjoy the arrangement we currently have, but I won't tell her that. It puts me, admittedly, in charge. And, given her out-of-my-league airs, my making more than her brings her nearer to equal.

"It's not just the job. It's more, a lot more. You really wouldn't get it."

I force empathy. "If something's bothering you so much, why haven't you brought it up?"

She's looking me straight in the eye, intently. "What do you think I'm doing?" I hear the wind. "I've brought it up. You choose to not listen." For a twenty-six-year-old, Brie can act pretty childish and worries about the pettiest of things. And she knows my buttons. She knows I feel less worldly, that I've lived in this town my entire life— meanwhile she's been pretty much everywhere. At least in comparison.

"While we're on this subject," I tell her, feeling judged, "did you ever consider the burden I might be feeling as the sole breadwinner of this household? Supporting both of us on one paycheck, the house, food, utilities. Your trips to the coast, your cappuccinos. Your car payment and student loans. I've been considerate of your feelings. The empathy you expect goes in both directions." I stop just short of telling her to grow up. Get a spine. Toughen up.

"I can pack and be out of your hair in a day. Just give me the word."

It doesn't just hurt. It puts her on top. And I don't like that. "I don't want you to move out. I'm trying to tell you, the situation, all of this, it's taxing on both of us. Not just you."

"You're not listening—turning this around to you is not listening. You bought this house without my salary, so you can keep this house without it. Meanwhile I'm flat-out broke and unemployed."

Windows rattle. It seems to be picking up.

"What are you trying to tell me, really?"

She doesn't answer right away. Instead, she lets me stew and agonize. "I'm saying that…a little selflessness would go a long way."

"I see."

"Staying here. And living with you. And finding another job here. It all requires a commitment on my part."

"It might."

"I don't know if we're up for that."

All I can do is stall silently while I formulate a response, which is just to rehash what she told me. I continue to choose words carefully. And in the end, I swallow my pride. "I want you to stay." I slide my hand on the bed, wrapping my fingers affectionately around hers. "I want you to. Won't you?"

It's dangerously silent for what seems an eternity. For the most part, she keeps her gaze down at our hands. Then, occasionally, she'll glance up at me. But she doesn't say a word. Which is fine, I suppose, because I don't understand what she's telling me. I have no idea what she's thinking. Sometimes I feel like I have her. Other times I worry that I've lost her. But that's part of her appeal and so much of what locks me to her.

Her bottom lip is fragile under my thumb, and I smudge it to remind her why we're together. But she doesn't feel the same, childishly rolling her eyes, standing up, and leaving the room.

❖

Brie

If I could be anywhere in the world right now, it sure wouldn't be here. And that makes me the most horrible person alive, doesn't it? Maybe so, but with this insight, I'm unapologetically optimistic. Maybe that's because I've been running on autopilot for too long, settling into this new role as domestic goddess, as her ill-suited girlfriend. Kept.

She's beginning to snore, Ryan, and the entire length of her back is pressed against mine. Once in a while she rolls, which tugs even harder at the spread stretching between us and it gets taut like a carnival tent.

I don't love Ryan. And admitting that finally, even to myself, is rather liberating. I'd even go so far as to call it redemptive. And I hardly led her on. So why am I weighed down like this, crushed in so much guilt that I can't even appreciate my newfound freedom? To my defense, for the past year, she's reiterated time and again that she's not looking for a commitment. That she has no expectations, can make no promises. So I have every right to up and walk out at my leisure, right? Sometimes I think she wants me to.

I think I'm beginning to regret all of those lattes today because I have killer insomnia. And whenever I get like this, I think way too hard on way too much. It'd be nice if I could call someone. I lean over and thumb-scroll my directory even though I know it's too late to dial.

And after Mom and Ryan is Hadley, my tae kwon do partner, one of my best friends. (Did I just admit that?) That girl has her own connections with my girlfriend, the common thread being Jessie Miles—Ryan's BFF. Hot, yes. And Hadley's infatuated with her.

As infatuated as I am with Chris, in fact, who's still right here on my phone. And it hits: if I could be anywhere right now, anywhere in the world, that's where I'd be.

With that square peg in a round hole, that rule breaker. Carefree. The opposite of me. I'm a complete control freak, I admit it.

When you meet her, she tells her story about being born the same day the world bid adieu to Andy Warhol. I think there's some meaning to that. I miss her soul. Almost as much as her perfume, which I wear incessantly because *wearing the same perfume*, she preached, *is like wearing each other all day.*

We were in tenth grade thirteen years ago when she passed the test and brought home her driver's license along with that faded red '55 Ford truck, a gift from guilt-ridden parents. She loved it. It was so big, she had to hop down from the seat, but still, she seemed tough. I can still see her, reclined against that silver logo with a foot tucked under her hips. She was tough in the way she took care of me. In the way she looked after me.

"Need a light, Bee?" she'd ask as her cigarette met pursed lips and a match struck. I'd watch her fingertips fall to her hip and her middle finger do that little flip to shake the ash off.

She and I spent every day together for the next two years. Still, by the time we tossed our tassels, that relationship remained cloaked under the guise of friendship to the outside world. She stayed up in Portland while I spent four agonizing years putting off growing up in college and then law school. I'm still paying off that loft apartment in the form of student loans.

Chris loved it, though, the loft, the few times she drove down. Me lazing around covered to my hips in a white cotton sheet. Her drinking coffee without a stich of sheet or robe. Watching her swagger to the bureau, the way she'd pull down that long-sleeved tee and up those saggy jeans as the morning sun reached its outstretched arms around her. She had the sweetest taste of cream with coffee on her breath. I can still taste it now like it was yesterday. As if I'm still lying beneath her, that knee weighing the mattress down as I sink in.

Between tenth and twelfth grade, our routine breakups consisted of coming-out panics, hormones, raging jealousy, and our need to please overbearing parents. Regardless, she always came out unscathed.

As for me, I sank into some serious bouts of depression. She said she went through the same. I doubt that. Still, neither of us could function apart, and we inevitably fell back into *going out*—over and over and over again. Like vinyl with a skip, I forgave her flings because, as she put it, "I was lonely when we were apart." So lonely that she dated half of the girls' soccer team.

Eleven years, two degrees, five addresses, a fresh set of friends, five J.Crew suits, a hot enough girlfriend, and a couple of unemployment checks later, I find myself smiling ear to ear just thinking about her. That is, until Ryan tugs at that blanket again, this time leaving me covered in nothing more than goose bumps. I go back to that number on my phone. I fixate on it, as a matter of fact.

I can't help but compare the two, and guess who wins? It's the same story every time I try to move on. I try to get over her. I try other fish in the sea. They're not as entertaining or they're way too serious, too yawn inducing or too gabby. They don't know me or just don't click. They don't have her soul. But I try. I am trying to move on.

I wish there were a finish line to denote the end of one relationship and the start of something new. I wish I had a thing, a symbol, something there to offer an actual conclusion. Just as there was no real end with Chris, there was no real beginning. We had a lot of ends and a lot of beginnings. A lot of firsts. Too many lasts.

Maybe we're supposed to hold on as long as we can, letting the past circle and flitter around us. Because I see Chris everywhere, in the eyes of strangers, the tastes and touches of new lovers. Maybe we're supposed to miss them every once in a while, even years later. Maybe that's part of this process.

I shimmy out from Ryan's bed and get to my feet seconds before she turns over and flops her arm around my empty pillow. At least I left it warm for her. At least I haven't woken her. If I had, she'd bark at me for drinking far too much coffee, and she'd be right.

Look at me. I'm breaking cardinal relationship rule number eight.

My Cardinal Relationship Rules

1. Never eat anything messy or bad-breathy on the first date. Or second.
2. Wait at least one month to drink red wine in front of her. (It makes my teeth look bad.)
3. Kiss her on the first date, but make her wait for more. (All right, so I've broken that one.)
4. If she hikes, bikes, wakeboards, snowboards, or performs any other form of outdoor fitness activity, expect that will be your next date.
5. If she plays soccer, rugby, or any team sport, trust that she's already slept with half the team.
6. Let her pay. If she wants to. If she doesn't offer, there's no need for a second date.

7. If she's not out to her family by the age of twenty-five, she never will be. Leave or live with it.
8. Never juggle two women.
9. Keep some things to yourself. It's not okay to know your girlfriend's type, or vice versa.
10. Never say I love you first.

All right, so I'm not exactly juggling two women. But I am responding to a letter from my ex behind Ryan's back. While she sleeps, at that. I can't tell her. I don't want to tell her. She just wouldn't understand.

And some rules are made to be broken. Regardless, it's all innocent. Chris made it absolutely positively clear that our last breakup was it—the ultimate, final, forever end. So it's not like I'm keeping anything important from my girlfriend. All lesbians are friends with their exes, right?

So here I sit in Ryan's comfy little home office while a blizzard whips us. I turn on her desk lamp, which casts a lemon chiffon hue across the walls, over the side chair, and arcs into the hall, and then I lift my laptop. When I do, the blue glare blinds me for a second.

As I wait for my computer to wake up, I twist and tie my hair up into a messy bun. I also work to convince myself that it would be healthy for Chris and me to remain friends. She's trying to make amends. And it would be very Buddhist of me to forgive her. I've just been putting it off. She wrote me a laundry list of apologies. Apologies for the way it ended. For how she treated me. For not appreciating me. She feels remorseful, as she should. And I've let her sit in that remorse for quite some time now. A few weeks, to be precise. After all, it's never ever wise to reply too quickly. What message does that send?

That said, I know what Mom would say. She'd say I'm crazy for responding at all. She'd tell me about all of those fish in the sea and how I deserve better. That I should step back, enjoy my youth, date other women. I know because that's the lecture she gave me every single time Chris broke up with me. But the way I see it, who has Mom ever gotten over? She married the first man she kissed, so she's not exactly one to dole out advice. Not on dating. And especially not on women.

Besides, Chris and I were kids. We were melodramatic, over-the-top, never surviving more than six months apart. It was all short-term. Brief. Like clockwork. I grew accustomed to waiting out my six months' sentence. During one of our separations, I even went out with a girl on the track team. That's when I made up Cardinal Relationship Rule No. 5. We didn't get far. She just wasn't Chris. Nobody was.

For the most part, though, I had zero confidence when we were apart. I mean zilch. Nada. I couldn't feign confidence with anyone, let alone laugh—let alone smile. She had to come back or I'd die. And when she did, I knew I'd cave. All of that pent-up pissed-off and pain, those exhaustive monologues that I'd rehearsed in my head over and over where I called her out and put her in her place and screamed, only to be roughly embraced in a perfect Hollywood kiss. All of that anger I held on to, it would all dissolve in a matter of seconds after hearing that voice again. Seeing that swagger coming at me. And I'd be hers again. Blissfully. Like nothing had ever happened.

When that kiss never came, I knew that after ten long years of being The Couple, she was done. Done with me. Done with it. Done. She wanted to see other girls. She didn't want to be *that* kind of girl, the one that meets the love of her life in tenth grade and stays for the rest of her life, never experiencing anything else. Anyone else. I know this because she told me so.

And the fact that she left me and still loved me in some sort of way, well, that crushed. She thought she could play the field. She thought she could come back when she failed to find what she was looking for. When she missed me again. I'd taught her that much. So I waited and sulked. I somehow crawled out of bed in the morning, buried myself in studies, and kept busy enough to hide my deflated chest.

But she was supposed to call me in six months, give or take. I could still to this day tell you how the wet air weighed the grass leaves after all that rain. The odd absence of birds as I woke. The yellow highlighting on my Day-Timer because I'd waited for that month. I can hear the sound of my phone, how I jumped when it rang. Maybe I survived that long only because I knew there was a light at the end of the tunnel. Maybe. But that month came and passed. And yet another. She never did call.

More than a year later, here I am. With another woman, so I really did heed Mom's advice. Everyone's advice, really. I think I'm strong enough, now, capable of maintaining an amicable relationship with my ex. She left this widening gap that nobody else fills. A friendship, possibly, perhaps, is just the thing to fill the vacancy in my heart. In my lungs. In my spine. At least enough to help me move on.

As I set my fingers on the keyboard, I notice light shining through the *S* key, a key that should be black. I wonder why I've used the letter *S* so often that it rubbed the keypad raw.

The arrow hovers on my screen as I click to open my email, typing her new address manually in the to field.

Dear Chris

No, too formal.

Hey, Chris

Too informal. How exactly does one open this sort of email?

Hey!

No. Way too peppy. She'll read fake into that faster than I can lose a job.

I think she started her letter with *Hi Bee*. So I opt for the same.

Hi Chris—

And with that, thoughts begin to flow.

It was great hearing from you. No apologies—I'm glad you got my snail mail address from my mom. And, no, she didn't tell me you reached out to her. I pause, tap my forefinger on the keyboard, and look at the corner of the room for inspiration, though all I see are Ryan's family photos. Outside, the snow heaps taller against the window.

Yup, she's still old school, I write. *She won't touch email.* I'm surprised, I think to myself, that she gave Chris my snail address instead of my new number. She does have my number. That's quintessentially Mom, though, trying to protect me from some random call out of the blue. Or trying to keep us apart? I'll never know.

In time, words and sentences and then paragraphs form. I analyze my tone. I don't want to seem too anxious. A nice mix of *I don't care because I've moved on* and *You matter to me* would be best. You know, so she gets that I'm cool with being friends.

Before you know it, I'm telling her everything under the sun. Once in a while, I scroll back and edit. I backspace and erase one entire paragraph because it's far too gooey, gives off the wrong impression, seems too clingy. I huddle under the lamplight enjoying the warmth it emits as more sentences expand into paragraphs. And then it hits me like one of those friendly snowballs packed with too much ice, hard. I'm crashing.

Bleary eyed, I glance over at the clock and see that an entire hour and a half has passed just like that. I guess that means it's officially tomorrow. Can I call it tomorrow if it's still my today? My email is too gooey. It's still not right. I'm too emotional, and I'm really, really tired and hazy and imprisoned by feet of snow in the middle of nowhere, which I think has done a number on my emotional well-being.

I add my close: *I'll leave you with my number just in case. We should catch up.* Then I sign it *Love, Bee* because that's how she closed hers, *Love.* I'd like to mull over the use of the word *love.* But I need to look at this and edit it another time. Like tomorrow—or should I say today because it officially is tomorrow—and after a restful night's sleep. When my head's clear. I hover over the little pictures of envelopes and arrows and trash cans to save it as a draft and then I close my laptop, click the lamp off, and make my way back into bed with Ryan. Maybe I'll wake up tomorrow and this whole storm and everything will be just a bad dream.

FRIDAY

CHAPTER FOUR: RYAN AND BRIE

Ryan

When I wake, I'm shivering and I roll over to find Brie's yanked the blankets over to her side and I'm stripped down to a cotton sheet. I'm sure she's toasty warm under that towering pile of down. Lucky her.

I hit the alarm before it buzzes, grabbing my iPad on my way back—thoughtful not to disturb her. She was up late. I know because I heard her banging around.

Wrapped in a throw, I let my inbox load. Just one lonely message drops. It's from Ella. I'm relieved, though, that she's keeping a skeleton crew. She never shuts down. This must be Sam's influence, the rational of those two.

I could head in if I had to. I heard the plow. But my mind's just not there. It isn't on work. It's on Brie. She and I could use a day together just to reconnect without our typical weekend running around—the buckets and mops and Comet and Simple Green. It's nice having her take care of that all week. And if we really did get as much as they said we would, it looks like we'll have a full three days to ourselves to do exactly that. Reconnect.

My drowsy eyes settle on her. Curled on her hip, ash-blond hair spread clumsily across the pillowcase and one arm tucked underneath. We're almost wifelike, though we fight like cats and dogs. But all couples do. She's like a tide, amazing when she's high but barren when she's low. I'm surprised she has stayed with me as long as she has. After all, we met at a toy store, and I'm not referring to the kiddie kind.

I realize this isn't the most socially acceptable place to meet someone, and believe me, that's not why I went there—to meet someone. And the fact that we did has hooked us into several awkward exchanges, you know, when someone asks that inevitable question: "So, where did you guys meet?" It doesn't matter how upscale or ritzy the place is. The only thing they hear is *adult shop*.

So it's impossible to be one hundred percent truthful even with friends. Even were I to share our rather refined introduction, they'd still concoct their own seedy account. So that would be why there are some aspects of my life I just don't share with others.

Besides, this was an upscale lesbian shop, women only, women owned. Not even gay men are allowed on the premises. But beyond the estrogen prerequisite, as far as patrons go, they're nondiscriminating. I ran into smug baby dykes, tough bikers, athletic hikers. Even hemp-skirted hippies who, I could only imagine, enjoy their sex pot enhanced. But one thing's for certain, there's always an overabundance of women on the prowl or boisterously chatting it up at the checkout counter. Waiting. Watching everyone who walks in. That type.

Even if I were to go with, let's just say, ulterior motives, I think I'd be one of the few who made her way out empty-handed. And leaving empty-handed was precisely what I expected as I pulled up to that concrete curb that day. I hoped to find a book is all.

I passed a vending machine anchored into the sidewalk, where a quarter can buy you one of two LGBTQ publications. I bought one. Inside the shop, rich mahogany and thick velvet chairs, studded and pink, arranged in a small circle. There's a desk, an antique silver register that doesn't work, tall ceilings, and drop lights. Lush, frivolous, seductive. A covert spot, out a ways, so you could visit with dignity half intact. Still, it's not like I went there regularly.

Nerves hit when I walked in. So I rushed past a shelf (clumsily) and bam, there she was.

That would be how quickly my day, my life, just altered. My heart ran away from me. My palms all gummy, brain in a fog. Lean like a tennis player. Hot like July. She just drew me in.

I had to remind myself that this was a lesbian shop, after all, so the inevitable question was already answered for me. No, she did not look it. And yes, she was alone, or so it seemed.

I glanced again, who wouldn't, but I did keep a distance assuming her drop-dead gorgeous girlfriend was surely around the corner ready to pounce. Sliding my finger on the spine of a well-stocked paperback, I sliced it out from the others. Then I flipped, finding page one so that I, too, could pretend to read.

It wasn't long before I caught her glancing my way, coquettish, and the mere thought of it sank my stomach. Then I smiled. She was euphoria. Really.

I took a (therapeutic) breath, and then I let it out to calm myself before wandering beyond peripheral views. And I felt a spurt of confidence, so I went with it. I held on to that charming smile until her eyes peered over the spine of her book, intentionally or so I thought in my direction. She was maybe into me. I was starting to feel certain of it. I was incapable of knowing where that glance could ultimately lead us. Here.

She continued her tease and I continued to muster the courage to slip in, reaching uncertainly across to choose another title. I do recall brushing against a bare arm not so subtly and she noticed. Our eyes settled in as if in bed together.

Eventually I said something under the chatter.

I saw her mouth say something back, sinking my attention to succulent pink lips. And her voice matched. It was plump like a fruit. I liked it. I thought about it for a little while. I lost gravity.

I flipped pages, standing as close as I could in hopes that I didn't appear overly interested or, worse, desperate. I was pretty sure this was something she got often. Me, this, like a cartoon with hearts spinning. But that silence, it eroded any fleeting sense of cool. Those jitters, they overwhelmed. And that's about when I decided to just walk away, give up, and stroll past the DVDs to calm the pounding.

As did she.

I still had both books in hand, but I picked a movie and she mirrored me. Then I put it down, backing myself into a fully stocked shelf of massage oils in every flavor imaginable. Cherry, vanilla, apple blossom—even milk chocolate. And she was next to me. I gave her a side-glance. She reciprocated.

"I'm Ryan," I said, extending a hand.

"Brie." I saw her lips pronounce her name like a kiss. Her grip hard; her skin gentle. She was over-the-top my type. And the longer I looked, the more I liked. Here we were, face-to-face, and she was unbelievable.

Unbelievable as in way out of my league, I knew that. But I'd just met her, so I felt bold. I had nothing to lose. I chose a flavor and read it. Out loud. "This would be interesting," I remember saying with my nervous laugh. "Don't you think?" Then I slipped in and said, "Sweet Honey Pie." Only when she smiled did her cheeks crease. I unscrewed its cap and, half serious, half mocking, recited what I saw. "Warm and provocative." It would be heavenly, I imagined, were it on her. Why was I mocking it?

I gave this performance. I told her, "Here, give me your hand," and she actually did. But this wasn't really me. She played along, we were onstage, and it was almost natural between us. She made me feel something powerful. Someone self-assured. So when I touched her skin, I lingered a bit. Her hand was delicate in mine. Her fingers just as slender as she. She drew me out. She still does. The oil glided along the length of her wrist. I asked if she liked it.

"I do."

I asked again. I wanted to know, chuckling.

"Yeah," she replied rather harmlessly.

We tipped our heads. I heard her laugh, at ourselves, at the situation. "So what are you reading there," I teased.

"Oh." She flushed and covered her eyes with those fingers of hers. "That's nothing." And she left that book on a cardboard box of somethings right beside her.

Soon enough we were at the edge of reading chairs sharing ourselves, both meaningless and deep. My elbows resting on my knees and fingers locked as she reached behind her head and wrapped that sunny hair into a loose tie. At what point I'm not sure, but it dawned on me that neither of us was listening to a word the other was saying.

"Could I make you dinner?" In truth, I was dizzied at the thought of her in my space. But we shared a meal. We shared more than that. It was on that couch where it all started. It was down the hall where her bra pinched open and she fell out of it and into my room and against that wall and then onto the bed. I had to tone her playful down.

That tie twirled around and around her wrist, tugging. *That hurts.*

She couldn't move. Her jeans were so loose that my hand slid into that gap.

She couldn't see when I left the room. When I returned, I kissed down her sides and up with ice between my lips that melted, dripping to the sheet. I watched her flinch as it touched. I let it pool. She was unzipped, and ice wet elastic as her hips rose and they pulled off and parted around me and water trickled down to where her thighs met. It melted against her and inside her.

I didn't much think of the consequences that night. She left my place that morning when the sky was still black, tucking my number into her back pocket. And I woke with the sun, drunk with sleep deprivation and desperate to hear that tangerine voice once more. The taste of her coconut lip balm still on my own lips, but she was gone. She was all diamonds and European vacations, and I had to have more of it.

And the hours and days fell away. She might've mistaken the night for something else. I didn't chase her. I couldn't. Even if I had the sense to do so at that point, I let her leave my house without taking her number in exchange. A few times, I went back to that shop just in case, departing empty-handed. I'd become one of those I abhor, the idlers and watchers at that adult shop, though not intentionally and not for the same reasons. I didn't talk to the same people. I didn't want to. I kept to myself. I was different somehow.

She made me wait six days for her call. She made me wonder. She made me think all sorts of things. She made me miss her, crave her. But she was worth that wait. I was punch-drunk.

And we were inseparable. We were adventurous. It's the nature of how we met. The expectation of impermanence stripped our inhibitions. The risk added that much more. And the stakes grew even higher. I certainly did not want it to be love. I had something better.

❖

Brie

It was some idle weekend in mid-July, I can't remember exactly. That time in early evening when the birds are screaming but melodic. I'm thinking two years ago, but it feels more like five. Chris and I were sitting on that swing that hung from her porch. The sun stayed up late along with us.

She had this way of sulking that begged for attention. Anyone's really, but it always got mine. She'd rest her elbow and chin on the armrest and pretend she was unbreakable.

"No really, what's wrong," I asked.

"I said nothing. Why?"

"You just seem distant, that's all."

Every night, her roommate would go off for a run. She slipped headphones on, strapped music around her bicep, and laced up. She'd just taken off.

"My aunt's coming up," I hear. "I probably won't have any time to see you."

I wanted to know how long. She said a week. It was a family thing.

She was nudging the swing with her toe on the rail and, once in a while, she'd glance at me with those sullen eyes. I'd study her lips, her unshaped yet perfectly shaped brows, that bush of hair that curled over her forehead, and the straggles near her ear. She had the face of a schoolgirl and a body that was far from curvaceous. She wore jeans even in the summertime. They were loose and cut for men; she had no hips to fill them. Her T-shirt was always well fitted, white.

I kicked feet over her lap. She reached around and pulled my knees against her chest, running short fingernails up and down my shins. I tried to kiss that pout but she wouldn't budge. I heard, "I don't want you to go."

"I want you to come," I said.

"I can't." She wasn't happy. "You've been gone. You're always gone. Why do we do this?"

"I don't like when you get this way," I said.

"As soon as you get there, you'll forget all about this."

Of course I won't, I thought. But I didn't say that aloud. I couldn't exactly quit at that point and work retail for the rest of my life, nor did I want to. It was just our summer.

While I stewed in frustration, she was tugging my hand around her. I couldn't look up though I tried. When I did, she wouldn't look away. She was somber and now I was, too. I felt sad lips on mine and then adoring hands down my shoulders. It was a gloomy kiss that turned away. She lifted a knee, clearly withdrawn. It felt like she was leaving.

I asked if she'd wait for me, just a year and then I'd be done. She didn't want to answer. Maybe she couldn't. Maybe I shouldn't have asked. Maybe I shouldn't have come that day. But she kissed me again, this time sweetly, but it was deeper than that. It was the kind of kiss that weakens you and strengthens you at the same time. My hands were over her shirt but hers were beneath mine. Her touch made my heart race. She leaned for me as if I were backing away, but I wasn't. She needed me more than I understood her. And our sounds were so heavy yet achingly silent and secretive.

The swing was gentle and then stopped as she steadied me; I was dipping, touching without knowing. She was at my ear when I heard, "Let's go," and she lifted me. Her voice tickled. We were outside and then inside and I was falling onto the bed and she was sinking over me on a knee the way she always did. That kiss was inexperienced, but I inhaled her. I felt my shirt hike up and her hair prickle my flesh. Her tongue at my breasts made me swell, made me whimper, made my knees rise above her.

Until she rose at the edge of her bed, tugging my shorts off lifted hips, and elastic clung to my ankles before they slid off. I spread my elbows and lifted a knee as her arms made an X and pulled over her head. She sank down over me, pushed me apart, and wet me. She was teasing me, fucking me until I moaned in her mouth and again. And she crawled down me.

I was gripping shoulders as hair brushed against my thigh and her breath felt heated and damp. It was an ache and a throb and then sublime and she held me apart and down and consumed me while restraining me. And I listened to myself, to those birds, to her muffled and moaning against me as she came.

My thighs like a vise trembling when I did.

When she fell beside me, we didn't speak. We glistened. The sun was still with us. The screen slapping and the shower surging through the old pipes as the house became inhabited again but our door remained shut. I crawled over her and kissed her until the sun fell asleep.

The following day, it was over. "I can't miss you again," she told me. And that was that.

❖

"Yes, you can…Brie Hamilton…It's our power. It's out…Account number? To tell you the truth, I have no idea. I'm so sorry. This would be under Gabriella Ryan, my partner…Okay, but can you be more specific? I mean, are we talking a few minutes, hours…Days?…I understand…No, that's all…Yeah. Thanks."

As I hang up, I'm shivering.

My hair's damp from the shower, and I can hear Ryan on the phone with her sister, cackling. I used some of her paste on the front of my hair to get it up and out of my eyes for once. I don't know how it'll turn out. I've never tried it. It smells nice enough, like her.

She wears her hair up, short on the sides. It's way thick, unlike mine. She's got her denim shirt on with the sleeves cuffed up, untucked. She grins at me occasionally around the corner, pacing.

That's when I start to wonder—am I one of those leap first, look later types? I keep asking myself that. I try not to be. I like to plan, ponder, weigh it all out—to a fault usually. I'd like to get through life without one stitch of regret. But I've already fallen short of that goal, haven't I? I have regrets, the biggest of which being this right here.

That small part in me, that part that was just a little too enamored, the part that was regrettably drawn in to the allure that is Ryan, kicked my rational side's butt. Because in reality, she and I are completely incompatible. She's obnoxious. Hard. Embarrassing. Insecure. Awkward. Stocky. Possessive. Gruff. Stubborn. Set in her ways. Controlling. Insensitive. And self-centered. Why did I not see this?

In stark contrast, I'm a pretty upbeat person. I'm a big-time problem solver. A great negotiator. And persuasive. I know how to work people when I need to. I'm excessively organized. And I think shit through, like I said. I find the problem, weigh solutions, reach a conclusion. Case closed.

At the comfortable age of forty-two, Ryan's proudest accomplishment in life is this house, and I'll bet you anything she plans to stay in it for the rest of her God-given life. Seducing one woman after another after another. Probably two at the same time, you know—that's how she lost her last girlfriend.

I will admit, she has a certain allure. A charm, at least in the beginning. And beyond the chemistry (which is indisputable), she offers a home that's already made—complete with a comfortable savings, a stable job, it's nice. Who isn't impressed with that?

It's a lot like home.

Were it up to me, I'd prefer to live downtown. A townie, she calls me. I like background noise. I need civilization and little comforts. The spa. The gym. The pub on Saturday night. And townies, I guarantee you, are enjoying just that. Shops are open. Food roasting and sautéing and simmering. Folks chatting over the brims of steaming mugs filled with Sumatra plus nonfat milk in cozy cafés that have condensation across their bright frontages. Happy people smiling as they pass one another on bustling sidewalks that are cleared and shoveled and crusted with salt. College kids pecking at their keyboards and hidden behind textbooks, moms strolling through racks and racks of crisp new trousers for the office, road rage and traffic jams and hordes of pedestrians wrapped in fur-lined hoods amid this milky landscape. Towns are open and lit, laborers are laboring, and plows are grinding trails for cars like mamas guiding their little ducklings. Sigh.

Meanwhile, out here in farmland, I can't even get two bars. The television's out. Internet's down. Heater's dead. There are no neighbors to even check up on us should something seriously go wrong, which makes me more than a little uncomfortable, and I don't even want to think about the predicament we'd be in if we ever needed an ambulance. We're cold, buried, disconnected. Isolated. And she's happy about that. She's actually happy. This is a good time for her. I know because she's loudly conversing and cackling about that right now with her sister.

So what's kept me with Ryan this long? That's the question of the day. Mom definitely wasn't on board with my decision to truck my meager belongings into this place. She wanted me to settle in and live a little. Not jump, essentially, from one relationship to the next. One long, heartbreaking, absolutely idyllic relationship to, well, someone I met in a porn shop. And, no, I didn't tell Mom that part.

I'm not jumping, I told her. *I need roots. Stability.* To the contrary, Ryan was so low pressure and, quite honestly, the most stand-offish woman I've ever known. That right there got me. It's all I needed. A distraction, someone to get my mind off this constant ache in my chest. Live a little, cut loose. And I could leave at any time and she wouldn't blink an eye. She didn't even have my number. She let the chips fall as they may. I liked that. I liked that a lot.

Still, what possessed me to tote my life here in that dinged-up old truck just because some woman happened to be great in the sack? Well, amazing, I'll give her that. But that's not enough. It's not.

So case closed, right? I need to get out. Get on with my life.

I pour myself a glass of cold water from the sink, still starstruck by this groovy kitchen. White marble up half the wall. Cracked plaster's freshly painted white by yours truly. Open shelving over the counters where plates and cups and that shabby teapot pile atop one another. The purple flowers I set out just a few days ago are wide open now.

I've paid my dues. I deserve this much.

As I listen to her conversation wrap up, I marvel at how communal it feels in here, the long island down the center and backless metal stools where we've chatted and feasted before work on scones and waffles. The ceiling's low exposed beams. And her rows and rows of spices, so colorful and symmetrical on small wall shelves under a large clock, which tells the accurate battery-powered time. It's the only timepiece in this house currently working. I marvel as if it's the last time I'm ever going to see it.

I wonder if her next girlfriend will be equally impressed. If she'll even deserve it.

I rehearse.

I'm sorry, Ryan, I'm so sorry. I, uh, I...

I've been thinking a lot lately, and I'm wondering if we went too fast.

No, no, no, that's not it. That's just patronizing.

"Ryan," I yell, not at all gracefully. Yet the minute it clicks that my thoughts have found a voice, I freeze up. She tells her sister she has to go.

They're such a close family. I've met her father. Not her sister, but at least her father. He looked me over as if I were disingenuous, yet he knew nothing about me. There's one who'll be pleased I'm out of the picture.

Soon her reply rounds the corner and walks down the hall. I see no backing out now. I could do without this dreaded anxiety nonetheless. I was hoping more along the lines of relief or even happy.

Ryan. We need to talk.

I pace the length of the kitchen nervously from stove to sink and back again, leaning against the island for a drink because I'm completely parched.

She asks how the call went. What call? She just looks at me

puzzled as I ponder the question. And that's when it dawns on me—the electric company. And I tell her in a long-winded sort of way.

"Okay."

I notice the way she's now concentrating on me. Her fist is supporting her chin. She nods. I rant some more. She listens, though slightly less engaged and a bit more glassy-eyed and drifting into disinterested.

"We need to talk." My words fall through the air like ash— unbearably slow. Here I am in the spotlight, and it's too much. As I heat up, I take another drink.

"What about?" She's nonchalant, digging around in the drawer for something. Then her attention shifts to the sink and the few dishes piled in it. I study her thighs as she walks over.

After some clatter, she turns on the faucet only to realize that we have but a few drops of hot left and she just used those up. She needs a haircut. It's scruffy. She washes a cup and a small pastry plate, setting them on the rack to dry.

"About this," I tell her.

She turns around, fingers curled under the counter just behind. "This?" She's small eyed now with a crinkled forehead. Haven't I tried for months to get her to listen to me, pay attention to me, hear me out—even support me? Now that I have her undivided attention, I don't think I like it. I don't want it. Brush me off again and give me a reason to fume. That would make this so much easier. But instead she listens, appearing confused.

I drop my gaze to the thick floorboards. "Yes," I say.

This is difficult.

I think my mouth opens a few times, but nothing comes of it. Then I'm telling her, "Maybe not so much *this* but..." I lose the flow, but do find two words. "I'm unhappy."

She jumps in to blame the job, concluding with "That's expected." I hear "I know" and something about hope. But she knows it's not about that job, and I tell her as much.

She looks confused again, making her eyebrows more pronounced. I notice the gray in her hair, which I like. She doesn't, but I do.

"It's so much more than that." I'm rubbing my eye. I'm just exhausted. "It's being away from everything—from family," I tell her. "I don't like that."

I'm accustomed to hearing appliances hum, the television, water streaming through pipes. But it's stagnant, and that clock is ticking persistently. "You know Mom's always saying she wants me to come back, that my room's—"

"Brie, you're not a kid anymore. You're a grown woman."

She makes my anger swell. Must she be condescending?

"What exactly are you saying? That you're moving back to Portland?"

"It's something like that, something I've thought about," I say.

"Since when?"

"Since…I don't know," I say. When she looks at me, I can only shrug my shoulders. "I don't have a job."

"But I do." Why does she have to be this way? I want her to understand what I'm saying without my saying it. I wish she'd be happy for me.

"We don't have that kind of…relationship. That kind of situation."

"What do you mean, *that kind of relationship?*" she asks.

I just roll my eyes. I don't even know what to say. This should be evident. This is not a question.

"Honey," she says, "I'm sorry I haven't been…Look, it's hard. I know you need time."

But it's not time I need.

"I don't know if this, this *us*, is what I really want right now. And I'm not sure…" I so don't want to say this. I can think of a million other things I'd rather be doing right now besides breaking up with my girlfriend. But I do—eventually—just say it. "If this is going to work."

"I don't understand," she says. "What are you saying?"

My hands are in a prayer over my mouth.

"No—why are you saying this? We get on about things, I know that. That's not how I am."

She's waiting to hear something different.

"You don't want to do this. Can we just get through?"

"I need to slow down, doll, figure things out." My throat closes when I say that. It feels final, and that final, for some reason, is feeling sort of sad. She looks sad. She must get what I'm saying now.

I didn't expect to feel so awful. I don't like who I am right now.

"I'll help you figure things out," she says.

"No, I need to do this on my own."

"You can't leave everything here."

"I've pondered it."

I'm watching reality sink in.

Then she says, "Don't do this to me."

There's anger in her words. She leaves the room.

Which means I need to leave. I know my 4x4 can get me through this, and that sure beats feeling this right here. It's claustrophobic, stifling. I guess I hadn't thought this through. Now I'm scrambling to find an out.

If I could just be alone. Once I reach the main drag, the roads will clear up. The plows are out. I can hear them. I have no choice.

I make a call to Hops and order a Caesar salad for pickup.

When I hang up, she comes back and rests on the counter. She's just watching me from across the room. I can't decide if she's livid or what. I notice her fingers, though, thick and creased.

She knows now. She's covering her eyes. My heart breaks.

"Tell me what I did wrong," she says.

I can't let a girl cry, I just can't. I go over and do this thing with my finger to lift up her chin and I say, "Ryan, Ryan…" I pull her in, but she's holding me tighter than I am her. "You didn't do anything."

"I don't want to do this again," she says.

I don't know what to say back. She stopped breathing. Her nose is brushing my collarbone.

I hear, "I love you."

"It's okay—we're going to be okay." But it's not okay. She's breathing into me. Her eyes aren't angry. Something settles, or does it?

And she's pressing her thumb across my lips. I feel the pressure on my teeth. She's so lost, yet she's never been this focused. I wonder how it would feel if she kissed me. I feel her pulse. I want her to. Maybe this will be our good-bye. I'm still ashamed that I'm not at all shying away. It's paralyzing.

Why think about it? I meet there, right in the middle of us. I don't understand why. But I want to help her. When I don't push her chest, when my lungs swell against hers, her lips take a part of me. I don't know what to do.

They feel like Chris and then they don't anymore. That's when my palms shove her chest away. That's when she falls into me.

I take a step back and wonder, why did I do that? She won't even look at me.

"I can't do this," I say. "We can't."

I do want you.

"Why?"

"I'm not sure," I say.

"I don't understand."

I don't say anything back. I just step into my boots. I get my coat from the closet. My keys are in the pocket, but I double-check.

I get my phone. I leave my water glass. It's empty.

She makes me angry again.

"You want excitement. You want newness," I start in. "You want butterflies and giddiness and the thrill of impermanence. You don't want complacent. You've told me that over and over and over again. Well, I hate to break it to you, but that impermanence you wanted so badly? Here it is."

The doorknob sticks when I turn it. Outside the cold stuns me, but it doesn't calm my temper. Why was I so mean?

It's secluded. There is nothing here.

My truck beeps as I approach. I pull the handle, and an avalanche tumbles down onto my hand. I side-sit into the seat and turn the engine, flipping the mirror to catch a trickle down my cheek. I feel it, too. It's warm, until I wipe it off, stepping out to brush off the window while the engine warms.

Past the hood are those painted steps and that *Circa 1856* placard I see every time we pull up. But the place looks empty. Did I make it that way? *She'll be okay.*

I don't love her. Why her touch can still do this to me—break me down, weaken me—it's unsettling.

❖

Have you ever wondered how much you could take before you actually break? Because I am right now.

And what I wouldn't give for a plate of breakup food and an excuse to stay in a pair of Abercrombie & Fitch sweatpants all day watching romantic comedies. That or a bottle of merlot celebrating the fact that I'm the youngest ever to experience a midlife crisis. But short of all that, I'll settle for takeout and a visit with my BFF.

As my ex's driveway (I like the sound of that, *ex*) fades in my rearview mirror, I head toward the 91, which takes me clear into town. But I'm doing so with a mess of tears smearing my face. It's my own personal pity party.

I'm able to make out a few painted arrows through the blur, past wipers flipping left to right, left to right like some sort of highway hypnosis.

To break the monotony, and since I'm a born-and-bred glutton for punishment, always have been, I click through my music and stop at that song Chris sent me. What kind of a person uses a love song to say good-bye? It's maddening. But the only way I'm going to cry myself out and face her (which I do plan to do) is to get over her—for good.

So I stop at that song, a good song, an old song, and the first chords are entirely drowned out by whining wiper blades. Then it repeats, and repeats again, and those vocals get gooier and that day is this day and she's leaving me all over again. It hurts like a brand-new bandage.

How'd I land myself in this mess? Just look at me out here trucking down an empty highway crying my eyes out. And I'm having a pretty good time at that, playing my heartbreak song and singing along.

At least until that intrusive ringtone gets going on my phone. Someone's calling in the middle of this moment, right during my therapeutic meltdown, and I'd love to just ignore it. But I can't, and besides, I need to grow up one of these days and get a thicker skin. Before answering, I clear my throat and find I'm able to speak without so much as a crack.

But the first thing I hear is Ryan asking, "Is it something I did?" Which is the last conversation I want to be in. Then she goes on to say, "Because if I did something to hurt you, I take it back."

But driving in good weather is tricky enough, and I wonder why this can't just wait until I'm not doing ten things all at once.

A street sign points me to the right as a pine tree flies by and I flip the blinker and steer around the bend.

I finally answer once my wheel's just about straight. "It's not you, doll." When I open my glove compartment to get a tissue, all I find are folded-up napkins from visits through drive-up coffee shops. Which reminds me, I could sure use a Venti right about now.

"Why'd you let me," she wants to know, and then relaxes her voice to say, "kiss you?"

Then I sense a little tug and glide, so I grip the wheel and pump my brakes.

"Did you want me to stop?"

Did I want her to stop? That's not a question I can even answer because, to be perfectly honest, in that moment with her back there, no. I did not want her to stop. I wanted her to keep going. I wanted her to unfasten and unbutton, open this blouse right down to this way too expensive La Perla bra. I wanted her to want me and hold me and do those things to me, persuade me, prove to me, coax me, make sense with me or just confuse the heck out of me a little more. I wanted to forget or maybe disregard it all. Maybe I wanted her one more time before I didn't have her anymore. But sharing that little bit of information with her is not the right thing to do. Sharing that would only take her and me and this in the wrong direction.

"Are you even going to answer that?" she asks into my silence. But my head's sidetracked by the actual act of driving, rapidly encroaching dangers, and frost that's now veiling much of my view and leaving a miniscule arch of clarity where the defrost hits the glass. "Could you at least call me when you get there? So I know you're alive."

"I'll call you," I say.

As soon as we hang up, I bite my thumb and shimmy a glove off, flinging it to the passenger seat. But, what the hell, this is a sheet of ice.

When I slam the brake, it kicks my truck into a tailspin, a move that triggers a huge and oddly unexpected rush of adrenaline. And I start whirling in circles, blurred circles, bracing myself against the dashboard and watching this scene rotate around me three hundred and sixty degrees until my rear dives headfirst down the wrong side of the road and I'm shoved into my steering wheel.

That's when I brake again, hard, and the ABS gets right at it. Soon enough, my head fits right back into the headrest and it dawns on me that I've finally come to a stop. I sure wish somebody would inform my head of the same.

And with my wheels spinning but taking me nowhere, I decide it's time to call AAA. They'll get me out of this, so I fish for my membership card and phone. Which is when I catch a glimpse of myself in the visor mirror, and—let's be frank—these eyes have seen whiter days.

Emergency roadside service. What's your emergency?

"I'm in a snowbank. I think."

In less than a minute, he's dispatched a truck to get me.

I decide to zip up and reglove and do my waiting up on the hood since the engine's warm and I'm feeling a little claustrophobic in this truck. Besides, as much as my situation screams helpless female, I'd rather not play that role.

Once I get situated, I pull out my phone and speed-dial Hadley, who picks up on the second ring and we begin as if continuing our last conversation.

"You were right," I say.

"That it never plays out like you script it?"

"Yup."

"So it's over?" she asks.

"It's over," I announce.

"I'm...just—ouch."

"I'm relieved. It's behind me. I said it. I *did* it."

"How? And when?"

"I don't know," I say. "About an hour ago."

"An hour ago? Is she there with you?"

"No, I'm on the road. I quite literally left her," I say.

"But the roads are—"

"The roads are fine. I'm fine. Everything is fine."

As fine as fine can be. As I say this, I sound as calm as a therapist asking, *How does that make you feel?* My words are mellow and monotone and you'd think I'd swallowed a half dozen Valium. "And you know what? I feel great. Like, really great. A burden has been lifted."

"Are you sure you're all right? You sound sort of numb. Nasal."

"I know, I know. I've been sobbing. But to be out of there. It's good. Tell me something, though. How do you deal with the moments right after when you actually live with someone? You know, it took all I had to just say it and do it and then I got all sentimental and I was starting to cave. So I took off. I had to."

"How did she take it?"

"Not good," I say.

"Oh, man."

"But you know? That's not my problem. I'm taking care of myself."

"You are. You did the right thing."

"Did I?"

"Oh my God, of course."

I breathe a sigh of relief. "Thanks, doll. Right now I really don't want to think about somebody else. I need to think about me and my happiness. Move ahead after riding this merry-go-round with her for a year now."

"Come over. We need to talk."

"I'm actually like twenty-five minutes away." Okay, more like five but I still need to get out of this snowbank, something I'm not sharing because I'll never hear the end of it.

"I crashed with Jess last night," she whispers.

"And how'd that—?"

"My car died. Oh, and by the way," she adds, "we lost power."

"So did we. You're going to tell me everything. But for now, can I pick you up anything? Lunch…coffee? I called an order in before I left."

"Just get over here and off the road," she tells me before we both hang up.

When Audrey arrives—that's the tow truck driver—I hop off the hood, flag her down, and try to help out, though I'm more of a distraction than anything. This is quite possibly, no positively, the first auto club save I've had from a female. Suddenly I'm more than willing to play the damsel in distress. In fact, I wish I'd totaled my truck so I could get a ride in hers.

This girl has the sexiest eyes, eyes I wish would keep looking my direction like that, and that square jaw, and when she gets on her knees to hitch the bumper, I catch those tight jeans and cuffs. She's soon able to lift me right up and out of the bank, and after a few maneuvers, I'm incredibly ungrateful to be heading back in the right direction as opposed to her repair shop.

Disheartened, I put in a quick call to Mom to square away my plans. Right away, she wants to know how we're faring.

"We're...okay. A lot of snow, but we're fine." She worries incessantly. I have to lie—even if I'm hanging off a cliff and ready to slip to my demise. "What about you?"

"Just a dusting." I can actually hear her sitting down, a combination of a sigh and a...something. I'm not quite sure what. "How's everything otherwise?"

"Oh, you know." She rustles. "As to be expected." Which is just the prompt needed to launch her on a diatribe about their latest trip to the casino, her blood pressure, the neighbors, her leaky faucet, and her Wonder Bread lunch, which Dad's busy making as we speak. "How's the job search?" she wants to know.

"Bad."

"No interviews yet?"

"Not a one." On the job front, Mom's surprisingly indifferent. It comes from having never worked a day in her life.

"Well, don't get discouraged. These things take time, you know."

And since the topic of work has been broached, the home economist segues into the latest happenings at Dad's office including his pain-in-the-ass boss and a new girl who's completely incompetent. So I ask about Grams and the line settles. I interpret this to mean she's within earshot. Then she's bemoaning the loss of her empty nest, their lack of alone time, how much she enjoyed it. Which is when I'm tempted to say my good-byes and abandon the next topic altogether.

But I toss it out regardless, testing waters to see if my room might possibly be available just for a few weeks. The woman couldn't be happier.

"So did you and Ryan—"

"Yes, we broke up."

"You shouldn't move in so fast. I told you that much," begins her sermon. "Does this have anything to do with Chris?" Every time she brings up the one that got away, I get unsettled and uncomfortable and want to wheedle my way out of the conversation, which is what I do.

By the time we hang up, I'm pulling up to the parking garage right behind Hops.

❖

Ryan

I'm relieved, no lie, when the power comes back for good. One minute I'm brooding in self-pity. The next a lamp is on and the clock winks *12:00 12:00 12:00*. The house is back, and man have I missed all of that hot air.

Which would be why I'm posed over a heating grate looking like someone who just got voted off a survival reality show. And then my head is filled with questions like, why do they film those shows on tropical islands? Would it not be more interesting if they threw castaways in the middle of a New England winter? Brie said once, while we were glued to the television watching a rerun, that she thought it was solely to encourage contestants to prance around barely clothed. Not that I mind. Make it *Lesbian Survival* and I'm in. I would love to watch ten to twenty scarcely clad and well-built lesbians trapped on an island, sleeping together in makeshift tents. Forget watching it, I would go on that show. But I digress.

Now that I've been officially discarded by the above-mentioned, my first order of business is a warm bubble bath with oatmeal soap and this loofah. And while this old faucet always sticks, I eventually get it cranked up to full blast.

Just hot. Scalding hot water, which makes the bubbles rise and rise and rise. In no time, steam eddies up like the white circling a candy cane.

Then I let that heat thaw the only part of my anatomy I'm brave enough to expose, and that would be my hands. Submerged in water, they start to throb and tingle, but I find the pain utterly rejuvenating.

Before the tub's full, I tune in to NPR, which is singing a brooding mix of blues tonight. How appropriate, I contemplate, as I listen to the deep baritone barreling through the record needle.

When I do finally dip a toe in, it numbs, yet with some fortitude, I submit and submerge. And it feels clean. I lean my head back against the curve, and I begin to ponder all the work I have ahead of me next week. I'll need to relocate my brain for it. I know I will, somehow. Then I sink even deeper and let the bubbles creep over my shoulders.

The blues. It's how humidity would sound if it had a voice on a sugar-sticky summer night. I'm done with winter already. Take me to June, and I'll sleep with windows wide open as piercing crickets harmonize across the field. The thought of sun and sweat and vegetation, it's so much more alive than I am right now.

My tiny bathroom is damp with a trace of sandalwood that shimmies through the air and beads on the walls. I pick up that pink razor from the side of the tub, soap my leg, and begin to de-hair myself. It's ridiculous that I need reading glasses to shave anymore. I'm not that old.

Eventually my legs are presentable, and the vents quiet to a mild gush. The scald of water, that relaxing burn, starts to chill. Bubbles burst. I rise from the porcelain and am toweling each arm when I hear the phone ring in the bedroom and I run to get it before it drops to voice mail. I answer as if I couldn't care less that someone called even though I'm glad someone did.

I hear, "Hey."

"Brie?" My voice is audibly inflected.

"Yes."

I'm actually surprised she called and find I'm speechless for a second. I've never been good with words, with writing, with talking. But that urge to crawl through the line, to be next to her and show her what I want to say.

"You wanted me to call when I got here." There's a pause, some rustling on the receiver, followed by a short-lived laugh in the background. One of those can't-hold-it-in-any-longer outbursts. "And I'm fine. I'm with Hadley."

I catch myself nodding, but I don't actually respond.

"Another thing. Jessie, we're at her place, she wanted to see if you maybe wanted to meet up for dinner tonight." Another frustrating silence and then, in a whisper, "She doesn't know."

This whisper feels like a secret we share, albeit an unfortunate one, and I can't help but find comfort in that. That she and I still have secrets. I allow myself to feel that. "I see." Back in the bathroom, I distract myself with an uneven lump in the curve of my nail, one that I need to file down after we hang up.

"I'll let you handle that."

"Okay," I tell her, reluctantly.

"Anyways, if you wanted to come, we'll be at Hops. Around four."

The medicine cabinet whines when I open it, grab the file, and close it again. My hazy reflection peers back at me, my freckled décolletage (as Brie calls it) yet to fade from last summer.

"It'd be nice," I finally offer. "Let her know I'll make the drive up."

As I end the call, I take another timid glimpse in the mirror. A drop of water has muscled its way off a strand of hair and settled on my cheek.

It's over, I tell myself. I'm starting over. Again.

CHAPTER FIVE: ELLA AND SAM

Ella

Chocolate biscotti with powdered sugar (plus no alarm clock): it's the best way to start your day. Especially on mornings like this. I grab a bite of breakfast before cinching my robe around my waist. Then I settle deep into my armchair.

I reach for my iPad, slide it on, and take another meditative sip of some seriously hot coffee. It tastes of cream, no sugar, just the way I like. Occasionally I hear bursts of air in girlish shrieks and muffled blades scraping the blacktop down the way. It breaks an almost religious silence.

Our news site loads on the screen with its obligatory weather warning: *A Winter Storm Warning is in effect through eleven a.m. Friday with heavy snow and periods of ice and sleet.* Eleven o'clock, they say. We have our work cut out for us. But the worst of the storm ends in a few hours. So I make a mental note to give my proactive wife this news. *Rapidly accumulating snow along with drifts may hinder travel, and residents are urged to stay indoors.* That's when I hear creaks in the floorboards, which would be Sam fixing our bed. *Snowfall will begin to taper off at eleven a.m., with main roads safe for travel by nightfall.*

Soon enough, the staircase creaks one weary step at a time. I rush to finish what I'm doing, expecting her typical morning interruptions.

After that time, travelers are strongly urged to stay on main roadways, where plows will be working hard to provide clearance for emergency vehicles.

I always check the news before my inbox. I have to know what happened in the world while I slept. And as message after message drops in, all I can do is watch in utter dismay.

I get a *good morning* from Sam, who's more than mildly groggy. She's carrying a full cup of coffee as she shuffles to my side.

"Morning," I mumble through a kiss.

Then I get, "Don't you look adorable this morning," a compliment I brush off with a Mona Lisa smile.

She wants to know how much we got overnight. Her words breeze my ear just long enough for her focus to fall curiously to my screen, which is when she offers a bit of advice. "Unplug, babe. Work can wait. The whole town's closed down." She's more than a touch delighted about this little snow day off, ambling away and grabbing a few bits of kindling from the pile to heat us up. Then she yanks her loose sweatpants with her only free hand.

"I need to reach Ryan before she comes in," I say. "In an hour I guarantee she'll be on that highway and that, right now, is downright dangerous."

My wife does hear me, though she's already cross-legged and lost at her woodstove. Amid the scent of wood smoke and scorched wood chips, I can still detect the hint of sweet vanilla candle wax. I compose my email on this tiny screen keyboard and eventually tap send. I lock it, place it on the table, and grab my mug as my wife returns with her own.

"So, tell me, how are things with our friend Ryan," she asks, sinking into our worn-down couch.

And this is just the opening I need to vent.

"Not good," I tell her. "Brie's in some sort of depression, she tells me. Insists on landing a job that's as good if not better than her last. Really. I say, drop those expectations." Then I add tentatively, "Or move. I'm not telling Ryan any of this, of course."

"She's looking, though, right?"

"She sits in that coffee shop every day," I say, taking an introspective pause. "And every day, I'm trapped with Ryan. And it's really starting to wear at me. I'm somewhere between wanting to help and telling her what I honestly think—which is, Break it off already. But lovelorn still thinks Brie is the be-all and end-all, and she takes herself as a complete failure for not making it work. I'm just trying to get a sense as to why that is. Brie doesn't come across, at least to me, as someone who…Let's just say, I overheard a conversation just the other day, at least half of it. Ryan was going off, clearly they both were. I went over a bit later just to check, what's up, you know? She didn't say a thing, so I didn't pry. I've never seen her this way, about anyone."

That's when my wife looks at me as if to ask, *How can I lighten your load?* Eyes that are just starting to mature. If you've ever met a person who could listen to you lecture about any yawn-inducing topic and never once get bored or distracted, you might as well have met my wife. She's an amazing listener. She really is. I could learn from her. I admit, I'm a good talker. Maybe that's why we fit.

"Hey," I say. "Let's not talk about work today, okay?"

"It's all right, Ella. Sometimes you need to talk it out." She's using her mug as some sort of hand warmer. I could probably continue on my morning tirade, but I'm ready to move on. I let my gaze travel over her scruffy morning hair, which presently defies gravity. Then I brush my own hair out of my face, wishing I had something to keep it off my neck. Which is when she states the obvious, "It's really coming down out there."

"Does that mean you're ready to shovel?" I ask, half joking. I'm sure not. I might need a whole pot of coffee today just for myself.

She curls both legs up under her. "When exactly are we getting that snowblower?"

"What—you can't handle this?"

"I can handle it. It's you I worry about." Those eyes are unconvincing as she puckers her lips to take another sip. She clearly does not want to shovel, and she doesn't seem remotely interested in letting me off duty either.

"I'll be fine today," I tell her. "Can't say the same about my back tomorrow."

"We'll take shifts. I'll get going just as soon as I finish this cup. You just keep that fire going."

So I smoked up the house once—once! I didn't know how much kindling was actually required to get a fire started back then. She may be a modern pioneer, but this is all new to me. That said, I think I have the concept of fire down now—at least keeping one going once it's started. Fuel, oxygen, and a source of ignition. Sam still seems to think she needs to take care of our heating source. She thinks without her, we'll perish. I'll let her go on thinking that if it makes her happy.

"When's the worst part of this over? Do you know?"

"It clears out this afternoon," I tell her. "In around four hours."

And the next thing I know, her mug's upside down on her face. "Well, I'd better get out there."

❖

Sam

I have this worn-out grin on my face watching Ella struggle to lift that heavy snowplowed ice at the end of the drive with that chintzy plastic shovel she bought. I'm waiting for it to break.

The fact that she won't take a breather means she's in some sort of imaginary competition with me. This isn't the Olympics. I don't know where she gets this from, her drive or whatever you want to call it. She thinks she can top me even though she knows darn well I'm the only one with the shoulders to take on that heavy stuff. Besides, I can actually do a pull-up. Several.

My wife's reminding me why I married her, wearing those threadbare Levi's with a little slack, the pair she's always threatening to throw out just so I beg her not to. She knows I love the way they fit, just right. That scarf I bought three years ago for her birthday. It was the thickest and warmest one in olive green I could find. Drove all the way to Connecticut to get it. I don't know when she got the biker boots. They predate me.

My wife is a ginger, and in the tradition of all gingers, she's forever in green—olive, hunter, moss, jade. You name it, her closet is full of it. I admit, I've encouraged it. The only thing I won't buy for her that's green is eye shadow. That should be left in the seventies.

My cheeks are starting to feel the flush of labor. My back the twinge of something else. I'm grateful this work has given me some relief, a reprieve, from real life. We've been at this for nearly an hour now and, at this rate, I figure we'll clear the drive just in time for lunch. But it's barely nine.

Maybe a short break won't kill us?

I stop shoveling and start listening. I take in the smoky cologne of fireside fused with evergreen, propping my shovel (the sturdy metal one *I* bought) deep into the snow mound next to me. Then I watch as flakes land on the hat of my industrious partner and on those frozen strands of orange hair.

This is what I fell in love with, this intensity. This is how she's always been, persistent. It used to be me. Now it's snow. Most often, it's work. This girl simply won't break unless forced to. Why is that? Me, I've got to take a breather here and there. That's why I have a plan that'll generate some much-needed R and R, and that plan involves some freshly packed powder in the shape of a baseball.

I haven't pitched in, what, twenty years? But I still have it. In my prime, I was unstoppable. Which is why I was pitcher in my softball days.

As I reflect on how naïve she looks right down to her amber eyelashes, I crush a good round mound between these mittens. I try to guess what's on her mind, but I'm likely wrong. Look at her, in a world of her own. So productive. For now, at least.

Until I crouch, army style, wind to the shoulder and *bam!* pitch that sucker as if she had a bull's-eye on her backside. And here it comes, a loud distinct smack followed by a scream. Sacked!

And then the sound of approaching danger throws my gut into a nosedive. I pause to consider the fact that I'm spooked by a sweet redhead in a fringed hat and green scarf, to boot.

I resolve to scurry away stealth-like, huffing through the slush pile, slow and steady until those footsteps cease. I turn my head cautiously. Casually.

"Act innocent with me?"

"I am innocent," I lie.

"Like hell you are." She points down at me all first grade teacher-like.

To save my bruised ego, I stand (feebly), brushing the snow off my knees and smirking nervously down at her. "I did nothing of the sort," I say, moving in closer and trying to coat up my charm. "Look at those kids over there," I say. "See them? Now, there's your guilty party."

"Really now? You're stooping so low as to blame toddlers?" I don't think she's really mad. She just wants me to grovel, which is not my style.

"Toddlers with a serious windup." I wink.

"Why then were you crawling away from me?" Those lips are

flat-out luscious. I just want to kiss her and get this over with because what could be better than a truce under flakes? I need a truce more than anything. I need acceptance even though she's oblivious as to why.

"Would you believe I dropped my mitten?" My wife, she tolerates me. I'm grateful for that. I reach around her hip, sweeping those stiff strands aside. She's starting to forget, so maybe I can. "Get in here and warm me up," I say, wrapping her in my coat. I'm starting to wish I could take this inside because she's really never looked more incredible. Instead I just watch as snowflakes settle on her shoulders. She isn't looking away, either. It's like she's daring me.

And I accept that dare because my only escape is distraction. She bites her lip to taunt me. Then she leans back against the barn, and my hips find hers. I feel lips brushing mine and fingertips slipping between two buttons on my shirt, but she never does this. And it's the kind of kiss that mends, or maybe I just want it to.

It's not until I come back, refocusing, that I notice she's still waiting for something. She's extending arms light as air onto my shoulders.

And eventually I lift her off the ground and give her a slow spin. When her boots settle back down on earth, I tuck my nose in her collar and breathe her in. And I can't seem to let go.

A few hours later, I'm cleaning off the front steps with a broom. On the upside, we've nearly dug out. And since Ella's at the mailbox gabbing with Anne (our sweeter-than-stevia neighbor), I figure I should probably head on down to be social as well.

And my steel-toes kick slush along their way, past the brambles, our ancient maple. When I punt a pinecone off the path, I'm greeted by a pair of seriously uneasy grins—and the best news all day.

"They lost power," Ella tells me.

"When?"

"About ten minutes ago."

"We haven't. I was just in there," I say.

"Were you using lights?"

"No."

"Why were you in so long?" she asks. She's just staring waiting for my response. It's not like she's ever been this skeptical.

"I was filling the woodstove," I finally say. "It was high, babe, I had to turn the airflow down and keep guard."

"Go check again," she nudges.

"Relax," I tell her before fast-tracking it back to the front door. Then I stomp my boots against the step before flipping the light switch inside.

Nothing. Seriously?

I give Ella the thumbs down and stand at the front steps as her hands meet her mouth and then forehead—then she up faces both to the sky.

So it appears we'll be spending this year's anniversary off the grid with no cooktop, no heat or hot water, no lamps. No ballet, even though I paid an arm and a leg for those tickets.

I should pause here to note that the last time we went through anything analogous to this, it took three arduous and unbearable days to bring the place back up because we're not exactly in the thick of town. Which is why we bought a piece of real estate complete with a working woodstove. It's necessary. So I do know what's going through her mind right about now—and it isn't pretty.

Regardless, I resolve to focus on the glass half-full angle because this could very well be a minor blip in the grid. Besides, we do have the stove and lumber and plenty of cuisine to get us by, two hundred and fifty dollars' worth. I stocked up precisely for this reason. We certainly knew it was a possibility.

And I think about all of this as their two voices grow louder and I'm back at the road. "You guys should come over," I say, joining in just as they're about to wrap it up. "Cozy up by the stove. It's burning up in there."

She offers a polite head shake, mentioning something about their fireplace. I glance at my wife's pinched brow, which lets me know her mind's still on the grid. Mine's on the price I paid for those ridiculous ballet tickets.

"Last time this happened—"

"Babe, that won't happen again."

Every time Ella goes all end-of-the-world on me, I have no other choice but to lie. And divert. "I've always wanted to cook on the woodstove. I plan to whip you up quite the treat for supper."

Our neighbor says, "She's probably right." She has my back. "We always get these little flickers and things come right back up. Enjoy some downtime. You don't get enough of it." That's when she turns with a beauty-pageant wave and power walks back through the calf-deep snow.

And my wife takes my hand. She looks at me, too, like she's reading my mind or trying to. Maybe this is where I say something. Or not.

❖

Ella

What's it like to lose power in nine-degree weather? It's not pretty.

The minute we get inside, we bring up two hurricane lamps from the basement to light the upstairs later on. Then I put in a call to the shop, which is now on life support thanks to generators. During that call, I guzzle an entire bottle of water, sprinkle talc down my shirt to clean up, and strip down a layer to cool off. It seems the last remaining task on my to-do list is dealing with this small tub of ice cream, now in danger of melting. And that's precisely what I'm about to do.

I'm feeling that good kind of exhaustion you get after a knockout workout. The glacial temperatures only quadruple those endorphins. But even though I'm basking in the afterglow of accomplishment, I'm really starting to get bored. I mean really bored. I mean need-to-pull-out-board-games bored, wherever those might be stored.

Sam has this over-the-top plan for cooking leftovers on the woodstove tonight for dinner—the woodstove! I've suggested to her that we prepare a cold supper, maybe cheese sandwiches with fruit. But she won't have it. Never having cooked directly on wrought iron in her life, she thinks she's perfectly suited to go all pioneer on me. And knowing my wife like I do, it'll probably turn out delightful.

I watch as the log she pokes falls right into place. "This is romantic," she tells me, "don't you think?" She's crouched on the floor peering up at me.

How a woman can even get muscle definition in her hands like she does? No gym could even do that. I suppose it's German genetics and hard work. She's out there all summer long picking and pulling, tilling and shoveling in the garden. It shows. She creates life with a simple push of two fingers into soil, knowing just how deep and how wet it should be to draw it toward the sun.

"Romantic?" I scoff, fixing chin-length bangs behind my ear. Then I get a little closer, tub in one hand spoon in the other. "Babe, it's frigid and dreary—and I'm starving and bored. How can that even be remotely construed as romantic?" I give that last word emphasis with air quotes. When my better half gets all happy-go-lucky on me, I have no other choice but to play devil's advocate and bring her back into life's harsh reality.

"Don't worry about the cold," she tells me as she props up on her knees. "I'll keep you warm. And I'll keep you fed. You'll love supper. I'm going to make this all up to you."

She has the most adorable way of hugging me from the floor, and my fingers always find their way down the nape of her neck, where hair is just getting heavy enough to fall vertically. That's where her faded tan dives beneath that shirt collar.

"I'm sure I will," I say. Then I savor my last spoonful of ice cream.

"That is, if you still have an appetite."

"Very funny," I say.

"Listen," she begins, "why don't we do something fun."

When faced with unscheduled downtime, which we all want don't we, it would probably be a good idea to get shit done. Organize the closet, pay bills, read a novel, make calls and catch up with people you never have time to call. But instead, I choose to focus mindlessly on her lips, now gleaming with a hint of balm.

"Like, what kind of fun did you have in mind?" I ask.

"Outside fun."

"Oh."

"Let's hit some powder—come on," she tells me.

"We're to stay off the roads, don't forget."

"This doesn't involve driving."

"What exactly does it involve, then? Two eyes made out of coal? A carrot nose?" I ask.

"Not quite."

"Scrabble and whiskey in the barn?"

"Not that either. It's better than that," she says.

"How is that even possible?"

"Remember when you said you always wanted to go snowshoeing—"

"Like when we met." How in the world does she remember this stuff?

"Yes," she says.

"I hate to be the one to break it to you, but, we don't own snowshoes, and—Why are you looking at me like that?"

"Hold out."

"Are you kidding me? You didn't buy snowshoes, did you? For one, we can't afford it, and two, you make me look like—"

"Just wait right here. I'll be right back," she tells me.

"—the worst wife ever," I mumble under my breath. Then I watch as she coats up, privately proud of the woman I hooked.

A quick glance in the mirror squanders what few minutes I have while she does whatever she's doing outside. My cheeks are still pink, which means I'm likely windburned. My hair's in clumps. But I leave it, powdering my nose to dull the shine and rubbing Brick Dust across my lips, at least that's what the manufacturer calls this shade. I call it the only color you'll see me in on a sunless day like today, the shade I wore that day, up on that hilltop. When she spread out that checkered blanket across a field of grass, and I can still see those cotton-ball clouds above as we feasted on grapes and crackers talking about our dreams. As she popped the cork (and the question) and slid two stems between her knuckles. Our newly ringed knuckles. And she tasted of bubbling champagne when she kissed me, warm and intoxicating.

Much like this woodstove, which is just where I'm going to stay until she comes back in.

❖

Sam

Retirement is sweet, especially when it's your parents who are doing the downsizing and you're the one acquiring stuff. It used to bother me that Mom was such a hoarder. Now, not so much.

Mind you, the pickup part of that acquisition process requires trips down memory lane, which can be a drag for someone like me who'd rather live in the now and forget my youthful—and not-so-youthful—mishaps. And the pickup part can be a double drag when it involves a few hours in the company of soon-to-be retirees who act more like newlyweds than I do.

Quite frankly I've heard more about aging in place and Palm Beach than I care to mention. I half expect to see those two spinning around on mobility scooters (they've been mentioned) and sporting Life Alerts. They've already joined AARP. And Mom has been asking for senior discounts at stores, in my presence. They have to card her. It's embarrassing.

On the plus side, though, they've finally gotten serious about cleaning out that attic, one that's warehoused bunk beds, yearbooks, ski poles, trophies, and I don't even want to know what else. Between my brother and me, we've acquired a heck of a lot of that stuff, like two pairs of snowshoes that have been stored in the trunk waiting for the perfect time to spring them on penny-pincher in there.

"Cover your eyes," I shout as I butt close the door.

"I can't believe you!"

"Are they covered?" I ask.

"Yes," she sighs. She's excited. I know she is. "They're covered," begins her lecture, "but I don't know why—because I know what you have and they aren't in the budget."

"I didn't spend a dime, sweetheart. You can have a look now. And you can thank Gidget." That would be Mother's nickname. She does have a Sally Field quality in that never-aging girl-next-door sort of way.

Then I get that moment I've waited for. I love springing stuff on this girl. She's still shockable.

And shocked she is when I shout, "It's adventure time!"

❖

Ella

Women fought over me. They used to anyway. Now I barely turn a head.

I'm not talking an all-out clash on the pool table. I'm not saying a physical brawl. Let's just say I'm dangerously good at playing hard to get. They bit. I dodged. They chased, many of them. I juggled them. It wasn't always intentional on my part, the playing; it was in self-defense because they craved the competition. Once they won me over, that was it.

Then who was doing the chasing? I was. I called. I left messages under the guise of *Let's remain friends.* I bought two tickets instead of one and invited them. I said my computer broke or friends were moving, could they help? Then I ultimately gave up. And that's when they usually fell in love with me.

I still catch myself doing it now, even with five years and a diamond ring under my belt. I don't think I could turn it off if I wanted to. I stay at the shop late without calling, say Jessie stopped by. I want her to be jealous, curious, appreciative at least. I know she won't leave. She doesn't need a competitor to love me.

What she does need, though, is a grocery list. Ask her and she'll say a Post-it's too much effort, that she'll remember. She likes to stroll grabbing anything that comes to mind. For me, grocery shopping is a weeklong competitive strategy. I use a meal-planning notebook with 100 percent recycled paper, wire bound. I outline the week's meals in advance. I clip coupons from Sunday's paper. I organize those by month of expiry and then by year. I keep an inventory of the fridge, the storage freezer, and the pantry to make sure I'm not leaving something out that I might need. Call it a carryover from work. An ounce of prevention is worth a pound of cure—or at least another trip to the store midweek, which I never have time to do.

We made another trip today because she didn't remember olive oil. While we were there, I'd like to say that we ran into her coworker but that would be an understatement. The woman mauled her. Maybe she didn't see me right beside. She wouldn't recognize me if she did. She doesn't know me, but she knew my wife. She hugged her like a linebacker. It made me wonder what goes on there if this is how she acted at Whole Foods. I don't even hug my wife that way in public.

"What was that about?" I asked once we rounded the aisle.

"She just thinks we're one big happy gay family, that type. That's all."

I'm not threatened.

"Is she the one they promoted?"

"Yes."

The unstyled hair and that ratty old baseball cap. Definitely not a threat.

"The one with marital problems?"

"Yes."

My wife, how could she cheat on me when she never notices the most obvious advance?

"The one who likes to watch you lift?"

"Oh, stop. She's not hitting on me."

She is. But I think occasional jealousy can be good for a relationship. Once in a while, you need a little reminder. And because of that far-from-subtle display today, I opted against buying another pint of ice cream, came home and spent a little more time on myself, put on better than average sweats, held her a little longer. Not like a linebacker, though.

❖

Sam

I have my paperback propped on my knees as Ella breezes into the bedroom bound in a towel, skin dripping and freshly scented of soap. Her toothbrush foams at her mouth. She talks through it, coming off as a grunting brute.

"You're spewing germs everywhere," I say. "Go!"

Then she exits, and I hear the sink.

"I got an email from my mother," she tells me. "Their power flickered. That's it. She said if we needed, we could sleep over for a night or two."

"You told her we're fine, right?"

"Pretty much," I hear as her voice grows louder around the door frame. "I told her we did too, but it's back. And, besides, we're set on food and have heat. I still think she wants to see us. I told her I'm just always so busy."

Then she shuts the door, which is generally the sign for...you know. I do realize that this is our anniversary weekend, but I hadn't planned—well—I hadn't anticipated that every night be that. Besides, we had that huge dinner and I'm overstuffed and she's been difficult all afternoon, and I'm still holding a slight grudge.

From the corner of my eye, I catch her dramatic towel fling onto the bed. Onto me. I set my book down. And my specs.

"So." She smiles innocently. Then she makes her way to the dresser in the buff. I can't help but admire her. "What's your book about?" The view is more than mildly distracting.

"This guy's lunch break."

She snaps the elastic at her waist. "And?"

"And all the things he sees. He took an escalator. He's going to buy a pair of shoelaces."

"And?"

"And that's about it so far," I say.

"And you're that far into the book?"

"Pretty much."

"I'm surprised you're still awake." She yanks a shirt down her torso. A rather loose-fitting shirt. "Sounds about as exciting as watching paint dry. Who is this?" she asks.

I just flip the cover her way.

"Why do you read this stuff?" she asks. Then she crawls beneath layers of thick bedding. Once that pillow heap is adequately propped, she gets out her iPad. This is her signal that I can pick up my book again, which I do with every intention of reading. But the moment I find my spot, I realize she's already interrupted my flow. It's kind of like when you're having sex and the phone rings or the cat starts scratching at the door. It's kind of over.

So I elect to continue our conversation instead. "Reading email?"

She scans her screen without responding. I suppose I could open the bedroom door at this point because this is not going to lead to anything. Instead I look over her shoulder trying to decipher chains of words across that screen through my I-can't-believe-I'm-forty reading glasses. And it's from Ryan.

"Business or personal," I ask.

"Both."

I start studying her expression secretly without looking, thinking I can catch anything out of the ordinary. My mind's on our argument earlier. Women forgive, though. They rage and fume, but come back— they always do. Her finger glides up that screen. It's not until she laughs, as slight as it is, that I reopen my book. And I pretend to read where I left off. Eventually I get to the line, and the plot thickens. I turn the page. And another.

I catch Ella flipping over to watch a documentary. "Everything okay?" I say.

"Some deliveries are delayed."

"Does that push orders out?"

"It might," she says.

"And you're okay with that?"

"I have to be." It's something she'd normally say with a vain attempt at acceptance, but not tonight. Tonight she genuinely seems relieved.

"Hey," I say. Then I touch her hand.

She's amused when she turns—her skin still dewy, framed by hair that's towel dried and combed. I'm thinking she's perfect this way. I lean in and press my lips against hers, desperately. I keep trying until she's kissing me back. I don't mean for this to be as tragic and anguished as it is.

"What was that about?" she wants to know.

I shake my head. "Can't a girl kiss her wife without raising suspicion?"

CHAPTER SIX: JESSIE AND HADLEY

Jessie

My alarm's out, so I roll over. It's damn cold.

She's got my favorite T-shirt on. It's long sleeved. The neck bows low enough to show some. The fabric's twisted like her hair. And my eyes get a mind of their own. It's not like anyone will know, but it's enough to throw my stomach in a flip dive, and I realize, what the heck am I doing? Really.

Thirty, sixty, ninety seconds later she's still sound asleep and I'm still stuck.

So I nudge her shoulder. She squints and makes what can only be described as a satisfied sigh. I offer, "Good morning," with my guilt-ridden grin.

She covers a yawn.

"It's so cold," she says. "Do we have power?"

"Nope. And I'm not getting up," I tell her, "but you can—I mean, that is, if you really want to. Get out of bed, that is."

She fluffs a pillow and glares at me from under that hair. "No thanks."

"I know, right?"

And I'm enjoying the way her eyes dart back and forth between mine. Her face is calm. I tuck my arm under a pillow. She tucks her arm under hers. Then she arches her back into a stretch and, mercy, is she this oblivious to how hot this looks? I watch her lean off the bed to get her glasses.

"I wonder," she says, pinching joints, "if my phone's even charged."

"Hey. Turn it off, okay? We may need it and, besides, I don't know how long we'll be here in Girl Scout mode." She reaches to check the time regardless.

"I work today," I hear. "Not until later. But still."

She rumples a brow.

There's that part of me that aches to keep her here, stay in bed all day. In reality, though, I can't do that. Work apparently beckons.

"Will I see you tonight?" she wants to know, giving me a once-over. "For the usual?"

I nod, hesitantly.

"How's this even going to work?"

"How's what going to work?" I ask.

"I'll need a shower, you know."

"Dude, it'll come back on." I slide in, fixing on her.

"But we don't really know—"

"Well, let's just say, hypothetically, that it doesn't. Can't you call in?"

"No. I wish, but no."

I see my own breath and that's just insane. "I'll take care of it. Don't worry. I'll give them another call. In the meantime, I think I can take your mind off this pretty easily."

"Do you now," she asks. But it's not what she's thinking. Believe me, I wish it were.

"I've got a couple bottles of Frappuccino in my fridge. It tastes like dirt. But I could get us some. I'm starting to get that lack-of-caffeine headache. Aren't you?" Her face softens as she sinks into a pillow. "I've got some blueberry muffins in there, too, good ones from Ella's." I tuck that loose strand of hair behind her ear. It never wants to stay put. "Hey, what do you say?"

Except she just sort of collapses on her back.

"What, you don't like blueberries—since when? You used to. I've got cinnamon rolls in there too."

I follow her gaze to the silver ceiling tiles, and I'm listening to nothingness. The sun wants to come out. It's moving shadows across the ceiling, up the wall. And I'm thinking pretty hard on breakfast when our phones ring. A few profanities come from the other side of the bed as I fumble and pat my way to hit the right button. And we listen in, blankets up to our chins, as a recorded voice from the town lets us know that—get this—there's been a power outage.

"No shit," I mouth, and her smile returns.

The outage has affected a wide area.

"Why do you keep looking at me like that," I ask, my voice wobbly.

Crews are working hard around the clock and roads are being cleared.

"I don't know…"

"You do know."

"It's nothing," she says.

"It's never nothing," I say back. I'm curious what she's got on her mind, why she's now walling up on me. But this droning announcement is so distracting. "What, what, what?" I snicker. "It's the hair, right? You like?"

And we're so done with our phones as soon as we hear: *Shelter in place.*

I sit, begging. "Come on. Please? Let me go make you some breakfast."

And she lets out a long-drawn-out sigh like I'm torturing her, tugging the sheet up over her head. I take that as a definite yes.

❖

Hadley

Sure, I'm relieved when she steps away. I could use a jolt of coffee right about now, preferably the warm and unhurried kind. But cold will have to do. And better her than me to walk around in a heap of blankets. Once I get properly caffeinated, I can maybe head off to work. In other words, our lives will get back to normal to some degree.

Besides, I'm not sure how else I should feel with her acting like this. There's a part of me that wishes she would go on and on and mean it. But there's another part that wishes she would stop because there's no sacrifice in it, no pausing or self-reflection. I think she can be so impulsive at times. Which is why I hate myself for reacting the way I did, getting all wrapped up and confused by her, preoccupied by crazy ideas I shouldn't even contemplate.

It's like she never actually hurts like I do. She never collapses from the weight of it, when that part of you is gone, so heavy you can't even breathe at times but you try. She never seems to lose what really matters.

It's not that I haven't caught a glimpse of it, those bits, a few words that slip off her tongue unplanned when I least expect it. And I know they're big, especially when she darts away like this, like she's worried about something. Worried about how I'll react. As if anything she could do or say would change the way I feel for her.

I guess there are times when I might venture to believe she actually loves me. I do think she might. Just not in that way.

Still, if she did (you know) love me, how could she do this to me, glance as if it means something. Pretend as if that touch was an accident, when I know it wasn't. Mistaking me for someone made of so much more resolve than I really am. More like irresponsible and inconsistent when I'm around her.

It's like I'm sinking again. That rush. Then I don't know what to say, and I get annoyed with her. Why do I have to get this way, stupid wishful thinking of me. Yet that frustration, my dependence on her, my always wanting to be near her, it's the best feeling I've ever had in my life.

But I will never be that someone else who keeps her. The most I can be is a mirage she keeps chasing but still never reaches. There are too many beautiful distractions along the way.

Distractions of my own, as well, because I have hassles I should be dealing with, like getting ready for work, which is going to be madness. I can't think of this. I can't be thinking of her.

And yet just as I'm texting another reply to Brie, look who dashes in and dives under the covers. And she holds my gaze. I take one of her bottles of too-cold coffee and study those familiar features, all the while she's reaching for that bakery bag. Then she hands me a bite of breakfast.

And she makes this adorable shivering sound before giving me that smile. "Wrap up," she says. She sets this plate in front of me and another at her side. And isn't this how it goes, that even in my silence, she knows me well enough to offer the best one.

And next this. She's tucking my hair back again. But of course it's a morning mess. Stop looking at me. Why does she have to be like this?

CHAPTER SEVEN: BRIE AND RYAN

Brie

This is the part that makes me regret stopping by in the first place. Hadley doesn't notice or just doesn't care (or maybe she's too engrossed in the fact that her shift is about to start), so she does this dry shampoo thing with her hair and just scruffs it up and is out the door. *Please stay*, I get from her. *I sure could use the company*, Jessie says. Had I known my girl had work today, I maybe wouldn't have stopped by. But it's too late now. I'm here. This is a shitty day all around.

So I take another bite of lunch, dreading the thought of spending several hours with someone I've barely spent five minutes with over the past year—alone, that is. Every time I've been around Jessie, we've had Ryan or Hadley as chaperone, or shall I say conversation orchestrator.

Why is it that none of us could stop talking, in fact we were overtalking, when Hadley was here? The minute she goes to work, crickets. The alternative, though, would be heading home, which I'm not prepared for or wanting to do. And Jessie does give off this genuine vibe. Let's just say, I don't feel I'm intruding in any way, quite the contrary. She seems to need me here.

So I finish my takeout, which is amazing by the way, and she's asking these questions, cautious I can tell to dodge anything remotely job related. I know everything I say could head straight back to my ex, so I don't bring up that ordeal earlier today. Instead I flip topics back to her life, which I only really know about through Hadley. But this one is so secretive about everything, likely the same as me, thinking everything she says will go right on back to Hadley. And she would be right about that.

Soon though she's tossing out some interesting questions; it's not small talk either. It seems natural, being here. She tells me she tried the grad school thing as well—stopped at a BS. She works at the hospital. Things like that. She wants to know what interests me. She's leaning off her seat and then stretches out. We start in on art and I learn we've both been to MoMA far too many times.

She's got a pretty deep voice. And the fact that she's devastating doesn't help matters. Still, she's my best friend's crush, so I'm uber mindful not to cross any boundaries here. Not that I'm *not* thinking things, especially when she saunters into the next room and I get a glimpse of her walking away and let's just say I'm curious, that's all.

Her wink is friendly enough. *She* is friendly enough. You know when someone sits on the edge of their seat, that kind of thing. So I rack my brain for harmless topics that I can bring up, and I wonder, does she know I know so much about her? Then I worry—does she know that much about me? It makes the room thick, at least for me.

"Is that good?" she asks as I crumple the paper bag that carried in my lunch. I guess she's been watching me eat while debriefing.

"Amazing, I was starving. I feel like I have such poor manners."

"No, not at all. I get that way, too. I'm sorry it's so cold in here," she says.

"Our place was the same. Made for a long morning."

"No kidding, right?" But the heat's back on and it's loud.

I get the sense she watches a lot of movies because she asks if I've seen this or that. I haven't seen any aside from a few really old ones she brings up, and then we get to talking about those. She has a rather impressive setup, the flat screen television and massive speakers—almost too big. Overall, though, this place definitely has a bachelorette pad feel. It looks like she might have tried recently, but it's not pulled together well. Let's just say that if you think motorcycle helmets are suitable decor, you'll fit right in. I don't even see a coffeepot in the kitchen, which should seriously be illegal.

"Do you have a trash?" I ask.

"I'm sorry, let me get that for you. Can I get you a glass of water or something?"

I could use something stronger, but I accept her offer. I follow into the kitchen, noticing she's my height.

"Your place is so cute," I say.

"You think? It's not much. Hadley helps. She's got a better eye. She did this rug thing. It's a bit much."

It's the only part that works, I'm thinking. "I like it," I say, "and I love this couch." That's no exaggeration.

"That was Hadley, too," she says. I take a drink of water and cross my legs on said couch. She leans against the wall casually. Which is when I come up with a seriously brilliant topic—the girlfriend. So I ask, "Is Alicia meeting up with us tonight?" But my question hits the floor like a sack of potatoes.

"We're...sort of...separated right now."

That would be topic two hundred fifty-five that shall not be brought up at all tonight. I tell her I'm sorry.

"Not at all."

"So you're single again?" I ask.

"I guess you could say that, in a way."

I'm feeling rather comfortable now, so I remind myself to keep my mouth shut or I'm bound to say something that will A, make me look stupid or B, get back to Ryan. She peels off her unzipped hoodie to the thinnest shirt imaginable. "Little hot in here, don't you think?" Then she heads over to the thermostat to adjust it. I'm just curious about her, that's all.

Once she's resting back on that wall again, I hear, "So, what do you do for fun?" But my mind's locked in freeze-frame from when she was undressing.

Chapter Eight: Jessie and Hadley

Jessie

Hops is busting at the seams. Some peek in, see the line, and leave. I'm liking the postapocalyptic climate. Brie and I wait our turn.

And the drama. I'm reminded of the saying, *Believe half of what you see and none of what you hear.* That area over there is reconfigged into an overflow corral, and the crowd's on edge. I cannot blame them. Given some of this bedhead, I'd guess most have another frigid night ahead. It appears I'm one of the lucky ones.

My dinner companion's agitated as well. I find this bizarre since she's been nice enough all afternoon, mysterious but not impolite, downright giggly at times. I hope I haven't said anything to offend her. My mind loops back.

"When are we expecting Ryan?" I ask.

"I texted a bit ago, said four, four thirty. Should be here any minute."

She makes no eye contact. Not sure what to make of her sudden rudeness, but a part of me accepts it as a personal challenge to turn her mood around.

"That's cool," I tell her hoping to lighten the air, wave a white flag, for what charge I do not know. Still, nothing but a nod back.

She keeps bumping this frame that dangles from wire on a nail. And we wait, along with everyone else, to be seated.

My shoulder brushes hers. She's dipping into my comfort zone, which I don't mind, to talk over the music. When she stops talking, I check out her slightly overdressed appearance, her wool trousers, her loose-fitting blazer that tragically fails in its attempt to cloak her femininity. She's taller than average with hair knotted in the back. Her sheer, shapeless blouse. The hand that never leaves a pant pocket. You'd think demure, but she holds her own.

I catch the more charismatic Hadley making her way through the swarm. At first oblivious, she finally catches a glimpse of us over here and waves through heads and backs and shoulders. Brie and I squeeze as two elders crouch their way past and out the door. Hadley grabs a couple menus and turns to escort a party of four to a table that's still being wiped down as they're seated. She pens something on her pad and flits away. I check out her tweed skirt and oxford shirt, which is (as always) buttoned conservatively.

"Let's hit the bar," Brie shouts. It's a sweet voice but a jolt from a rather enjoyable daydream about hemlines. I lead the way and motion back, and we soon secure two stools. Cushions exhale under our weight. She's at my eye level. She rests on the padded edge, shoulders slumped and more at ease. Then, when I spot what might be a smile, I naturally assume it's my doing.

"I can't believe I'm even hungry already," she tells me. "Have you eaten?"

"Before you came, lunch was an entire container of cold Chinese takeout in my fridge that wouldn't make it."

"Sounds yummy."

"Delicious. But cold."

I must confess. As I ate that, I tasted nothing given my mind was on Hadley showering. That clear curtain, especially when wet, left little to my imagination nor did she when parading through my apartment in a wrap and towel.

Brie spins a paper coaster. I let my gaze amble from her fingers up her arm to her face, and I reach an eyebrow, arched as if to scold me. "So," she drags out like a long puff on a cigarette. "You guys have a good time last night?"

Why do I feel like some sort of criminal when she comes up in conversation? "You could say that." I wink. "She's notorious for this. She puts shit off until she can't anymore. This time, it's her battery. The car's still here—it's in the back lot," I say with a nod in the general vicinity of that garage.

"That's unfortunate," she says. "Isn't that a fairly new car she has?"

"It is. I got her fixed up, though."

"Did you, now?" I notice her smile again. It's nice—when she uses it.

"I always do."

But she has no more comebacks. Instead, our attention swings to our pal over there, who's finally heading in our direction. "Won't be long," I say. "She'll put us up first."

"Thank God." Clearly she's ready to chow down. But my appetite's somewhere else, not here. Until she mentioned it, I wasn't even thinking about food. Guess I'm running on autopilot and adrenaline.

"Tell me," she says, adopting a critical tone, "because I've never really asked you. I know you two go way back. Like, how far? I'm curious."

"Way, way back." I can feel my eyes roll. "Like, way back. We actually grew up together. First grade, maybe?"

"Seriously?"

"Seriously." I twist my fingers in a knot for luck.

"I haven't kept up with many from back then."

"Don't tell me," I say. "You were that popular girl, right? You smelled powder fresh and all the guys wanted to go out with you and all the girls thought you were bizarre because you didn't date the homecoming king. You probably wore skirts until you got sick of guys checking you out, so you traded those in for pants. And I peg you for an only child, which means you have an unusually close relationship with your mother."

"You're pretty damn close. It's actually eerie how much. Just off by a long shot on the popular part. Why would you take me for popular?"

"You just have that aura."

"What aura would that be?"

Does this require explanation? "That unapologetically gorgeous aura." Did I just make her blush? And laugh, it's a rather cute one. "You know, that popular girl aura."

"You're a doll. I don't have a personality for popular. I'm no chameleon, and I'm far too temperamental." I notice she doesn't actually address the *gorgeous* part. "I was more of a recluse if you can believe that. Dated the same girl on and off for years."

"Really. Where is she now?"

"That's complicated."

I nod.

"As for others, I've tried, but, you know?"

"Things do change," I say. "You change. That's what I love about that girl. We've grown together. It's wild when you think about it."

The bartender whizzes over, pouring some blue liquor into a glass while propping a beer stein under a tap. The foam edges its way toward the rim. "What can I get you gals?" She's Asian, which means I have no clue how old she is. She could be forty. She could be twenty. But given the modest bumblebee tattoo I catch on the underside of her wrist, I'll assume the latter.

"Give me something strong," Brie says, raising her voice over the crowd. "Strong and sweet."

Seldom do I see this girl drink. But, outside of a few get-togethers at Ryan's pad, I imagined she'd be a martini gal. Sophisticated. Cultured. Stylish. Old Hollywood-ish. I remember when Ryan introduced us. The instant we shook, I thought, *helpless female*. I was wrong then, too. Plus from the few bits and pieces I've gathered from Ryan, she's pretty racy where it counts, but you'd never know it from appearances.

The bartender offers a suggestion. "How about Sex on the Beach?" Then she drops her eyes. It's her once-over coming next that makes me question whether that was a drink or an offer.

"Never had one."

"You've never had one?" I ask. Is this not the biggest pickup line ever? The drink we've all been handed at one point in our bar-dwelling lives?

"I spent seven years in school—fourteen-hour days," she says.

That's when the bartender jumps back in and says, "It's vodka, cranberry juice, orange juice, peach schnapps…"

"You should get one," I nudge.

And the look I get back.

"I'll take it," she says without shifting those eyes from mine.

"And for you?" the bartender shouts, glancing down to my lips to read them.

"Whatever you have on tap."

That's when Brie leans in rather intrigued. "So, high school." Now that she's being friendly again, I've already disregarded her earlier rudeness. "Care to elaborate? We have some time to kill."

I laugh. "Hadley's really the storyteller."

"Oh, I've heard some stories from her," Brie says.

"Have you, now? Why does that worry me?" And there's that downright giggle of hers. But she doesn't actually elaborate, which worries me even more. Well not really.

I muse over which factoids are safe to share. "What do you want to know?"

"You know, tell me how you guys met. That sort."

"You haven't heard this from your girlfriend? She's the worst gossip I've ever known."

Her laugh cuts off short. "Nope."

"Well, let's see, that would have to be the time I saw her toweling off after practice one day…" She actually buys it, so I play along nodding lecherously. Then I backpedal. "Totally kidding. Nothing even remotely like that. We grew up a block away from one another, and like I said, we went to the same school all the way up. Rode the same bus. Usually in the same class. It wasn't until high school that we got close and I liked her. You know"—I wave my hands defensively—"in a friends way. I can't say that we got along that well in elementary school. Honestly, I think I hated her. She had a clique—I had mine. But in high school by some fluke, we joined the girls' softball team in our…I believe it was our sophomore year. After-school practice, you know? She was catcher. I played first base. That lasted three years, and we kicked some butt. Anyway, that's when we started to hang out a lot."

She nods, clearly engrossed.

"Am I boring you yet?"

"No, not at all."

"We're kindred spirits."

"Are you?"

The bartender slips our drinks into the conversation, and we both slide bills out to pay. I cover her hand and tell her, "I got this."

"All right. Hey, thanks," she says and lifts her glass. "Toast?"

"Toast."

"To lifelong friends," she says.

Our drinks touch and then she takes a sip with a flush of absolute pleasure. Then she takes an even bigger swig—as do I—amid bells and tings and rustles. The songs of liquor and ice being shaken and poured until foam tops beer mugs and salt rims the lips of margaritas. I watch in awe as a zester peels a lemon into a coil of yellow, which the bartender presses into a glass under ice and clear liquor. His beard fits right in.

"Kindred spirits, you say. You guys never went out?"

I feel a tinge of guilt and almost shame again, as if maybe she can see right through me. Has she noticed something I'm not sharing? And the noise escalates, making it more difficult to continue our conversation.

"We never went out," I say. "It's my philosophy that hooking up destroys friendships."

"I respect that. I do. But that hasn't been my experience. I'm thinking, and disagree if you will, that there's something to be said about a girl who sticks around that long through thick and thin and, as you say, grows along with you. It's less superficial that way." I don't know if I agree with her. But she continues, "I could pick a girl right now and go home with her and that'd be great fun, but it's not the real deal."

"You sound like you're trying to convince yourself."

"Maybe I am." I can't translate whether she's curious or still disagreeing with me.

While I try to interpret, the seat opposite her empties, filling in seconds as if a queue or line was waiting. Our conversation lulls, so I watch our bartender juggling glasses in a variety of sizes and shapes. Folks around are huddling in groups of two or maybe three. Across the room, I catch that hemline again as she rounds chairs to set down plates piled high.

Then an unfamiliar voice says something beyond my bar mate, and our heads turn in unison. The woman crosses her wrists and looks Brie over.

I holler across in classic third-wheel fashion, "Hey!"

"A little crowded here tonight," the woman says, shouting above the noise and leaning in with an inviting grin along with an accidentally deliberate touch.

Brie offers an apprehensive grin. "You could say that."

"You here alone?" She excludes me from their conversation.

"Yes, you could say that." Brie's obviously flattered but still rather cagey. Based on appearances, these two could be climbing the same career ladder. The bartender slides another drink in front of Brie as the woman pulls out her billfold.

"Let me buy you a drink."

Wait a minute.

This is not okay. We were having a nice conversation, one I'd like to continue as we wait for her girlfriend to show up, someone who could walk in any minute. This is wrong on so many levels. And not just that—I'm getting perturbed by the fact that my companion here is acting disrespectful just by entertaining this woman's overt come-on. I scan the room to see if I can catch any signs of Ryan, but I don't see that hair or coat anywhere.

The two keep at it, lip to ear, giggling, drinking.

"Hey, I'll be right back," I tell her because I've decided to walk around near the entrance even if that means losing my seat at the bar.

Excuse me. Pardon me. Can I get through here? Thanks.

When I reach the door and step outside, the breeze is so energizing. A car splashes past. Roads are glistening from piles of salt, mirroring the glare of headlights. Shops are open, illuminated, and warm.

Then I hear my name. It's panting behind me. When I turn, I see a puff of breath bobbing before Ryan's face registers. "You're a sight for sore eyes," she tells me.

I just shrug. I need to get to work on a distraction. "Listen, the line's out the door, kid. It's a madhouse. We won't have a table for a while. Say we hit the mall for a few...kill some time?"

"Sure. Let me run in and tell Brie I'm here. She's here with you, right?"

Oh, this is not good.

"You'll never get back out," I lie. "Seriously. Can't we just? I really need your opinion." We link elbows, and I (forcefully) guide her down the walk.

She's clearly conflicted. Another puff of breath settles between us. A man and woman bolt past us heading for Hops. Voices barrel out the second the door opens. "I've got to defrost," she tells me with a tug and in no time my arm is being dragged between two doors and they slam on my heels.

The girl's fierce, barreling into the crowd, and I'm in tow, my pulse off the chart at the thought of what she might discover. What's going on with these two? From the look on her face—hopeful and, dare I say, gooey-eyed—I have a sinking suspicion she's not anticipating the scene I just walked away from. Unless she's into threesomes, which would be news to me given she's morphed into that annoying jealous type with this particular girl. More than once, she's jumped to conclusions even when there's no conclusion to make.

She beelines for the bar. I bow my head as an apology to those I've bumped until I ram headfirst into her back not ten feet from Brie.

I glance up at her shoulder and then catch her expression, which is empty and drained of that childlike giddiness going on a few seconds ago—and she's transfixed.

Let's face it, this doesn't look good.

It's like a slow-simmering nightmare. That woman's working something on Brie. This scene's going to get ugly if I don't get Ryan out the door, which I do.

And then she cuts loose on me. "What the hell'd you do that for?"

"Because I'm your friend."

"Like hell. You could've warned me."

"I tried," I say. "You wouldn't let me."

"How do you figure?"

"Dude, quit the yelling. I'm trying to help you here. Don't let off on me when you know damn well you're mad at someone else in there. Shouldn't you be yelling at your girlfriend right about now?"

"That was the plan."

I bring it down a notch. "Which is why I pulled you out. Can't you see that? Don't make a scene. What kind of friend would let you loose in that frame of mind? Think rationally for a moment." She's just stiff. "Don't do something you'll regret." I don't get any kind of agreement back. She's trembling. "Let's take a walk," I say.

We head toward the center of town. Our path is narrow, so the side-by-side thing isn't working. I wait for a green. That's when she shoves both hands in her pockets like she's cold.

She wants a line by line. There's not much to tell. Did she talk about me? We talked about art. Was she mad? No, she was pleasant.

"I don't know what's going on," she finally says.

I want the rest.

"It's like we broke up. But where'd it come from? Do you know?"

"When?" I ask.

"Today, I guess."

I rewind.

"I wanted—I thought *she* wanted—something lax, you know," she says with a grunt. "The thing you do." She swallows, to stop from choking up, apparently. It works. Then a few steps back. What's astounding is through her broken speech, I get what she's getting at.

"What I do never lasts a year. They don't move in," I tell her.

"This wasn't supposed to happen." And then we're walking again. "I meant to tell you, but..." Her head drops. She's just heavy. She's too unhappy. "This wasn't the girl to stick around, anyway. How do you do that, Jess?"

"Do what?"

"Not let anyone get to you," she says.

"You are kidding, right?"

"They never faze you."

"They do get to me. Trust me on that."

"She's flipped on me, won't talk, won't tell me anything, pushes me away. I'm trying to be supportive, you know? It's fucked up. It went too fast. From day one and I took her home. That, right there."

"What's wrong with that?" I chuckle.

"Heh. Not this one, I told you that...consider—"

She just lets me hang.

"Never mind," she says eventually.

We pass the courthouse. A drugstore. A closed bagel shop. And then the shoe shop. But I walk away without showing her the pair I want. We crush heaps of slush along our path, never pausing to look at the imprints.

"You want her back?"

"Who wouldn't?" she says.

"Give her space, then, time to figure it all out. That's what you do."

It's not just a brush-off nod I get back.

We pause at those bulky doors. I look over at her. Then I give her an elbow. I get a crooked grin. "Let's do this."

CHAPTER NINE: RYAN AND BRIE

Ryan

I'm starving—correction, absolutely famished—and I realize I haven't had a real bite to eat all day. It's nice when the grilling and frying and sautéing bring back those cravings. Admittedly they also send my patience out the door.

I've spent most of the day paralyzed, pondering my girlfriend's misery—with me, with life, with everything. And it makes no sense. Not long ago, I was the venerated adventurous girl she went out of her way to please. What gives?

Just look at me, dressed to impress in her favorite getup, the cuffed denim shirt, the khakis, the Fluevogs, the paste that lifts, the leather-strapped watch. And sandalwood.

But as doors part open, some serious doubts set in. That I just may not pull this off. That I might not get her back. And this lump in my throat just recalling that display, her giggling like that, desired like that. I consider her insecurities and want to throw them at her like darts.

"Be right back," Jessie says. She heads over to Hadley, who's busy at the hostess stand. I back into the corner and hide on the bench. I'm beholden to her for yanking me out before I made a humiliating spectacle.

Still there's no sign of my girlfriend from here.

It's nice being tucked behind a menu stand beside this cooler full of take-out brew. I don't know how I'll react when I see her.

Jessie pouts her way back. I must look pitiful, feet flat on the floor, an elbow on each knee, fingers woven.

"Ten minutes and she'll have a seat," she says, intentionally bumping elbows as she lifts my half of the bench like a teeter-totter.

"I can live that long."

"Hope so," she says.

I grab a menu from the stand and start flipping. I'm ready to try something new. Something super bad for me. Something my highly reserved girlfriend would never even consider. I deserve one night of debauchery, if you could even call it that.

How well, I wonder, do I even know this woman I'm revolting against? She's a puzzle I can't ever finish. There are too many missing pieces.

I glance at my nails, now filed, and rub palms on either thigh.

But a hostess rushes over just then with a, "Hey guys, follow me."

Jessie's hand is warm on my knee as if to repeat her mantra, *It's going to be okay*. Boy, I must look like an inconsolable wimp right now. So I toughen up on the outside and swagger to the table like I own the joint. Like I couldn't care less. Like life is glorious.

We're seated at a small table less private than I'd prefer. We occupy two of its four chairs. And while I'm pleased to soon be ordering, I can't help but wonder where my girlfriend might be hiding, or if she's even here.

She could be in her truck in the parking lot, windows steamed up. She might not be alone. I know how she operates, how she did with me, at least. Is it wrong to assume? It makes me angry again. Maybe I should take a walk, find that truck. But I'm too afraid I'm right.

I scan the noisy backdrop, landing across the table on Jessie, who's uncharacteristically pensive. My girlfriend says I'm selfish. Tonight she might be right because look at how long it's taken to recognize someone else exists.

"So how's life?" I ask, attempting to save some face.

"That's a loaded question. You know, same drama, new girl."

She can see I'm waiting for details. Then her lungs swell and she answers with a shrug.

"Alicia?" I ask.

"I can't go into it here. But if you see her and she asks about me, not a peep, comprende?" Hand language tells me I should change the subject. Then I catch her little visual excursion across the room. I follow around past open mouths and licked-off lipstick. She leads me to Hadley behind the counter fingering an order on a screen. The girl's oblivious, but my friend's fixated.

I squeeze lime into the water glass and take my first sip. I wonder where Brie is.

❖

Brie

Get used to it, Mom would say. *It comes with the territory.* But really, these overly insistent, arrogant, bullheaded sorts—they like polite. Well-mannered girls feed their ego. They steamroll nice.

A pinch of apprehension would do wonders to your attractiveness quotient. It's like fine art. Sharp needs blur. A dab opaque, a touch transparent. I should be grateful, but I'm not. They only understand rude. Or at least passive-aggressive, which is what I chose tonight.

And I'm relieved to see my extra-long visit to the powder room has worked exactly as intended. I meander past bar stools now swiveling with new billfolds. Pushy is nowhere to be seen. I share a nod with the bartender and find myself swooped into Hadley's arms.

Just beyond her shoulder, my dinner companion sits at a table scarcely large enough to support the rose vase, let alone dinner. My ex is there, and I watch from a distance as they break bread, taking in a lungful of courage before making my way toward what will surely be my second most uncomfortable encounter of the evening.

And I'm tables away when my ex catches on, dragging a chair—a *we're still together* tactic. As gazes turn to me, I have to wonder what words were said in my absence about you-know-what.

"Hi, guys!" I announce.

Given my ex's chivalry has always been something that's appealed to me, I'm a bit swooned, I admit, and the flush of those drinks, they've done nothing for my self-restraint. So it's good she doesn't even catch me trailing down her shoulders to thick thighs in pants that hug those curves too well. She looks so good. I can't help but notice. Then I chastise myself for such a thought and huddle into Jessie. "Why didn't you save me?"

"From that? I didn't think you needed saving."

"I hope you two haven't been waiting long."

"Long enough to order," Jessie says handing over a menu. "What'll you have?" she asks, flagging down Hadley.

"Anything you'd recommend?"

I'm taken aback by her response, a moan of debatable interpretation though, I'm certain, unintentionally sensual. I study her features, which are surprisingly girlish given her posture, which is quite the opposite. She nods as she gushes about the dish, lips describing it in far too much detail. So I lean in. "You spend a lot of time here, don't you?"

"A lot...that's relative."

"Well, you seem to know a great deal about the menu," I say.

"That's because my wife over there is the manager." She motions to Hadley. "And it's takeout or canned Campbell's at the moment."

"I need to show this girl her way around the kitchen. The way to Jessie's heart is through her—"

"Sh," Jessie says, putting her hand over Ryan's lips. "G-rated. Please."

"You can't live on takeout," is followed by, "and how do you stay so thin?"

"Cooking? Oh, she's horrible in the kitchen," Hadley interrupts, flipping her pad.

And Jessie's water glass makes for a weak shield, though I've got to hand it to the girl for trying. "Harsh," she says. I watch as her lips pucker around the curved rim before she crunches down on a small piece of ice. Her eyes flit over to me. "Order, just go ahead and order already."

"I'll try the Veggie Hop." I smirk. "It comes highly recommended by your wife here." That's when I catch a moment between those two. Their restraint, it's almost painful to watch.

"Won't be long at all."

As she leaves with my order, my ex dives in with, "How'd you two make out without heat?"

"Blankets. Lots of them." If things were so innocent last night, why's she smirking like that?

"I see."

I stay out of it, creating a pretty intricate origami figure with my straw wrapper.

"Oh, but listen to this. She's quite the Girl Scout."

"Girl Scout...our Hadley?"

"Yes," begins Jessie, now hunched over adolescent style. "So picture this. We spend a few hours catching up. You know, that sort. Alicia comes by." She grunts. "Then we decide we've had it, crash. So here I'm in bed. She's on the couch. And the next thing I know, no power. In the middle of the night, mind you. So we call it in, and as you know, the whole damn town's down so they don't even have a time. We figure we'll go back to bed and tomorrow things will be normal again, right? Wrong. So she tells me this cockamamie story about how she made a homemade heater to get some Girl Scout badge and she wants to try it. I'm thinking, lovely. We're nearing frostbite and this kid wants to make a heater. But no, she gets way excited and goes on this hunt through the apartment, searching drawers. Tells me she needs tea lights and a brownie pan—"

"What the—"

"I know, right? So oddly, I actually had it all. And she lights this candle under a pot. Shuts us up in the bedroom with this contraption. And hey, I mean, it works."

That's when I get the nod, which means she wants my input.

"Didn't you think so? I mean, it's not a heater, but…"

For some reason, my ex really likes this story and she gets this half smile going, you know, I guess just one side of her mouth is happy. That's when the Girl Scout herself leans between their shoulders to offer coasters and mugs. Still crouched over the table, our storyteller follows her around, though nobody notices but me.

They both grab their beer. Conversations swim around us. Then the Girl Scout visits the next table and Jessie tries to center her mug in the circle pattern imprinted on the coaster. I'm taking her as rather introspective now and a bit smug. "Here's something we talked about last night," she shares. "Give me your take on it. It's kind of trivial. I don't know. I mean—"

Ryan cuts her off. "We get it. Just get on with it."

Hadley, Hadley, Hadley. Can we talk about anything else? I guess not tonight. It's better than the weather.

But Jessie goes on about their Twenty Questions, which start with, "What's the best part about winter?" She laughs, taking another swig. "Besides the obvious." She levels palms on the table in a *Don't look at me* or *I said too much* way. "There are perks, right?"

Then I get the look, which means she wants my answer first. And

I try to push away a few unwholesome thoughts jumping at me when I catch her peering from her drink, raising an eyebrow as if to proposition me. I just shouldn't have had that second drink.

I guess I pause too long (or make my ex uncomfortable) because she jumps in. "I could answer that one for her."

"No, I got it. Nothing, nothing at all."

"Don't be ridiculous." Why she hasn't moved to Antarctica is beyond me.

"Nope."

Jessie leans in, her posture telling me she thought Portland girls were born with boots on their feet. I tell her Portland girls could surprise you. We lock eyes, and seconds feel like minutes. I linger on that soulful expression, the way her hair falls unevenly on her forehead, the green tinge in her eyes. And then I grow rather self-conscious when I drop to her lips and I sense the start of what will soon be a full-fledged blush on my face.

"One Veggie Hop," I hear from behind, saving me from the consequences of one too many inebriating beverages. Maybe the warmth on my cheeks isn't a blush after all. I raise my finger, relieved for the distraction, and he sets a plate in front of me on what's now an incredibly crowded tabletop. Three drinks, three waters, three place settings, and not an inch of space left for three plates.

"Let me get you girls some elbow room," he offers, dragging a vacant table our way.

We shuffle seats and spread out. I savor a bite of finger fries. As he leaves, he carries with him a surplus of condiments but ignores two small candles, a pepper mill, a saltshaker, and this half-empty plastic bottle of catsup.

Ryan takes this opportunity to scoot beside me, and though I'm mildly perturbed by her lack of respect for my personal space at this particular point in our relationship, I'm too famished (and polite) to do anything about it. And whereas the downside of a few drinks is that inappropriate glance at a platonic friend, the upside is a rather okay-with-it attitude toward the still-in-denial ex-girlfriend.

We watch everything except each other. Catsup is squeezed. Mugs emptied. Eventually I thank Jessie for the recommendation.

"Anytime." And again, she fails to look away, giving me that devastating grin and yeah, no. But I do smile back.

"So," Jessie broaches, bringing a napkin to those lips, "Ryan."

"What?"

"How about you? The best part about winter, for you?"

Ryan

Mind if I sit here? She sets her fork down, wipes her quarter smile (daintily), and folds a napkin. Fingers balance a bowled glass with a wrist that slumps from its weight. It touches her mouth.

I hear nothing but myself. I'm not involved in this discussion. I'm not even listening. I'm wondering if she regrets me or if it's a new revelation. Has she met someone already? Does she want to? I'm wondering if she found a job, where she parked her truck. Has she told anyone? I want my jersey back.

I take another bite, oblivious (but not) to this perfume-spewing goddess inches from my wrist. All I can taste is rejection. It's sloppy and awkward. Jessie flips hair out of her eyes and looks my way. They both do. It's a conversation I don't want to join. I'd rather yawn through one of her cucumber spa retreats than endure any more of this.

But it beats lounging around the house in my bathrobe. I don't feel like reading a magazine or sticking in a Blu-ray that I've already watched umpteen million times. It'd probably remind me of her. I don't feel like speculating on what she's doing, where she is. I'd much rather watch it firsthand. So being here is the most logical thing right now.

Mind if I sit here? she wanted to know. Why would I mind? Have I ever minded? She looks over just long enough to get a smile out of me that I instantly regret. *Humor us,* her eyes say. She wants me to join in, but they're doing just fine without me. Then heavy voices, the rise and fall of pleasantries.

I twist my mind into a tight wad. I swirl my cup. I catch the hint of lime. My hand stops in midair and I get far too engrossed in the table tent advertising Sunday night's musical guest.

Until, beside me, "You okay, doll?"

I'm thinking, Why would you say that?

Things get still for a while. Brie takes another drink. I watch without watching. Then I hear, "I'm with you."

Jessie says, "In my truck, I'm on top of the world."

They're on something that has to do with work.

And then, "It's not like she didn't know, either."

And "I don't know about that."

And "Do you really think?"

And "It takes one to know one."

Hadley jumps in before too long and wants to know how everything's going. I raise a finger. My mouth is full.

She turns her attention to Jessie, whose elbows are propped on the table. They exchange glances. A kid's clearing the table just past her, and a band sets stage on the platform. Brie's watching that woman carrying speakers, then a mic stand, instruments, and equipment. The woman only takes a break to check her phone. Brie checks her own. I'm wondering if she wants to go home with her.

Then Jessie's freaking out. She unfolds a menu and ducks.

That's when I rejoin. I ask what's wrong. I scoot closer.

"Don't look now, but guess who just walked in," Jessie says.

I turn halfway to see.

"Nonononono! Don't make it obvious. Just be cool."

I just look confused. Alicia spots us. It's unavoidable, but I don't tell Jessie.

"She can't see us," she tells me. "Keep it that way."

I tell her I think it's too late. She grunts. I turn around and then think, Why am I being so adolescent? I don't like it when Jessie acts this way. The last thing I want to do is mimic her.

"I so don't want to talk to her," she says.

But she's already sauntering over in those cargo pants with far too many pockets. They exchange glares.

"Care to join us?" I ask. I get up and pull over a chair.

She thanks me but doesn't. "I'm meeting someone in a few. No need to avoid one another."

"No," Jessie says.

I ask how she's been. I've missed seeing her around. She gives me a hug. Her reply's pretty empty, though. She's not interested in talking to me. She's fixed on Jessie.

"Maybe I could steal you, just for a second? I owe you a beer, and…there's something we need to talk about."

I sense this wasn't the outcome Jessie had hoped for. So I'm naturally interested in her next move.

I'm also relieved when she stands up. "Sure." She's still reluctant. They make their way to the bar.

Unfortunately she's left me alone with Brie and here we sit in silence. So I decide to do the only thing I can do: I people-watch. So does she. We watch the band tune up. She's enjoying that much. She likes that girl, but she won't get what she wants in that package.

I feel like a chaperone. I'm liking the beat. It makes our silence a tad more tolerable.

❖

Brie

Could I be as entertaining as Jessie? I'd like to think so. We're still getting on dreadfully well.

So I grab the spotlight. Then I take a gulp of ice water. More like warm water, given all that ice has melted. I try to include the dark cloud beside me.

Jessie lounges in her chair. "Have at it."

"You know those women," I begin, "who have kids?"

It's like someone smacked a laugh out of her.

"I mean, I'm curious. Do you know anyone who's done that? Like, had kids. Without adopting?"

"You mean the turkey baster?" Ryan has a way of being a little too blunt. "Mail-order sperm?"

"Yeah, like the turkey baster. How exactly does that work?"

"It's expensive, for one," she says.

Jessie's getting engrossed. "And creepy," she says. "I mean, really, you're putting some dude's stuff up you—or her—whichever. It's creepy, if you ask me." She looks like she just bit a lemon.

"I don't know," I say.

"I'm into women," she says. "Not dudes."

I'm more than mildly offended when I ask in all seriousness, "And you have to do it a lot to make it take, don't you? I would think."

"I'd think so." Jessie ponders.

"So do you get a few batches from the same donor, like a twelve-pack? And then what? Like afterward, do you have to stand on your head? And does that mean your kids have half siblings all over that they'll never know about?" It's a serious topic, but I'm admittedly giggling at this point. "Sorry, guys. How'd we get on to this subject?"

"You brought it up." I think my ex enjoys stating the obvious.

"Oh yeah. I did, didn't I?"

Then, "I knew a couple once, drove clear on out to Boston to get it from a sperm bank. I didn't want to ask how it worked. That's rude, you know? Do you put it in at home or there at the clinic, or both? And, like, how do you transport it—in a Styrofoam cooler?"

"Did they, you know, get pregnant?"

"I don't know what happened to them, to tell the truth."

Jessie's shaking a finger. And these two try to remember. I get distracted through this part until a hand slaps the table. "Laura and Kim."

"Yes!" My ex is rather inebriated and shouting over the music. Not in an offensive way. She's just leaning in pretty tight. I'm glad she's loosening up. "What happened to them?"

"You know, I have no idea. They just sort of dropped off the face of the earth."

"Maybe it worked," Ryan says. "Maybe they're off at Lamaze class or baby yoga. Maxing out their MasterCard at babyGap and Toys"R"Us. Having playdates."

"Imagine if," I toss out, "both got pregnant at the same time. It's like twins but not. Different mothers. Same donor. I bet it's happened. And what about women using friends as the quote unquote *dad*? Some couples, you know, have people they know donate. Like it's an honorary thing up there with godmother or godfather. Look at David Crosby. He donated his offspring to Melissa Etheridge and what's her name. So are we just at a dinner party sitting around, sharing a beer, serving mashed potatoes and can you pass the gravy and oh, by the way, would you mind filling this turkey baster?" I can tell they're both thoroughly amused by this conversation, though they don't care to admit it.

Jessie rolls her eyes. "Two women preggers simultaneously. PMS times two is bad enough."

Personally, I think it'd be cute.

"If you know the donor, what happens when that friend wants parental rights and takes you to court?"

"Maybe I should start my own practice." Now there's a way to solve my unemployment problem. "Have you been screwed by your donor? Did you carry for nine months only to be served and ordered into court for child custody matters?"

Jessie cheers me on. "Do it. I'm totally serious."

"Don't let your kids suffer. You need strong legal representation to get that donor off your back for good. Call Hamilton and Partners. Experts are standing by."

She tosses me a wink. That look says something I've only seen from Chris.

My ex grabs the table tent to read. Without taking her eyes off the ad, she says, "I could never go there. Just the thought of being pregnant, really, no way. Not a friend. Not a stranger. Not for me."

"You don't want kids?"

"Not in my body, no. And I haven't really thought about that, to tell you the truth. Now that you mention it, I can't say that I want them. I can't share someone with a kid. And I'm too old—I'm forty-two. Besides, I wouldn't know the first thing. I know I wouldn't carry one. I mean, cravings for dill pickles and Cherry Garcia at one in the morning?"

And that seems the consensus.

But Jessie says, "I dig tots. I could totally get into teeny toes and booties and stuff. And I'd deck them out in little flannel shirts and lace-up boots. Teach them how to ride a bike—"

"Jessie is redefining the term *baby dyke.*" Ryan thinks she's funny.

"Hell yeah. And I'd pick a genius, too. I think you can scroll through their catalog, right, and narrow it down by nationality, IQ. Right? When you think about it, our community could already be breeding a superhuman race of geniuses." She settles on me. It's the kind of air you just need to fill with words.

"So, I would." Did I really just say that out loud? They're going to think I'm weird.

"You would?"

I suck water up my straw. "I would. On both accounts."

"You mean get preggers?" Jessie asks.

"Yes, I mean like carry a baby and all."

"Seriously?"

"What, you can't picture me at soccer practice?"

"Quite honestly, no," she tells me. "Not in a bad way. Don't take that wrong. You just don't look very mom-like."

"I'll take that as a compliment from you."

"Totally. It is."

"I'd love to have a kid. And I'd love to carry it. It's not that I'm hip on the turkey baster part. If there were another way…" I crease a straw wrapper in triangles. "But I would like to know what it's like, you know, to be pregnant—feel what that's like, give birth."

Ryan's been listening. "I didn't know you wanted kids."

"You don't know a lot about me, doll."

She doesn't take that as an insult. I think it was intended to be, though.

Hadley dips a shoulder in, sliding the check across the table. "Whenever you're ready."

Before I can even register what happened, Ryan has it. She bends forward to fish for her wallet. "I got this."

❖

I followed her taillights long enough. Then she hit the blinker and turned off because she likes to take that shortcut home. I don't. I'm fine with the long way. I actually prefer it, not that you can see the scenery when it's dark like this.

I'm sure that upset her. She probably spent the rest of the drive racing, rolling through stops just to make it home first, to prove her point.

I find it rather liberating to drive myself and not sit in her passenger seat. We pull in together.

That's when she gives me the cold shoulder. We walk up the porch. We step in. We run through our routine. She hangs her keys in the mudroom. I lock the door. She opens the coat closet, which squeaks, and sets her wet boots on the rubber mat just inside. She leaves it open so I can hang my coat. Then she goes into the bathroom. I hear a flush. We don't say a word the whole time. The clock is the loudest thing.

I'm in the bedroom getting nightclothes when she comes in. It's rather awkward around the bed. She tries not to touch me. I try even harder. I'm wondering how I'll fall asleep tonight.

We change in separate rooms. I start to miss her. Maybe not her in particular, so maybe *miss* is the wrong word. I don't want this to be messy.

If she asks me again where this is coming from, I'm not going to lie. I'm going to tell her the truth. That I'm too young to feel this old. That the more I think about who I want, the more unclear it gets. That every woman I see anymore appeals to me. Every one.

I'll tell her that I do want a daughter named Sylvia and a tiny lawn in town. Maybe not this town. Maybe a coastal town. That my wife will work with her hands and shoot hoops by our garage. She'll dress for family dinners and business socials, griping constantly about collars (like Chris did). She'll like my suits. She'll take them to the dry cleaner for me and pick them up. She'll take them off me after work. We'll have sex in the daylight. We'll summer in P-town. We'll winter abroad.

I pick up my clothes from the floor and pause at the hamper. It doesn't feel proper to combine our clothes now. They should go in a bag or a box or suitcase for when I leave. So I carry them out instead, and the door to the bedroom is still shut. I don't want to knock, so I put my clothes beside the hamper to deal with tomorrow.

I'm glad to be in sweats. I head to the living room and turn on the television using the remote. There's nothing on apart from a few cooking shows and infomercials. I've already seen this episode of *Modern Family*. I don't care to watch cartoons. But I find this documentary on pyramids, and I can't turn away. So I leave it on. It seems interesting enough.

When she joins me, she takes the couch. She's on the other side of the room. She just walks across, takes a seat, and flattens a pillow to her chest. She looks blue from the TV. She's glued to the show, not me. I'm wondering what she wants.

I think that maybe I should give her back that necklace, but I wouldn't know how. If I did offer it, how might she take that? I don't want it. I don't want anything she gave me; I'm too sentimental. What would I do with it? Maybe she wants me to keep it. Come to think of it, I should take the lawn chairs. I bought them.

They've interviewed a curator and are excavating now. I'm always intrigued when they brush particles off to keep artifacts intact. I could never be that meticulous. With some things, yes, but not that.

Maybe I'll happen across an archaeologist, like this woman. That would be nice. She'd come home from work and tell me about digs and I'd be so fascinated. Definitely someone who works with her hands.

CHAPTER TEN: JESSIE AND HADLEY

Jessie

Hadley's closing her shift.

Meanwhile I scroll through recipes labeled *Easy*. Pasta and herbs with broccoli. Veggie tacos. Stroganoff. And I begin to fancy myself as a culinary god. Emeril meets Ellen, slicing and dicing and sautéing in a kitchen adorned with Williams Sonoma, Le Creuset, and *oui oui oui*. At least until she materializes in the seat beside me and punctures that thought bubble.

Her voice is gravelly, translation exhausted. Her breath hints of cinnamon gum. She slouches like me except skirt style, knee over knee. Then she leans to see my screen.

"Planning a soiree?" she asks.

Next she kicks back, exhausted-waitress style. I try not to notice (but do notice) the arch of her back as she rests her head on her palms. God, she's hot. And she's turned me into a bundle of nerves anymore, tonight being no exception. When did this kid become my Achilles' heel?

"No, I'm not planning a soiree, as you say. I'd like to learn how to cook."

Two of her buttons struggle to tug apart but don't. It offers a glimpse of lace. She's hiked her skirt unusually high on the thigh and I have to wonder, is she doing this intentionally? I fixate on those calves just beyond the rim of my screen, but she's clueless.

In time I get back to "Six Easy Meals for When You Don't Feel Like Cooking."

"Don't laugh," I tell her. "Really, what's there to it? You just toss a bunch of stuff together and put it in the oven. Or stove. Some macaroni, this says, spices, a pinch. It gives how much. I could be good at this."

"Oh, you think," she says, doubting my culinary mojo.

"Yeah, this looks super easy. It even says it's easy, see? Says it's ready in fifteen minutes. Doesn't this look delicious?" I tilt my screen for her.

"It kind of does." The poor thing. She can hardly keep her eyes open.

"I could cook for you," I say, adding an empathetic pout and putting my boots down.

"What would you make me?"

"Let's see. I could make macaroni and cheese with these little breaded things, here."

"Zucchini?"

"Yeah," I say. "Zucchini."

"You think you could make breaded zucchini?"

"Sure I could."

I get a cheeky grin out of her. "Okay, Jess. Anytime you want to make me macaroni and cheese with breaded zucchini, I'm game."

"Good."

With that, I sit back again satisfied. I could start small, say with these easy fifteen-minute concoctions, and I could build up from there. Maybe in a year I'll hit the intermediate stage. I could make homemade pizza! I need to get grilling down, too. Campouts and visions of shish kebabs dance in my head.

Until Hadley pierces yet another joyful thought bubble with, "So what'd Alicia say? I saw you two talking."

"She's stalking me. I'm not kidding."

"Stalking you, really?"

"I saw less of her when we were together."

"I don't know," she says studying ceiling tiles. That beneath-the-button lace rises.

I divert the topic by changing it. "Busy tonight?"

"You could say that. It was worth it."

I just raise my eyebrows.

"I think my tips alone were well over two hundred bucks."

"You should buy me something with that," I tell her.

I want to carry her home.

"Like what, Jessie?"

"I've always wanted a sugar mama."

"Of course you have."

A finger slides under the rim of her glasses. It tugs at her lid. I look out. It's like double-exposure on glass. I can see inside and outside at the same time. And I just don't want to go out there. The apartment's heated up, but hardly inviting. I just hate cold sheets. It's not jibing for me at all right now.

I give her a nudge before she falls asleep. "Hey, let's get out of here. Test that new battery of yours." I get up before she can say *yes* and get my coat off the back of the chair. "I'll follow so you get home in one piece."

"I wish you could drive me."

I shrug. I wish I could, too.

She slips away.

I wonder why horns are honking out there. It's disconcerting.

I drop my phone in a pocket. She returns wrapped in her coat and scarf, pinching mittens delicately down each finger. She flings that backpack over a shoulder. She changes from flats to boots.

I zip up.

The garage isn't far. We don't say much with the wind. It's a fast walk. Her car seems lonesome. She wakes it up with the remote. That wind cuts through me. It must her, too; she's in a skirt.

She slides in, drags that bag over her lap, and offers me another (torturous) glimpse of knee. I hang against the car door awhile. She has too many keys, but it turns over fine.

"Wait here," I say. "Warm her up." She tucks her coat in as I slam the car door. Then I hike to the second and third floor. My bike's next to an Explorer under fluorescent blue. I hop on, rev her up, and straddle down corridors now vacant.

She pulls out and leads. She's driving slow, too slow. Roads are slick like water, salted and manageable. We pass a few reds, then greens, then she makes a left and pushes headfirst at the brick building. It's an old mill converted to apartments. It was all over the local news. She's one of the first to move in.

And this is where I could head home. I do consider it.

But I make my way over to her car instead. She's kicking that bag over a shoulder. It's a nice night, and all I want to do is run through this snow fog. But I don't. I just keep to her pace. Then she turns the key and we get inside. It feels unbelievably good and warm. Someone's cooking or did. Mailboxes line an entire wall; they're black. There's a table with books and a sign taped on it that says: *Take one. Leave one.* It feels open past midnight like Denny's. She checks her mail, but it's empty.

We take the carpeted hall and pass a window to the laundry room, and someone inside's shaking sheets. She uses the square key to the front door. She flicks a wall switch inside, and the room's lit.

We're on the first floor but it feels like the second or third. The windows are bare and they stretch across and up. I can barely see the cliff just beyond, let alone the river. She lets the darkness in. I head over, look down, and catch the river, which is high and crusted in ice.

Behind me I hear, "Have one of these." She's coming at me with a nice little grin and a plate full of powdered somethings. I'm apprehensive at first.

"What is this?"

"Just taste," she tells me.

"Poisoning me?"

Then an eye roll. She airplanes two fingers to my lips. "A neighbor brought these over. I couldn't possibly eat them all."

Not bad. I didn't expect fudge filling.

"Help yourself," she says.

"I will."

The place is tiny but tall. Brick gives it an industrial feel. She kicks off her boots, and I mean literally kicks them off, and then comes back to the futon and starts groaning about her aching feet. I tell her I can relate, that she needs a staycation.

"I know, right?"

This is my second home, the one with a much better decorator, I'll give her that. She makes tiny work.

This futon's always my bed. It's too many years old, but the bookshelves are new. They're not Crate & Barrel like the rest of the place.

I'm happy that she's finally unpacked those books—so many

jacketless hardbacks horizontally sloped and vertically stacked. A few black-and-white pictures in between. I pick one of those up.

"I haven't seen this," I say.

It's her brother. She's in it, too, hot from the sun. It's one of those striped bikini tops with strings that tie around her neck. Her shorts tie as well just under her tan line. Sunglasses, and sand stuck to bare feet. They rent that cabin at the lake every summer.

She tells me when these were taken. That's when I try to rewind and shift as nonchalantly as possible to another topic. I wipe the back of my hand across my mouth. Why'd I pick this up?

"I let that film roll sit, undeveloped, some years. I found it in a drawer when I unpacked, and with everything else going on..."

I try to shut her up, tell her I'm sorry.

"No, don't be, really. I can talk about her."

"The kids are getting old," I say.

"Like weeds. I can't keep up."

A picture is propped above a textbook; it's her parents. They're at the counter in the kitchen holding cookie cutters, a brush of flour on her mom's face.

"You look so much like your mom." I slip in next to her. "Same eyes. Same smile."

She mouths, "Thank you." It's nice.

Then I tell her, "That's exactly how I remember them." I said the right thing. It's how she's looking at me. I can tell. "How is he?"

"Oh. He asked about you—"

"No kidding," I say.

"Last time I called."

"I miss your dad."

"Maybe you can come next time."

"I'd love that," I say.

"Maybe. We'll see."

"We're getting an Airstream, you and I."

"You wish. You're so *Golden Girls*. Don't be that way."

"You've never been in one. They're incredibly cool. We could deck it out like this. I could make another bonfire."

"Tempting."

"And s'mores if you're lucky."

"You're a humungous nerd."

And you're a humungous tease, I think. Because it's hard to have any sort of posture on this thing. Any way you cut it, you're reclining. She stays at a comfortable distance—not too close, not too far.

She says, "I can't even remember when we last had time like this." I tuck my knees. She, on the other hand, is sprawled out.

"We can now. Until you meet someone."

She shakes her head. "I might start to annoy you."

"You never do that," I say. Those legs, and those patterns on her stockings winding around and along and up. Does she ever wear anything simple, I think. She yawns like a reach. Her palms become pillows again. Mercy me, don't do this to me, not tonight.

Then she does her, "So…um," thing and she starts interrogating. "Tell me about last night."

"You were with me all night," I say.

"We didn't talk when you came in."

"Oh, that."

"You hashed it all out?" she asks.

I don't respond right off. "She tried to. That's kaput."

She sits like me. The windows become our television.

"Not to change the subject"—but to change the subject—"our girl Ryan took some orchestrating this evening."

Her knees drop like she's interested. That arm stretches across the back of the futon, behind me, and she slides in. I'm reminded of her cinnamon.

"One word—awkward," I say.

"There's a lot going on behind that," she informs me.

"Like what?"

"She was probably, I don't know, confused or something, right?"

"Did they really split?" I ask.

"It's kind of a lot of things going on."

"Like what things?" I want to know.

"Like the ex—sort of, kind of—came back. You know…"

"Oh?"

"Ryan didn't tell you?"

"Ryan doesn't tell me anything anymore," I say. "Since I gave her a hard time about—"

"Well, you shouldn't have done that."

"Whatever," I say. "Did you catch that woman at the bar?"

"No. What woman?"

"Hitting on Brie. I had to excuse myself—"

"She gets like this, you know."

I don't know. My arms cross. We get quiet. I'm thinking about Alicia—and then Ryan and those two. Then my wires cross and I get on Casey and I'm tensing up about it. So I figure, why not bring that up while we're on the subject of exes. So I do.

"Let me ask you something."

She's thinking this is another harmless question but she's wrong. She'll be upset in a second.

"If you don't want to talk about it, that's cool. Tell me if it's not-okay territory. I just…well, how's Casey these days?"

Her deer-in-headlights expression tells me plenty. "I'm not sure I understand."

I could wiggle around the subject. But I choose matter-of-fact. Like a cop. "She stepped out on you, and I mean, you seemed—to me at least—to handle that all right."

"That's good to know."

"Well," I say, "you went back."

"I told you I shouldn't have."

"Why?"

"Seriously? She cheated on me, Jessie. You don't go back after that. It's disgusting. I couldn't trust her."

"So there's no chance…?"

She's studying my eyes.

"You two, you know, getting back together."

"It's been a year, Jess."

"You guys don't even talk?"

I retuck that strand of hair behind her ear.

"Of course we don't. I don't even think about that. And honestly, I don't even know what on earth I saw in her."

I'm glad I brought it up, though. I believe her. I rub her knee to say, "It's cool." I'm smiling at her. I can't help but notice that she's more focused on my lips. Would I blow it if I kissed her right now? Like just leaned in and screwed everything up between us. She wants me to. I could. Or maybe she's just tired and not quite here.

I squeeze her knee instead. Then I tap it and lean forward to get another pastry.

"You know," she hints, "things settle. You settle. It all gets settled and you fall into the…that ho-hum scheduled once-a-month thing." I don't turn my head from the window. But I do question her. She wants me to commiserate. She's uncomfortable now. "Bed death, you know."

I (ineffectively) hold back a chuckle. "I don't know, sorry."

"Don't tell me you've never—"

"Can't say that I have. What you have to do is—"

"Okay, stop," she shouts with a groan.

"You want me to stop?" She's trying to win this stare down, but she never does. So I ask again, "Do you want me to stop?" Eventually we can't help but laugh and look away.

I personally cannot understand why anyone could sit within a football field's range and keep their hands off these thighs and still insufficiently buttoned blouse. My smile is, I hope, endearing. "You're so cute."

"Everyone goes through that," she insists.

"No. It's a bad relationship thing."

"Well, I attract bad then."

"Don't let it happen."

If we keep eating like this every time the conversation gets interesting, we might just finish them off.

"Which brings me back to—"

"Yeah, Ryan," she says. "Far from LBD."

"Well."

"That's so not me. How can they do that?"

I shake my head.

"It's too much, come on—"

"Can't you just—"

"Before I jump in bed with just anyone…You know I don't do that. That's so, so…" She grunts, clearly worked up about this. "I would feel used."

"What's so wrong with it? Have some fun for once. And don't judge people like that." I clear my throat. "Haven't you ever wanted to…loosen up, slip out of those morals? It's not like anyone needs to know. You get to know a lot about a person—"

"By sleeping with them?"

I snicker. "It's one way."

"Then what if they're not even into you?"

"Oh, they are."

She's disappointed by my answer.

So I add, "I can't think of marriage on the first night."

"I'm not even saying that."

We grab another pastry, and then the futon finally gets its way with her. She gives up, propping feet on my lap. We always disagree on this subject. I don't even know how it keeps coming up. I knead into those calves. She seems to like it. I change the subject for her sake. "So, you're off tomorrow?"

"I'm off for four days in a row. Then six on. But I'm not even wanting to think about work. I'm jazzed to see everyone Sunday—and beyond ecstatic to have someone else serving me for a change. I hope I never have to do this again."

"Five years," I say. "They've made it that long."

She lifts her head.

"Don't look at me like that," I say.

"Why?"

I laugh. "You're so behind the times, aren't you? She and I are good friends—that's all. Just like you. Ella is ancient history. Maybe we need to do more catching up."

"Maybe we do."

My hand slips just above her knee. She closes her eyes. I take her in. She reaches overhead, which makes the seam of her shirt rise again to reveal that midriff. I just follow the patterns, back to her feet, stalling on ankles, and back up where thighs meet. That's when I see an intriguing grin curl up her cheek.

SATURDAY

CHAPTER ELEVEN: RYAN AND BRIE

Brie

My head hurts when I wake up. I self-diagnose these symptoms as one too many drinks last night and flat-out stress. It's not a hangover. I definitely know what a hangover feels like, and this is not it.

I squeeze the tube of toothpaste and push my toothbrush on, waiting for the timer to tell me when to move from quadrant one to two, three, and four. Then I step with some hesitation onto the scale like I do every day.

I look fat or bloated or something. I can see it in the mirror.

And I'm brushing quadrant two when those zeroes on the scale turn into real numbers and all I can say is this. You know what can turn the crappiest day into something adequately almost okay? Finding out that you're a whole two pounds lighter. There are some serious benefits to breakups.

Suddenly that pouch doesn't look so pouched. And I'm thinking, with this sort of luck, I should go out and play the lottery. Or maybe dial Chris by accident, who knows? How I would love to hear that voice.

Chris used to say that for every ten bad lucks you're due one good. I don't know where she came up with ten, but she swore on it. She'd count them down, like, every day. *Bad luck number three hit today*, and then a long diatribe about how she was late to school or work or yelled at or something or other. I'm thinking I've had far more than ten bad lucks to get this one good. But I'll take what I can get.

Hadley's right there with me when it comes to those last five pounds. She whines incessantly. So I send a brag text.

I dropped two pounds and didnt even try.
I hear back immediately: *youre an absolute bitch*
Me: *i know, right?*
Hadley: *i have at least 15 in my bra alone*
Me: *stop bragging*
Hadley: *what am I going to do?*
Me: *about what?*
Hadley: *what else? jessie* :(
Me: *she's hot…you should make a move* ;)
Hadley: *can I call u?*

That's when I text her *yes* and duck into the only quasi-soundproof room in this whole house—the attic. It's cold, but it's fixed, which means it looks more like a family room. Ryan has a couch bed up here and a couple Restoration Hardware floor lamps, a shag rug, some children's books and toys for her nieces and nephews. It's saturated in sun. If it wasn't so cold, I'd probably live up here. I pick up on the first note.

"I'm such a nerd," she says.

"Tell me something I don't know."

"She came over."

"Last night?" I ask.

"Yes," she says with a sigh.

"And?"

"And, you know, nothing. We hung out. I fed her pastries and she had her hand between my thighs. She went home pretty late."

"Wait a minute, doll," I say. "She had her hand between your thighs?"

"Okay, exaggeration. More like between my knees, only higher and…you know."

"What'd you do?"

"This is really horrible. I didn't do anything. But when she does that, I just—I don't know."

"You didn't do anything? What are you, a complete pillow queen?"

"No! I don't know. I don't think so."

"You're adorable," I say.

"Not really. She didn't stay long after that. I had a long day, and maybe she took it personally or something. She went home."

I sigh. "Why'd you let her do that?"

"I know, right? It's not like I wanted her to. Would you with this girl's hands between your thighs, really? Don't answer that. Maybe I need to let this go."

"Just kiss her already."

"I can't do that."

"Why not?" I ask.

"She's my friend, and we've always done this."

"She routinely runs a hand up your thighs, doll? That's not *friends.*"

"She'll meet someone probably tomorrow—probably already— and then it's good-bye to me until her next breakup. That, or she'll get back with Alicia and call to tell me how hot it was to literally rip her shirt off, buttons and all." Hadley's clearly angry—if she could ever get angry. Then I hear, "I'm not her type."

"It's painful to even watch the two of you. She wants you. And she's no prude, and neither are you—though in some ways…Well, look. We just need to figure out…*you* need to figure out. You know her better than I."

"I know—that's the problem. We know each other too well, and I think, if this were someone I met anywhere else, it'd be different."

I'm trying not to laugh. "Do you see how she looks at you?"

"I can't screw this up."

"You won't."

"Look," she says, clearly trying to change the subject even though I know she's beaming over there. The girl's infatuated. Then she asks, "How are things with you?"

"They're great. I lost two pounds."

"Between you and Ryan!"

"I'm currently trying to focus on the positive aspects of my life," I insist.

"Are you ever going to read me that letter?"

"I'll snap a picture with my phone. How's that?"

"Did you email back?"

"I haven't sent it."

"Why?" she asks.

"I'm not ready yet. I don't know if I should," I say.

"You can be friends with your ex. It happens all the time."

"Are you friends with your ex?" I ask.

"Not exactly. It never worked out for me. But that's not the point—"

"And what if I get all obsessed again. What if she wants me back?"

"Yes," she says. "Exactly."

"I already want her back. Is that bad? It is bad. It's all I can think about."

"Don't tell her that."

"I know that," I say.

"So am I going to meet this girl?"

"I hope so. I'm getting packed today. I'm trying to avoid you-know-who—which isn't an easy feat—so I can commit this whole day to packing. I don't have a lot. She made me get rid of pretty much everything when I moved in here."

"Want me to help?" she asks. Then she tells me, "I'm off," meaning work.

"No, it's all right. But thanks. Are you off Monday, though?"

"I'll help you load the U-Haul," she says.

"I don't even know if I can get one that fast."

"You will. There aren't that many lesbians in this town."

As we hang up, I fall back into the chair and tell myself that I'm going to stop obsessing over Chris. Stay in the present moment, I think. Which means I should be focusing on this silence, how cold it is, the square pattern of sun slanted on the floor—right here, not there. Today not yesterday. This attic not that loft, not lounging in bed squeezing a lifetime into one perfect weekend.

But I'm thinking about the way she sang to me a cappella accompanied by juvenile giggling, a song that's now permanently ours. I was wearing that extra-large button-up I slept in. I couldn't have sung along regardless of how hard my mind pushed. She was too thoughtful, endearing. I was too uncomfortable (in an ecstatically good way). It's always so positively difficult with her.

Today, I can't not think of yesterday—the way her body smashed behind me as her fingers clasped like a belt around my hips. The sound of thunder and gushing gutters. The hiss of bus brakes below. That cool touch down my neck and then that thick messy hair of hers—it was crazy up like that every morning. The way she does that, it's how I imagine candle wax must feel as it liquefies just before it drips over the edge. How desperately I wanted her because of nothing at all.

Why did she always do that? She went excruciatingly slow or I went excruciatingly too fast because I was there before she caught up, before she could even touch me, really. Before I felt the tips of her fingers down the front of my body. It was so easy with her.

I was there when her lips barely touched my spine. Weak-kneed as she reached around and down and underneath. I was there when her palms felt my ribs and my shirt came up and over, before I could turn to her.

Where her words just ached. *You're so beautiful*, she'd say. *I can't even stand it.* Because I knew she lived and breathed me, and then palms warmed my cheeks as I closed my eyes.

Everything I had to do so I would not be done when she touched me. And when it ended, the song began again. She must remember, too. It was all over the bed. It was hours and days. It was her scent that lingered on my skin. It was the way I could taste myself on her lips.

But I'm trying not to think about that.

❖

Ryan

Here it goes again, *Surya Namaskara B*, which means another morning led by that monotonous DVD.

You're going to bend your knees, looking forward and touching your fingers to the floor. Bring your hands up, breathing in and aligning your breath with the movement.

Now stretch your fingertips high above your head and exhale as you fold your body forward.

Place your hands on either side of your feet.

And jump back into plank.

"How long with this silent treatment?" I ask, breaking her meditative state. I'm beyond annoyed at this point. She's dodged me all morning. It's time we talked—about living arrangements, about when, about this. I won't bring up *Why?* again. I promise.

Elbows in, shoulders back, and into upward dog.

"Can't this wait? I'm working out right now." She's winded. "I got a late start."

"You're avoiding me."

I lean on the door frame. Why does she have to look so damn hot in this dog pose? Even when I'm pissed at her, dismissed by her, crushed, I still want her.

Exhale into downward dog.

Step your right foot forward and bring your hands up, reaching, stretching.

"We need to deliberate. I know," she says meeting my eyes for the first time today. "In an hour, I'm yours."

I'm yours. Don't I wish.

"All right," I concede. At least I've been scheduled. I glide pocket doors halfway shut to muffle the noise.

Exhale. Bring your hands down to the ground and step back.

Then I leave the room. I don't even understand this whole yoga craze. Why exactly would anyone voluntarily twist themselves into pretzels?

I make my way down the hall toward our bedroom, at least what used to be our bedroom, squinting past the bathroom—it's all just too impeccable. Hospital clean, in fact. Crystal jars sparkle. Chrome. The new day shines off marble and porcelain. Past the next door frame, a vase overflows with that bouquet I bought her just last weekend to cheer her up. They're yellow like sun because she hates winter. I can be thoughtful. Bedsheets are tucked military style. Wood polished. I certainly never kept the place this nice.

She has too much bottled-up energy. She needs a job.

The hall dead-ends at our bedroom. It feels like someone else's. I scope out her washed and dried and folded clothes atop the bureau. Her shirts, a few I've worn myself quite comfortably, they're like relics in someone else's house. They're hers, and not mine-hers but just hers. Same with those books, which I've insisted be kept in the drawer out of the way, not cluttering the top of the end table. Now I'm wondering why I complained at all. Could I not have been a bit more accommodating?

I griped when shoes were left at the threshold. When crumbs were left on the counter. The crowded closet and the not-quite-right dinners. But I love them now. I've not told her that. I'm not going to, either. Not now. Even her sunrise yoga and those Valium-induced vocals that drone down the hall. It's like an alarm clock. It's going to feel hollow here without it. The house without her in it.

I don't want her to move out. Move on. Move away.

I plop on my bed, grab my iPhone, open a senseless game. I have an hour of relentless mind chatter ahead of me. And with a brain that wants to stay right where it is, I let it do so, practicing my speech, predicting her response, and directing the next scene. It's designing quite the dialogue until my screen blinks crimson: *Defeat! Try again?* I don't know how long it's been blinking.

I think my fingers are too cold. This room, actually, is too cold compared to the rest of this house. Why doesn't the heat ever manage to get back here? I should call someone about that.

I part the closet doors. On my toes, I shuffle through a pile of wool sweaters on the high shelf until it dawns on me that this might be the only part of this house left in disarray. Our closet. My sweaters overlap hers, one atop another, in a towering mess of yarns and tweeds and patterns.

I stretch as high and far as I can because, naturally, I need the one on the top of the heap. It's the only one that matches. I push one back gently, tugging another until I can reach my favorite navy pullover.

A sweater at the top bunches, wanting to come down. That noise gets brasher, like a serving plate sliding across a table, until it crashes, sending paper in a flurry like confetti around me. Envelope confetti.

Four sweaters come along with it. I fish out a box. A battered cigar box, upside down, inside out, on the floor. It's next to my running shoes. I'm thinking I need to clean this mess up.

I listen to her yoga coach as I crouch on my knees. I reassemble the envelopes into a neat stack. I work quickly, peeking occasionally. And I see a pattern in it all: Chris.

I look over at the door and then the clock, reassured I'm alone and that I have another half hour until I'm caught red-handed. I take a deep breath, hoping to delve into some interesting reading. At least my mind clutter's at bay.

Each envelope is cut crisp with a letter opener, postmarks a decade past.

Truth be told, I've seen this box. I didn't know it stored letters. Come to think of it, I don't really know what I thought. That it was empty, maybe? It was Brie's, that's all.

My girlfriend hardly talks about her ex. But here she is. Sloppy, slanted, blue-inked penmanship and all. Like she's writing to me. Is this what it's like to open someone's diary?

I pick a letter, unfold it, and get sucked in. She calls her Bee, like the flying kind, and she's sweet like a teenager. She says things like *I mean it* and *I wish I could show you*. She's over-the-top dramatic.

I pause midway. Who writes like this? I imagine this kid with my much-younger girlfriend. High-school younger. Next to metal lockers with padlocks that dial.

When I'm done, I tuck that letter in its envelope. There must be fifty more just like it sprawled across the floor, and I file each one back into this deep cigar box. I cannot possibly read them all, though I'm tempted. Why did she keep these? And why hasn't she mentioned them? She didn't have to keep this a secret. It wouldn't have bothered me. But it does now. Sort of.

She knows all about my exes. I've shared pictures; she wanted to see. I took her to that inn, the best in P-town, the six rooms I've stayed in—the rooms I wanted to reinvent with her instead. We've shared waffle cones together with them and cups with cookies and cream, and rocky road. She knows them. Why didn't I know this? It's oddly charming to read.

I clean the mess. Some opened prudently, others ripped roughly or anxiously, taking the whole return address right along with it. Each in shades of age and beige. All with perfect penmanship. The pile in my hand gets thicker, envelopes corner to corner.

Until I spot the one that's out of place. It's like-new white. The postmark is peeled away. This letter came here.

A thumb makes its way through the slit until I pinch a single sheet. The crease is raw, so raw it'd cut if I'm not careful. I read.

My hand shakes, which surprises me.

And in two brief paragraphs dated two weeks ago, I lose myself. On every word, on *T*s and *B*s, on those neat flat lines like a ruler set below each sentence. And on its unhurried almost-poetic wording. This is written to my present-day girlfriend. I jump to the signature and a word tugs my heart: *Love*.

That's when a huff startles me. It's not mine. My house is hushed, almost deafening. The DVD is not playing. She's incensed and behind me asking, "What are you doing with my stuff?"

I turn to her, half angry, more ashamed, hunched over a pile of sweaters and letters. "Were you ever going to tell me?" She pulls my gut like the evening tide.

"It's nothing," she says. Then she squats beside me, frantically stuffing the remaining letters into her box. Can she actually hear my heartbeat? I can.

"This is why you're leaving?" I ask.

"No."

She continues (tap-tap-tapping the floor) to stack.

"I didn't write back," I hear her say.

"She knew where you lived."

"That's my mom."

It really wouldn't matter what she says, now. "Why didn't you share this with me? I mean, really, how do you even justify this?" I'm pissed.

"Why were you snooping?" Her voice is sprained, loud like mine.

"Far from," I shout. "I pulled a sweater down. Sorry if I was cold sitting here waiting for you to finish so we could talk—translation, do the adult thing and figure out what happens next, what we're even doing, whatever this is that we have. Nothing, apparently. And this thing fell on me. It fell all over me. So I have to wonder, why couldn't I know? What else have you kept from me?"

But the room's mute after my tirade. She doesn't give me the decency of a response. I stare at her on the floor next to me, but she won't lift her gaze. Her shoulders slump. She swallows. Gray yoga pants ripple across her crisscrossed legs. She looks guilty as hell.

Then my girlfriend says quite matter-of-factly, "I'll be out this week."

What do you even say to something like that? It's not like I've considered how things would end. But I trusted it'd be kind. Shouldn't it be kind?

"I'm not kicking you out," I say.

"I know you're not kicking me out."

What are my options? I have no options.

"Can we not do this," I say. "Things were fine two days ago. Now you're packing up and moving out. What the fuck am I supposed to think? I don't even get it."

She puts her letter in the box and opens a palm so I'll give her that last letter—the heartbreak I'm still holding on to.

"I'm so sorry," she tells me, "for putting you through this. You don't deserve this." And that's when she finally raises her (damp) eyes to me and I feel like I've broken through. But this is not at all what I wanted to hear. In fact, I've heard this intro enough to know its trajectory.

I'm connecting dots. The not touching. The not talking. The not trying. *Chris.* I don't want to stay open anymore.

I take a deep breath, choking a sting of my own tears down as I watch hers. And I hear myself pleading with a woman who no longer wants me.

The heater kicks on.

"I'm not over her."

The single sentence I really wish I hadn't unearthed. It hangs between us.

She looks at the letter in her hand, folds it, and slides it in the envelope. I'm speechless. She doesn't look at me again. She doesn't love me back. But she's crying still. At least she's given me that.

❖

Brie

If she wants to let off some steam by reshoveling that already plowed driveway, who am I to stop her? She's right, I bet all that slush could refreeze into a sweet sheet of ice if we get down to thirty tonight. But that's what salt's for.

For what it's worth, I could use this alone time. Actually, I think we both could.

Plus I do need to pack and would prefer to do so without her drama following me around room to room. I'm already short-tempered as it is. Those letters were not hers for the reading. They were never meant for sharing, let alone for someone already seething with revenge tendencies.

I guarantee one thing, nobody else will ever see them because they're going in this monstrous plastic storage bin, way at the bottom under dry-clean-only trousers and blouses. Above that, I pack pajamas and tuck two textbooks down the side. I'm trying to balance light with heavy, so it's not too hard to carry.

I've already taped up the entire contents of my dresser and bedside drawer including my hand lotion, a pack of Trident, and a bottle of valerian root; it helps when I can't sleep—which is too often. So I'm crossing my fingers I can live without it tonight.

All that's left is this phone and charger along with three complete outfits I'll need for tomorrow, the next day, and the day after that. Something formal for Sunday and old jeans and Henleys for the rest—things I can bend in.

I kneel on the box to shut it. Then I refold her sweaters on the top shelf of our closet, which looks pitifully naked with its three lone hangers dangling on a half-filled bar. On a positive note, I've freed space that she can fill up with a fun-filled excursion to J.Crew.

I wonder if I can even get this out to my truck on my own. As light as I've packed, the thing's beyond unwieldy. Which would be why I'm going to drag it down the staircase (let it drag me, more like), and it's loud, but I pause halfway at the porthole window to check status. And the coast is clear. She's still hard at work, chipping at that ice at the end. It looks warm out there, at least for this time of year. Clouds are dark even now at high noon when things are supposed to be bright.

I eventually lose sight of that coat behind the pine tree, which offers the perfect opportunity to slip on my boots and drag this tub to the truck without her even noticing.

Out the door, I lift with some serious oomph and hustle, coatless, breathing plumes along my path. My truck's half full. It's deep, which is good. I can probably get a few more bins in along with those suitcases and my laptop, which will go in the passenger seat. I'm starting to get excited. I cannot wait until Monday. I'm so out of here.

And it's not until the latch snaps that my stomach starts arguing with me. I'm sure Ryan's famished as well, and it certainly wouldn't kill me to make a little something for the both of us to eat. Even though she's not the biggest fan of my cooking.

There's enough for breakfast burritos of sorts, which will make good use of what little food is left: a pepper, an onion, three tortillas, and five large eggs. And it's sizzling in the pan when she stomps in, carrying with her a blast of winter air.

❖

Ryan

This kitchen smells surprisingly edible when I step inside, boots dripping. I tug at my fingers, hanging my coat on the wall. Then I warm my hands on my thighs only to notice, those jeans aren't supposed to be low-rise. But they dip seriously loose on those hips of hers. She's lean and tall at the stove, shirt tucked in front only, a chunky leather belt strapped around her waist, hair half down her back.

Then I hear, "I'm making more than I need—if you want some." My girlfriend's civil, and my stomach's more than delighted by her offer.

I thank her. "I'd love that," I say as I gather a few napkins and set them on the island. The pan makes an obnoxious crash in the sink before she approaches with two plates in hand, setting one in front of me. She seats herself at a distance.

I'm too hungry to talk, so I let silence settle amid the sounds of utensils. I do this fork-cut thing. She unfolds the newspaper with a shake, refolds it in fourths, and then begins to read to herself. Between bites, I try to read over her shoulder.

It's twelve forty. If this were any other Saturday, we'd both hit the grocery store and I'd make a few meals to get us through the workweek without hardcore cooking. But it's not any other Saturday. I don't know what we'll do today, tonight. I can't make plans, exclude her, unintentionally offend her. I also can't include her, assume, and do the same. She's not exactly communicative.

Once my plate's half empty, I ask her myself but first break the silence with small talk. "Do we have enough food for the week?" She's still reading. "I'm guessing I should've gone Thursday night. I didn't expect we'd get this much."

"There's not much in there," she tells me, glancing over the newspaper at the fridge. "This is about it."

"Okay." I admit, it feels nice that we can talk. Without yelling, that is. "I'll head out and get a few things. Is there anything you'd like me to pick up?" And then I risk, "You are welcome to join me."

"I have some things to take care of here and then my haircut. I should be fine. Thanks, though." She seems to be striking a balance somewhere between courteous and irritated. But I do sense she's ready to wrap this up. The thing is, I'm not.

"What time?" I ask.

"What?"

"What time's your haircut?"

"Oh. Four thirty," she says.

"All right. Well, I can have dinner ready when you get home…if you'd like."

"Sure."

"Is that a yes?"

"Yes." Her eyes are glued to the front-page story. Time passes, mutely, and I find I want to know more about this Chris. I have a couple more bites in front of me, a somewhat captive audience, and a conversation that was promised this morning which never actually transpired. So I dive in.

"I never did get that talk this morning that you promised."

"What's more to talk about," she asks, setting the newspaper down.

I try not to read into her newfound attentiveness. Then my mind sidetracks me. Even I think it all sounds more like an excuse to prolong a less than authentic dialogue. Even I'm starting to get annoyed.

Then I mumble under my breath, "You don't plan on vanishing while I'm at work, do you?"

"Of course not."

"You two back together?"

"It'll probably be sometime this week," she says. I'm not oblivious to the fact that she's avoiding my question. "I still need to pack. I need to rent a trailer, and they're not open until Monday." Then, as if reciting her to-do list, she says, "That's when I'm calling. I have to load it all."

"So this week," I say as I take my last bite. They're hard words to say. They're even harder to feel.

"Yes, most likely."

"I'm just curious about something," I toss out, mentally backpedaling right after the words leave my lips because I'm not sure how to phrase it or if I even want a real answer. When she turns back to her plate, I lose that fleeting attention she'd given me earlier. "What's her deal?"

I figure I'm transitioning into platonic, but I guess I've instead hit another nerve that I didn't know she had because she stands up in a huff. "She listens. She knows me." Her voice is raised, her arms crossed again in front of her.

"And your grandmother, apparently."

"Reading a few letters behind my back hardly makes you an expert on my life." She walks over to the sink and starts washing her plate. "In fact, you know very little about me after, what, a year now. Chris and I aren't back together. She wrote me a letter, weeks ago by the way, for closure apparently. I haven't even responded to her. Maybe I wasn't going to. Or maybe I was."

"So you and this kid dated in high school, right? She calls your mom because, what, she's like family. How sweet. Your mom gives her your address—my address. She writes you. She thinks—even your mom thinks—this is totally okay going behind my back, your girlfriend. I saw enough of that letter. If you think it means nothing, you're flat-out blind and you know it."

"Fuck you," she yells.

"No, fuck you. Really," I say. "Because I would never do that to you."

"No, you'd rather parade your exes in front of me so I can sit across the dinner table and make small talk with women you used to fuck. Like that's so okay. You don't even know the meaning of fucked-up."

"I'm over them. At least my head's in the right place. Some of us move on before they move in with someone new."

I don't even know if I've cornered her, but it feels to me like I have. She says nothing back and I'm satisfied with that, for whatever it's worth. Then I think aloud, "I know. You *thought* you were over her." The racket over at the sink comes to an abrupt halt once she puts the clean pan on the rack to dry. Joining her by the sink, I wave a white flag. "I didn't ask to start an argument." I twist the faucet on the sink to wash my plate, glaring at her.

"But why would you want to get back with someone who already screwed you over how many times?" I'm sincerely befuddled. She shakes her head. "This weekend, I was seriously looking forward to it, thinking maybe it'd bring us closer. The exact opposite happened." I catch a tree being blown to bits outside. "Why are you treating me like this? Like complete shit. No matter how much space I give you. No matter what I give at all. Why didn't you tell me? Why did you have to keep it from me for—what?—weeks, as you say? So I could find out this way? What'd you think would happen?"

She's staring outside blankly. She's thinking about what I said. I can see it in her eyes, in her lips that part just enough to let air pass in and out. This is the scene where she confesses everything. That she said her good-byes, that she missed what they had. That it's me she loves. This is the scene where I forgive her.

Instead she says rather calmly, "How many times do I have to say *I'm sorry*. You act like I planned this. Like I knew I'd hear from her, and then I had to let it sit and figure it out. And still I haven't figured anything out. Why—how could I tell you? It's why we can't talk at all anymore. You're suspicious—if I talk too much about someone, leave at a different time, who've I met? Imagine if I told you this. Imagine what you'd do. I knew you'd react this way. And quite honestly, I'm tired of defending myself. Being questioned all the time over nothing." She pauses. "It's ridiculous."

She flirts accidentally, I've watched it. People misconstrue. It's not jealousy, it's life experience. It's her naivety. Protective does not equate to jealousy.

She scrapes her nails together. "A woman hit on me last night at the bar. Did you know that much? I wasn't even interested in her, but she got me a drink. The whole time, I kept thinking: Ryan's going to flip the fuck out. I was so worried you'd make a scene. That you'd embarrass me. That you'd come in raging mad and unreasonable. So I ran into the bathroom and hid because she wouldn't leave me be."

CHAPTER TWELVE: JESSIE AND HADLEY

Jessie

I yank on the stuck dryer handle and reach in. It burns inside. Glaring back at me is a screen that wants another twenty-five cents for ten minutes. Visa, MasterCard, and American Express accepted. The air's pungent with commercial detergents, fabric softeners, and lint. At my right, zippers tumble. The room's dirty but cleaned. I tuck heated clothes into this canvas laundry bag and tug at its drawstrings. Then I haul it over my shoulder the few steps to my one bedroom on the first floor.

I pull a shade. It's gloomy out. T-shirt after denim after hoodie, I shake and zip and stack and sort until piles of V-necks nearly topple. Sock wads go directly in the drawer. Jeans are hung in a closet that's too crammed to jam even one more pair, but I get it in.

I fit in white earbuds and turn the dial. The scroll seems endless. Then I drag out the vacuum, starting in the kitchen.

I'm pretty into my *Fuck The Man* playlist when my phone vibrates at my hip, so I answer.

"I'm bored," Hadley tells me.

"I bet you are. You have four days off."

"I know."

"Paint your nails," I say. "Take a nap. Download a zombie podcast."

"Is that what you're doing?"

"Not exactly."

"I wasted the morning surfing the net, reading news, commenting on social media, and making pancakes," she tells me.

"Real maple syrup?"

"Of course," she says.

"Yum."

"You?"

"Domestic stuff," I say. "I'm hitting the gym in a bit."

"Can I join you?"

I'm less than thrilled about this idea. So I don't respond. Then I hear, "Or not. But I'd like to come by and abduct you."

"This could be interesting. Do elaborate."

"Are you dressed?"

"Do you want me to be?"

"Yes, smart-ass. Stay where you are."

When I hang up, my cheeks literally ache from smiling.

❖

Hadley

Is there any use trying to understand how I feel, let alone predict or plan or steer left or right or otherwise? When I think back, most everything I thought would happen, didn't. And now this? In fact, almost all those plans—how I'd look, the money I'd make, how I'd spend my day, who I wanted to be—either didn't happen or just slipped out from under me. It's too unpredictable, life.

I lose Mom and everything around me and inside me crumbles. It was too unimaginable at the time. She'd been there, nudging me, loving me. It's as if, now, I'm finding this new chapter. Maybe I've simply stepped into it by chance. I didn't find anything. But she's not here to see it.

This is a time I would call her and slant my story into that perfect serenade, and she would read between the lines. I can hear it now, quibbling about how reckless I am to not even consider whatever it is. But she encouraged me, nonetheless. It's not a good feeling or bad, not having her. It's just different, that's all. It's a big frightening blank but freeing at the same time. I'm ashamed to admit there's an upside, but it's true. There were things I wouldn't do, wouldn't say, just to please her.

I'm remembering this along my drive. I don't even play the radio. It's just the loud sound of solitude. That heat's roaring, anyway, not drowning my mind, but still. I don't want to. And I'm wondering why I've never thought this much about it before.

What I miss most of the time is not having that voice always telling me that I can do it. That I'll make it through. The one who could convince me of anything and everything, who could talk sense into me when I made none. If it was okay with her, it just was. End of story. I'm not capable of finding that without her.

As I make my way to Eighth and up Maple, I can see the same buildings through my window. It's all frosted now. New trees have been planted since, with old trunks taken down. Boards fixed and Benjamin Moore glossed over to give it all a brand-new shine. But it's still all the same underneath. The roads are still narrow and snaky, which makes it impossible to see just ahead. They spend summers repaving but never take the time to add a few lines over the asphalt. So we make our own, me to the left and that Subaru heading straight. It's as if we remember where they used to be.

I wonder if, when you lose someone, part of that person becomes you. I'd like to think that was the case. And as I pull into the lot, I remember something I must've filed away in my pile of disregards. All those things I never cared about, like that film and her old perfume. How old was I, dangle footed at a pew and then kneeling. *This is where I'll be,* she said. I don't even remember the context. Maybe I was afraid to lose her if I went off to find Dad or go to the bathroom. Just the way she turned to me, held my gaze a second or two longer, and told me that. *This is where I'll be,* she said, *when you need me.*

Chapter Thirteen: Ella and Sam

Sam

I should be brewing coffee and heating up this place, but I'm pestering my wife instead. After I've whispered, "Good morning," too many times, she's finally objected, rolled on her side, and covered her ear. This means she's had enough. Two of three pillows have met their demise on the floor just beside. I could give up, but instead I tuck my knees into the crook of hers.

"It's Saturday," I say. It's not like I want to be alone. I don't think that's needy, pushy, selfish.

I hear a groan. "Another hour," she asks and then, "just one more."

My hand makes its way up her shirt, a faded jersey in white and gray reminiscent of high school locker rooms in the seventies. And she rolls to her back, ginger hair sprawling out like she went to bed with it wet. Nowhere near *Vogue*-ified.

"What time is it?"

"Nine forty-five," I say.

"Just one more hour."

But she resumes her back-to-me position, disappearing into fluff. I tug the comforter over her shoulder. Then I slide my feet off the bed, slipping cold toes into wool slippers. I glance back at her, sound asleep. I guess that's just enough time to warm that dessert loaf and scramble some eggs.

After sneaking out the door, I shuffle downstairs and into the narrow hallway, mechanically switching this heater off, which says it's sixty-four in here. I feel tired, heavy. But I need kindling—that and several sheets of newsprint and this pack of matches. I stoop at the stove as the heater empties itself one last time before a day of hibernation.

My mind's a haze as I roll newsprint into cylinders. Knuckles curl. Roll and repeat. Obituaries become kindling. Real estate becomes kindling. The latest on the select board, the school board, the library board, the planning board, the zoning board. Nationwide protests.

Above this layer, I overlap sticks and top my masterpiece with the most substantial log of them all. Then a flick of the match and paper ignites into flames that crawl leisurely forming a trail of black singe that glows orange at its edge.

I shake open yesterday's paper, flipping past the crossword puzzle and comic strips in hopes that Ms. Abigail Van Buren, which is now her daughter, might possibly offer some advice. But the only letter I find is WORRIED WYNNE IN NORTH CAROLINA, who has just discovered inappropriate text messages from her boyfriend's ex-girlfriend.

A scenario that sounds like Ella in there, who stands true to the lesbian pact that we all must remain friends with our long string of *not quite into you*s. That's never actually been my modus operandi. If you've slept with her and it's over, in my book, you never speak to her, look at her, Facebook friend her, or think about her ever again.

In fact, my better half has kept in touch with most of her has-beens, even though most have been demoted to mere sidewalk nods.

Jessie, though, not so much. When the title *ex* was not yet registering, she was the embodiment of inappropriate to the tune of stopping by that shop a few times a week—and not for bagels and cream cheese. I'm pretty sure my then-fiancée half enjoyed the attention—to hook me (which it did) and to make me jealous (which it also did).

And just like WORRIED WYNNE IN NORTH CAROLINA, I found those messages. That phone was rattling across the kitchen counter while she was indisposed one morning. They were glaring at me, provoking me. Innuendos. Inside jokes. Who did this has-been think she was? Her intentions were crystal clear right down to her winking emoticons.

I could've looked away or left the room. I could've placed that phone in the drawer, where it usually lived. I could've trusted her or, minimally, confessed. But I didn't. And that was (undeniably) unforgivable.

Fast-forward a few months to a lovely day when my wife and I were still overnight bags and three-hour daily conversations.

A farmers' market. Town center. Sunscreen-scented air. Relishing that vitamin D infused sunshine. Picture sunflowers and asparagus. And her index finger led me past those vegetable bins up and across the stretched tent to a slender (strong) androgyne in her midthirties perusing produce. That's the first time I saw that winking emoticon in the flesh, and it shot a surge of possessive right up my spine. Her long-short haircut, the strands that tumbled down her forehead. She thought her tan made her hotter than the red habaneros she was eyeing. And she was right.

I watched as my competition brushed along, scanning chalked signs, pausing to listen to street musicians. She wasn't the sweet type nor the cute type nor even the pretty or handsome type. She was Ella's type.

"Let's go say hi," I heard.

Can we not?

Her hand dragged me—past pigeons, along tables and backed-in pickups, and beyond plastic buckets of sheared flowers—to introduce us. We shook cold hands, me sporting my horizontal smile and her holding two cantaloupes to her flat chest.

Then came that husky voice.

"Hey, Red, how've you been?"

Seething, I was. My tongue found its way to the top of my mouth and I took her in as she conversed with my girlfriend, intimately. Her ease. The slack of her shirt on her small frame, and those biceps. But as soon as her attention came back on me, I softened into a convincing enough fake smile.

Why am I still riled by this woman? It's absurd. It's every time they speak or even so much as look at one another. It's who they were. It's someone else. It's more than me. It's never platonic.

I roll up WORRIED WYNNE IN NORTH CAROLINA and toss it in the coal bed, now fluttering like the wings of a monarch butterfly.

❖

Ella

I'm sound asleep when the aroma of brewed coffee and something sweet spirals up to the bedroom. Leave it to her to turn this epic fail of a weekend into days and days of bliss.

I confess. I never do this sort of thing for her. She's making me look like a bad wife. I think I've given her flowers once since we met, and those were lilacs plucked from our own yard. It gave her a massive sneezing attack, so they met their demise in the compost pile pronto. I did make her a chocolate marquise when we were dating, which apparently sat in the car too long in eighty-eight degree weather and, well, imagine that. I could probably write a book about failed romantic gestures. I have far too much experience in that area. But why try? Nobody could outrank my wife. Samantha Lasley: the last of a dying breed.

And now just thinking about breakfast is making my stomach growl. I can actually hear it amid her banging and clanging downstairs. Something sounds like it's sizzling over the occasional *thunk* on that cutting board. She's up to no good. I honestly blame her for these ten happy pounds I've put on since we wed. It's enough to make a girl long for the days of heartache.

I stretch.

In the background, the distant melody of my wife humming a tune. How cute is that?

I hobble out of bed, cursing to myself that she woke first and left me to fixing this mass of linens all by myself. Which is precisely when I spot the clock, and damn. All of yesterday's shoveling, the snowshoeing, it must've really done me in. I haven't slept this late in ever.

I fix the bed, though, and feel heat once I hit the staircase. As soon as I reach the kitchen, I tell her good morning. Then I do that little *ahem* thing to get rid of the scratch. The house smells of sweet and hickory.

"What?" shouts the chef as soon as I reach her side. "No!" But this is not the response that I had envisioned. "What are you doing up?"

Did she not hear me moving around up there?

"I couldn't sleep with this racket."

"This was supposed to be a surprise."

"It is a surprise."

"No," she whines, eyes welled with disappointment. It's almost pathetic. I can tell this means a lot to her. "I was going to bring you breakfast in bed."

"Oh."

She motions me over to the other side of the kitchen, away from her. That means I'm crowding her space. I oblige and step back. "Now that you've ruined your surprise."

"Babe, this is a surprise. This is amazing. Are you kidding me?"

A loaf of gingerbread's warmed, its cup of molasses and half cup of sugar obviously the scents that lured me down in the first place. She's also scrambled eggs with her to-die-for secret recipe which she won't even share with me on her deathbed, so she says. I guess I'm stuck with her, happily, if only for the eggs.

She's squeezed two glasses of orange juice, fresh. Like, really squeezed. There's even a pot of fresh-brewed coffee, which she pours me along with a hint of French vanilla creamer. No sugar. A colorful snip of evergreen's propped in a vase on each tray. She bought trays! I feel grateful with a dash of Methodist guilt as I recall my bed-fixing bellyache not five minutes earlier.

"I need to get silverware and napkins and…How big?" she asks placing a knife on the loaf.

"I'm starving. It's nearly lunch."

"It's not nearly lunch. How's this?" Still I move that finger over just a tad to widen her cut. Then I brush up behind her, resting my arms around her hips. "Not while I have a knife in my hand." Once the first slice falls to its side, I fork a bite of her amazing eggs and gush about it being the best I've ever had in my life. And I mean it.

"Whatever. You're biased. You're married to me."

"God, I don't know what you put in these, but—"

She chuckles. "I said that very same thing to you the day we met. Remember? I recall kicking myself for being so unoriginal."

I'm touched she remembers.

"What in God's name did you see in me," she asks. "I'll never understand. You made me such a wrecked-up bundle of nerves. You know, I just wanted to be near you that whole night. Instead I had to work and listen to Aunt Annie and Gidget share medical stories I wish I could unhear. At the very least, it did give me a nice angle where I could check you out. That tight shirt and black pants, dressed up like a penguin. And that ponytail couldn't hide this," she tells me, running fingertips through my hair. "My brother told me you were drop dead—"

"Whatever."

"He was right."

"Not."

"Why is it straight people think they can play matchmaker if they meet another single lesbian—any single lesbian. Anywhere. Like we're all somehow into one another. It's pretty absurd."

"I know, right? But you really shouldn't have been hitting on random caterers."

"As I recall, you hit on me."

"Not quite."

"Quite," she says.

"How do you figure?"

"Babe, you saw me checking you out and you nearly dropped that cake."

"And who was checking out whom?"

"I was watching you set up," she tells me.

"No, you were checking me out."

"*Where does this go?*"

"How was I to know," I say.

"Babe, you were obvious. You were hitting on me." She gives me an oh-so-charming grin and then says, "Not that I minded."

Back to our familiar silence, we dole up plates full of all things delectable and eat in the living room on our little wooden trays that she bought specifically for this occasion, though they were intended for use in bed I now know.

And we ramble through our breaking-the-ice topics: the storm and the weather and shoveling and our aching triceps and, "Did you sleep well?" I sniff this evergreen, which offers a hint of Christmas. And I ask about her family, which predictably gets her fired up and chattier than a ten-year-old on a shot of Mountain Dew. If it wasn't for me digging, she'd happily sit back and listen to me hemming and hawing, ranting and raving for hours.

Sometimes her silence is nice. Other times it makes me wonder what's in there. It's always a relief to learn that it's just family stuff, which leads to some work stuff, which segues back to me. We finish eating around the time my eyes begin to glaze over. That's when I get up and collect our trays, carry them into the kitchen, and load the dishwasher as she silently tends to her fire.

❖

Sam

I could think of better ways to spend the day, starting with a trip to Lowe's for a snowblower and ending with a night on the town. I'm wondering if I should've called up United months ago and booked us a flight to Aruba. Hindsight, they say, is 20/20. Right now there's the matter of our roof, which is going to collapse.

What's worse, I've never used a roof rake in my life. I just need to steady myself, I suppose, while extending this wobbling twenty-foot pole overhead and balancing in knee-deep snow. It's so far from suave. My wife's more engrossed in shooting a video of it on her phone, which she'll post and tag for our entire world to see—folks I grew up with, went to college with, currently work with.

"I'm glad you find this amusing," I shout as a *whoof* of snow tumbles to my feet. "This isn't exactly easy. You could help, you know, like clear some of those icicles before I get impaled."

She peeks around her phone without so much as a word. I tug down another thick avalanche, crawling to the next section. Rake, chop, pull. Then a call comes in, and she ducks into the garage to take it.

I'm finally getting the hang of this when I catch her struggling toward me, hair peeking out from that gray hoodie that frames her face. She's not even wearing a coat, so her cheeks are beginning to match that lipstick. In her typical urgency, she plods through, stumbling to her knees as she nears. I'm thinking this is what should be on video.

And that's when I hear the unexpected (yet expected): "Work beckons."

"What!" You've got to be kidding me, I think—sniffling and tucking from the wind. She buried what little pleasure I had beneath a heavy mound of disappointment.

"It's not like I can leave it all to that thin crew."

"How hard is it?" I snip, unable to mask my agitation.

"The line's out the door. Busier than we thought."

I peer into those soulful eyes now seeking my approval. But that's just not something I can offer.

"They need me," she says. "Like seriously pronto."

I need you, I think.

"I won't be long, I swear." She offers a tight-lipped kiss. It's unfeeling, or so it seems, and it leaves me incomplete. I don't think I'm unreasonable or moody; she's wrong about that.

With knuckles tucked in those stretched sleeves, she balances back like she's on some sort of tightrope. And soon enough, she's backtracked all the way to the garage. The door slams. The engine starts. She waves good-bye, and I stuff heartache into bottomless pockets.

I listen to her wheels crunch off, half tempted to follow. Get in the car. Turn the engine. Park and step inside where it's toasty and she's orchestrating, slipping into that corner unnoticed and unforgiving. Didn't *Hey, Red* do that? Would I make her excited like that, or just hardened and still uptight? Because I would insist, stewing and stubborn. I would wait for her to finish.

But I don't do anything of the sort. Instead I step inside this silent house. One toe forces off the heel of my boot until both are dripping on the rug. I hang my wet coat. A glove slips off, still in the shape of my fingers. This is the perfect age, I think, when the leather's soft and pliable and worn. Molded to my hand.

I entertain myself for hours before she finishes work. Who doesn't want to spend her anniversary on her knees and up to her elbows in Bon Ami cleanser? At least I'm dressed and ready to go by the time she even gets back.

"What are you doing up there," I shout, "sewing the dress yourself?"

I'm picturing scissors, ribbon, and spools—and that way her tongue wets the strand before she threads it. Sure, patience is a virtue. But I'm reaching empty. I've already quadruple-checked the tickets, balmed lips, vacuumed ash, and started the car so it's heated when we leave—if we ever do.

"I'm coming, I'm coming. In just five minutes."

And my high-maintenance wife is still getting ready.

"We still need to eat, you know."

After the bathroom opens, I hear her scrambling room to room. At least she's moving faster now. "We need to get going. You said the roads are slick. And we'll need parking. On a Saturday night. Downtown." Her pace slackens with each creak of the staircase. Why do I feel like an awkward kid waiting for a prom date?

"I know, I know," I hear in a voice now abundantly louder. When she appears around the corner, arms overhead, fingers fidgeting with that honey-colored hair of hers.

"My, my, my, my, my." I sigh, leaning back against the dining room table.

"Oh, stop it."

"You. Look. Hot." I peer into my phone screen and snap a quick photo, moseying my way closer to this bombshell.

"I don't. Stop it." But she does. Her hair's cinched somehow in a low, messy knot sort of thing with a few strands falling down. Add nude lips. And that dress on those curves with that neckline that only she can pull off. And legs. Damn. This does something to me, is doing something to me, and she knows it. But she hasn't worn anything even remotely like this in too long, if you ask me. There's been no reason to.

"You're my new wallpaper," I tell her, finding the right button.

"You're nuts. I thought we were running late. Who's procrastinating now?"

Select, save, and into my coat it goes. That's when my hand makes its way down to hers. "I'm not nuts." But I sound pretty feeble about now. "And I've been ready to go for nearly an hour." The bow of her hip, it makes my mind wander. Something that always happens at the most inopportune times. "So you're ready?"

"Got the tickets?"

I (loudly) sigh, leading her to the coat closet. I love it when she answers my questions with her own. "They're in my pocket." I get her coat down, suspending it in midair. Once her fingers find their way through the sleeve, she does this pivot thing to pull it up to her shoulder. Afterward she points her toe into knee-high boots that cinch with a zip.

"This is exciting." She's hunched to secure her second boot.

"Had that storm hit two days later," I say. We would be playing Scrabble or Parcheesi instead.

That's about when the door lets in a fierce chill and that procrastinator bolts to the car before I can even lock the house. Getting out will do us both some good. My wife is beyond self-absorbed—stuck on that shop, even though she's spent half the day there.

Fortunately as soon as we hit the highway, our ride into town gets surprisingly smooth, restoring my faith in the public works department. It never ceases to amaze me when we get hit with a blizzard like this one day and then—poof—roads are wet and salted the next, totally drivable. At least throughways like this one.

"Don't put me to sleep," I tell her as she scrolls and settles on a playlist. And while she does her DJ thing, I take in the scenery. All of this fresh powder's making everything festive. Pearly fields. Farms glow under a setting sky as if Monet smeared it all in smoky, silvery, ashen. It's starting to put things into perspective, at least for the time being. It makes everything feel okay.

And we make the bend past a church steeple piercing the haze. Snow, like cotton, lit in azure blue. Pint-sized houses nestled in a nook, the glow of ginger peering out their many windows. Smoke billowing from stone and brick into hills sheltered with barren trees.

It's tranquil. About as tranquil as this music my disc jockey just turned on, which I'm not at all into.

"Can we not listen to whining folk music tonight?"

"What's wrong with my music?"

"It's not very…upbeat."

"But this is my *fast* folk mix." I give her the eye. "It's upbeat." I furrow my brow to add emphasis.

"Normally okay, you know that. Just not today." With that, she buries her nose in the screen, scrolling. "Do you remember when you dressed like this every time you saw me?"

"Are you disappointed?" she asks, even though I know she couldn't care less.

"No, I rather like you in a pair of Levi's," I say, slipping my hand to her knee. "But I like this as well."

"Watch the road."

She's tugging her hem above the knee and crossing those legs of hers. That ought to keep us out of an accident.

As soon as we reach town center, we hit a red. I glance over at her and then again. I watch the way her lashes fall and flit. It's so everyday, yet unfamiliar. I don't know where we fell into this…settled, overlooking so much. She did, and I did.

And I guess that's when I shift the car into park because I'm letting off the pedal now and leaning over, feeling her warm thigh beyond the hem of her skirt. And we're sinking into this kiss and it twists and ascends and dips. It falls into me, steadfast and relentless. And I guess that light turns green again because I hear honking behind and she's offering such a curious smile as I put it back in drive.

Now that it's warm out (with barrels of salt on this blacktop), roads have glossed over. It splashes all the way up Main Street. Above, rooftops drip to gutters, which are weighted by icicles.

"How's this?" I hear. "This is my coffeehouse mix."

"This is comatose," I say with a wink.

We drive across rainbow-speckled blacktop. Streetlights, headlights, shop lights streaking across the windshield like a kaleidoscope. A pedestrian enters a crosswalk. Downtown's desolate for a weekend and just beginning to wake.

I pull up to the parking garage, veering up its concrete lip. My window hums as it falls, and I fetch a stub. Past the wooden arm, fog crawls up the window becoming dangerously thick by the second. That's when my wife hits defrost.

We take curve after curve after level by level to the tune of concrete slabs. Then I center the car smack-dab between two white lines. We settle into our comfortable routine.

"Don't forget the tickets," I hear for the umpteenth time. "Do you have them?"

"Yes—the show tickets, the parking ticket, your phone so you don't have to carry it, tissues, your lipstick…" I slam my door before I finish, finding my way to her hand. And I walk to the beat of heels clicking on the pavement.

On Main Street, the clamor of rubber and exhaust drowns us out. We make our way through the crosswalk to a sidewalk on the opposite side, which is dimly lit by those gothic posts.

I pause to peek in the music store past my reflection to those guitars. She wants to keep walking away. This is about the time I drift off. I'm tuning, singing "Drive," telling bad jokes to a small dive crowd, breaking strings, sleeves cuffed, and then she breaks in with, "You're no Melissa Ferrick, but I love you anyway."

I just give her a look.

"Keep practicing. I have earplugs."

I would be insulted if she wasn't so smitten by me.

We've reserved seats at the nicest restaurant in town. That's not to say it's uber high class. But it's as high class as we're ever going to get. I pull the door and follow this goddess in, where our hostess stands by a pedestal. Her eyes meet mine, though my wife's the one vying for her attention.

"Party of two. Lasley," I say. "We have reservations."

❖

After signing a credit slip for our whopping one hundred fifty dollar meal with drinks and sweets, I tuck the pen in the binder and slide it over to the edge of the table. Ella takes one last drink of water, ice tumbling, before she stains her lips strawberry—something she always does after a meal out.

"I hope you got enough to eat," I say, rising to help with her coat.

"I could've skipped dessert."

I just shake my head.

It's a shadowy restaurant. Crystal chandeliers drop from elegantly high ceilings and sparkle across pressed tin ceiling tiles. I hold her coat as she slips an arm delicately into one sleeve and then the other. Coated up, we wind our way through the maze to the front lobby. I pause to grab a mint from a tray before slipping mittens on.

"I think we're early," I tell her. Then we push through the door together. The snow's returned, resting along fine limbs up above. I can feel flakes featherlight as they melt on my skin. We huddle together, heads ducked, down the sidewalk.

"I love you," I say in the most unromantic voice imaginable. "Your hair smells like coconut."

"You like?"

"I kind of do," I say. "You have my permission to buy this stuff again."

I get the same expression back that I give her. Then I finger loose strands of hair that have fallen across her forehead.

"There it is," she says.

A scrolling marque reads: *Friday* and *7:30 p.m.* and *Giselle*.

"But is that the line?"

"Doesn't look open yet."

The place is pretty out-there. Picture neon red meets violet on brick. An angular facade, a touch of Neo-Renaissance, with prominence suitable for tuxedos—at least, in a more cosmopolitan region. And that line wraps and crawls around it. I follow the smooth tempo of heels until we reach the end. That's when my shivering companion inches forward past anchored benches and a glassed-in cast list.

I whisper privately, "You know what this reminds me of...?"

"*The Nutcracker*," my wife says.

"Have I told you this story?"

"Only a million times."

I feel dejected, which must show on my face.

"It's cute. Really, babe."

I'm thinking about women wrapped in fur-lined capes. Perfectly choreographed plies and pirouettes. "We should do that."

"Do what?" She sounds so disapproving.

"Have a tradition every winter, like now—"

"I don't know about that. Traditions can be kind of, I don't know, monotonous. Don't you think?"

"Tradition doesn't mean boring. Just familiar. That's not always bad."

"Tradition is doing the same thing over and over and over," she says. "How is that *not* monotonous?"

I continue to harp.

She raises her eyebrow.

I twist my lip.

She rolls her eyes.

I wink.

"What time is it?" I ask.

"It's six forty-five."

Then we opt to listen to conversations as opposed to engaging in one of our own.

And eventually we step inside, my fingers tingling. I marvel. The ceiling. That carved wood. It's antique right down to this worn carpeting at our feet, which we follow, guided by ushers, making our way to a staircase leading to our own balcony—and we're hidden above rows of chatter.

"Can you see?" I open the program, sinking into my seat. An ankle settles on my knee.

"Yes, perfectly," says my shadowed companion, leaning headfirst to watch a crowd of heteros file in just below. The program's barely decipherable under jewelry light and tells me tidbits of absolutely no interest. Though they would be to her.

And soon enough, the room dims and heavy drapes are lit. A conductor enters and bows. Applause soars into a hush. A dramatic pause, a shift in the seat. A page is flipped. And the melody begins. Flutes dance in leaps and lulls. Violins flitter until a second curtain rises, gathering section by section until it unveils a quaint autumn day. A cape crossing before troops of loose skirts on laced slippers.

I turn to my wife, lit and entranced, and I'm more entertained by her than the show itself. I feel for her hand in the darkness, finding her knee instead. And there are no butterflies, for her or me. She doesn't even acknowledge me. I'm not holding my breath or flexing or tense. She's not pretending. I'm not wondering or worrying, tortured or longing. There is no apprehension. It's really the most wonderful thing. This.

CHAPTER FOURTEEN: RYAN AND BRIE

Brie

You can let life change you, or you can change your life.
Waiting, like this, has never been my strong suit, but fifteen minutes is acceptable as long as it's done in the waiting room of the best hairdresser in town, without question. That's what I get for taking his last appointment of the day.

I choose an outdated *Vogue* and begin flipping pages creased with Photoshopped beauty standards, settling into the aroma of perfume and perm. A mix of ammonia and vetiver, sandalwood, and rosemary. The baby boomer across from me is reading *People*. I sense her eyes on me and, when I let myself peek over the top of the page, those suspicions are confirmed.

I scan sans reading, as my ear strays into another room. The gossip that's shared in the presence of a hairdresser. I can make half of it out over the buzz of electric clippers and hair dryers.

Kevin smiles and nods as he lifts thin strands of hair over foil and brushes each with a creamy white paste, nodding to his chair's rant about her man, her boss, her boys. I watch as my fashionable hairdresser imitates her outrage, and I flip another page. Her head is soon a figment of a midcentury science fiction flick.

He hollers in passing, and I gesture as if to say *okay*. I set *Vogue* down on the table in front of me. This is Ryan's salon. And finding it was one of the few upsides I can take from that failed relationship.

"I'm so sorry you had to wait," he tells me. And I reflect on the fact that, sometimes, there's a great deal of comfort in a Hollywood hug. "It's been a madhouse," he gushes, combing through my tangles. "What are we doing for you today?"

We talk to each other through his oversized mirror. "Actually," I say, pulling out my own magazine clipping, "I'm going to need a change, doll."

My guy squeals and begins talking in staccato. "Oh. My. God." Then he studies my reflection as if I were bar prey.

"No more Disney princess," I say.

He chuckles, shaking his head. "So we're taking it all off?"

I nod.

He latches my photo to the mirror all the while dousing me with praise. Tipped back, hair under the spray, with warm lather draining down my neck, I fall into an aromatic coma.

He asks me what I'm wearing. "Is that a new shampoo?"

Chris wears this better, is my unspoken response. "An old perfume," I say.

When he asks about Ryan, I redirect the topic like a boomerang, more than happy to just listen and not talk for the next twenty minutes. I wonder, as I always do, if he also talks about me once I leave.

With a towel across my shoulder, I make my way to the chair and my chatty stylist snaps me in plastic. I guess the rubber band makes it more efficient, but it still feels like an evil sorority pledge.

"Ready?" he asks, positioning his shears.

"As I'll ever be."

The cut does tug, and my hair, my gut, my ex-boss, my ex-girlfriend, my femininity, my passivity, my stupidity, my misgivings, my dependence, my anxiety, and all my disappointments fall to the floor in one fell swoop.

I look through my bangs, which tickle my lips. I sense cold steel behind my ear, a razor on my neck, a comb across my scalp. I rise with each pump of the chair. I face a wall, a mirror, a chest. And I'm tilted this way and that.

When I return to the mirror, it's 1968. And I'm Mia Farrow.

❖

Ryan

I once read that Saturday night just around right now is the most common time for couples to have sex. I'm happy for them, as I curl up on the couch in flannel pajamas, alone.

Which reminds me, I need to get online and renew my gym membership and Netflix subscription, two luxuries that make this single thing immensely more tolerable. In the meantime, at least for this evening, I'm choosing from the few DVDs I actually own. I pick *The Tudors*, season one, and slide it into the tray. There's something to be said for corsets and busts pressed up like that. Of course, the downside is murder and men—but that aside.

With remote in hand, I squeeze the pillow into my chest and wrap a throw over my toes. I keep the volume high to give it a movie theater feel. That racket might be what's brought her in. I can't say I'm disappointed.

In fact, it's difficult to look away and I stare well past the turn-away point since I've had but a few hours to get used to this unexpected new look of hers. And as much as I'd prefer to see her in a breakup-appropriate robe and frumpy slippers, it's more like loose and sleeveless, a tank top with pants of some kind of knit that of course cling too well over those curves. I'm thinking she's deliberately torturing me.

I try to act indifferent as she makes her way to the chair. It makes a noise when she plops down. I'm thinking I probably should've worn something less modest given my current look is more Subaru Outback than Jeep Wrangler. It's hardly going to win her over or back or anything else for that matter. It's probably what frightened her away.

She settles in, lit in screen glow, as His Majesty enters to the sound of trumpets and bellows an argument for war.

That's when I ask, "Is this okay?" We don't normally agree so easily. She and I, we have rather distinctive tastes. She's more Cannes and subtitles. Then I add, "If you'd prefer to watch something else…?"

That's when she turns to face me. "I like this show. I forgot how much actually." It's nice that we have some common ground. But I find myself wondering when she saw this. It wasn't with me. I glance over without looking, her knees tucked to her chest with a fist around them.

I turn down the volume. "Listen, I'm really sorry about everything," I tell her. "I know I haven't been here for you."

She's listening. I know she is because she nods.

"Can I get you some coffee?" I ask, thinking, *You can drink as much coffee as you want. I don't even care anymore. It's so petty.* Then I say, "If that's behind this."

"That's not it."

"We could see someone like a therapist or counselor. I can change, you know. I'm far from perfect. I know that more than anyone."

She sucks her lips in. Then she shakes her head.

"No to the counselor," I ask, "or no, you think I'm perfect?" I get this look from across the room. My wink is probably flirtatious. *I love you*, I think.

Her half smile lingers long after she returns to the screen.

"You don't have to rush the job thing, you know. The right one can take time. But if you wait, I can take care of expenses. I already am. Like you said, I was fine before you. It's not even an issue."

It's a simple thing, that smile, but complicated. And she turns to me again. "But I love my work."

"Then let me help you find a job. I'm sorry that I've left this up to you—it wasn't fair. Of course you're overwhelmed. Who wouldn't be," I say, talking as much to myself as I am to her. "I can do so much more with that. I will. I want to."

"But I've already tried that. My résumé's everywhere—don't you see? I need to be near family. I don't think you realize how important it is to me."

She turns back to the screen; so do I. I need to back off. If I give her space, she won't get upset. She'll stay like this, right here with me, all night. She won't walk out. And I do stay quiet, staring mindlessly at the television for at least fifteen seconds more.

"Well then, what if I moved with you?"

"Moved—to Maine?"

"We could find a place together. I want to. I have equity here and there's a down payment," I say. It feels genius, absolutely brilliant, a feeling that's reinforced when she drops her fist and stretches out a single leg. So I add, "I'll do anything for you."

"You already have your life, everything you need here."

"It doesn't matter to me anymore. You do. I'll do whatever I can to make this work."

"I'd never ask you to do that."

"I can find another job," I say. "Anywhere really. Just think about it, all right? I won't screw up again. I can make this up to you."

Her chest swells as she turns back to the show. I'm fine with that. Besides, I've run out of things to say. So I turn the volume back up and try to act like I'm in this room watching with her. In truth, my heart's sinking at the thought of moving. Selling. Packing. Starting over. I don't want to. But it's exciting to think so.

CHAPTER FIFTEEN: JESSIE AND HADLEY

Jessie

I never expected the day to turn out the way it has. How could I? There's a lot I don't know about her. There's a lot I do.

We learned that, in the dead of winter, there's little to do in this rolled-up town—especially after all this, when everything's closed up with the exception of a few family-run delis.

We finished some errands just before lunch. She had things to drop off at the postbox. I picked up coffee beans because I'm out. We passed the mini-mall and decided that would be our next expedition. I felt like a celebrity, or how I imagine it'd be, when they unlock just for you. But that's where the comparison ends because half the shops were closed. It was our empty playground. I bought my boots. She found candle lanterns for outside.

We wandered down the hill to Ella's. She was out back but caught us and came out to see us. She should be home with her wife; it's their anniversary. I told her that. She told the woman at the register to waive the fee when we ordered. We wanted to pay. We insisted. But she wouldn't have it.

Which leads me to this parking garage, which is empty with its entry gate up. Less a surveillance camera or three, we could run a marathon up and down the ramp and nobody would be the wiser. We've chosen not to. Instead we walk leisurely down the slope.

The rest of the afternoon is still a free fall. Our conversation has descended into overtalk about stuff that doesn't want to end. It isn't about anything in particular. It isn't about anything at all, really. It's about everything. Gender reassignment. Our shitty jobs. Her shitty car. Vegetarianism. Sexism in STEM. Priests, atheism. Democratic Socialism. It twists all over the place like an overpass.

And while most of the town is shut down, there's this church. Churches are always open. They're heated, too, which is why we duck in. I'd forgotten the smell of church, a stuffy blend of aging wood, dust, Sunday-best perfumes, and coffee from a can. A different kind of quiet sits inside.

The double set of parted doors, that makes it feel accepting even though I'm far from religious myself. I sit in the back, flipping a hymnal and closing a kneeling bench. She's up front being Catholic.

Humble people have gathered here for hundreds of years wearing pins on their Sears brassieres, sock suspenders and bowties. They took care of one another. That does appeal to me—the forgiveness part, too. Why is religion so ugly yet so beautiful on her?

As we leave, that same solitude follows us for a couple of blocks, swapping overtalk for voyeurism, past a local art gallery and theater, which is already prepping for tonight's performance.

"Do you want to head home?" I ask.

"And do what?" She's clutching my hand and speeding her pace. Tugging me. "Come here. I have to show you something."

We leave the sidewalk and take over this roadway, crossing the street but skirting the crosswalk. An entire block passes before I know it. The alleyway's narrow with barely enough space for one of us to slide sidelong. That's when I realize I'm borderline claustrophobic.

"Where exactly are you taking me?"

"You'll see."

I'm relieved when we reach another pair of doors. They're nearly twice our height. She rattles the knob. "Let's go around."

I trail behind—am dragged, rather—to the side where more slender paths are carelessly cleared. When she turns this knob, it opens. We look at each other. The air's stagnant inside, like that church, and we make our way toward the spiral staircase. It even smells of church. My thought is that it might be the chapel. It echoes.

"We can't be in here," I say in a loud hush as we wind up flight after flight.

"Sure we can. I know someone. It's totally fine. We won't touch anything." Her smile is devious. I kind of like it.

Our steps repeat vertically. We're not discreet. And if it weren't for daylight streaming in from up above, our path would not be lit.

I'm winded when we get to the top and…awestruck. I realize that we're in a clock tower. I've never been in a clock tower. I did not even know this one existed. Numerals are Roman, brass, and reversed against round glass, and they dwarf us. Brick is painted white inside, but chips.

"It's so cool, isn't it?"

"I'd say." I lean on a ledge, close enough to touch the glass. There's a lot of dust. I feel like nobody can see me.

"It's even better at night," she tells me. "The lights shine out." She shows me beacons near our feet.

"How many times have you been here?" I ask.

"Not much. Maybe three. Four now."

"I'm the fourth girl you brought up here?"

"No. You're the first." She looks beautiful in this light. She looks amazing in any light, but this especially.

I walk the perimeter, my heels making a noise that I try to (unsuccessfully) muffle by slowing down. I don't want to get caught, but I like it up here. I wonder who's in this building downstairs. I wonder if they can hear us and simply don't bother. As I make my way back, I catch her profile with the backlight. A glow's cast on her skin by frosted daylight.

"Up here, it's like there's no world out there."

I approach. Her lips are glistening. She must have just licked them.

"It isn't every day," I say, "that the world just shuts down like this."

Then I hear, "I came up once after Mom died."

She says it so bluntly. When do you start talking about this? I mean, when is it okay? It doesn't feel okay to me yet.

"It's like one more thing she won't know. The stuff I can't show her—and I want to. What do you do, Jess?"

"I don't know."

"I was so selfish, you know, with arguing. We were always arguing. Why is that?"

"Because she's your mom," I say. "You do that. You just do. Even I do. We all do."

"Yeah, yeah." I get an eye roll.

"Yeah."

"Yeah, you're right."

"Of course I am."

That grin. That side-eye. I follow it to the clock face, which says it's nearing three in the afternoon. Where has the day gone? Why did it take so long to do nothing? To do everything, really.

"Hadley?" Her gaze meets mine. I steeple my palm against hers, gliding my fingers between each gap until all I can see are overlapping knuckles. I can't help but marvel at the shadows cast under her cheekbones, in the crease of her eyelids. There's some really interesting light in here. "This was a really cool day."

"It beats sitting at home, right?"

Her smile is inviting, and I find my attention darting around to her bangs and those lashes, until her chin drops in a don't-look-at-me way. I can hear the mechanical rhythm of this clock, which fails miserably in keeping pace with my own heart. When I pull her knuckles to my lips, she's wearing my exact same smile.

"You're cute," I say. "You know that?"

"Don't say that."

"Why?" I ask.

She looks away. Light streams in. Her hand falls back on her lap. She brushes aside a strand of hair. Tick-tock.

"Curious," I say. "I almost hate to ask."

"What's that, babe?"

"Does this thing ring on the hour?"

I've startled her.

"You're so right. We'd better get down. It's a little loud."

Hadley's voice can be heard over the dishwasher. Meanwhile I'm wondering what would be on today's soundtrack, if it had one.

"Well, just cut it here, like so," she tells me. I follow along as she slices clean through the center of that green pepper. It snaps.

Behind her, I watch and learn. And she's surprisingly patient, given I'm not the most adept or practiced pupil. I like to think I make up for that with raw enthusiasm.

"Take the seeds out," I hear her say, pinching inners in a heap on this cutting board. Her fingers are wet and glistening.

This evening she's agreed to give me cooking lessons in exchange for a double feature on my surround sound home theater. But we had one complication. I had no spices or pots or mixing bowls or... anything. So we hit her place and then the grocery store to buy all of these whatevers she said we needed for this dish we're making. Stuffed peppers. I've never had it, but I'm game. Anything beats another can of vegetable barley soup. Anything would. Besides, a few more meals out and I'm sure to lose these abs, and I don't want that.

After demonstrating, she passes me the blade and steps aside. "Here. You do this one."

"Why no seeds?"

"We don't use those."

"Why?" I ask.

She eyes me as if to say *don't ask* as she fills wineglasses with Lambrusco. She pours mindfully, fingers curling around that narrow bottle. She's wearing eyeliner, which is now smudged from those arctic winds this afternoon. And that tousled hair.

She sets my glass beside me. Hers, at the edge of the counter. Then she moseys on over to the door, where we left soggy boots and some bags of belongings she took from her place. Her nightclothes and robe, an outfit, an excess of toiletries, even more cooking things.

"I'll be right back," she says, bag in hand.

"Where are you going?"

"I'm setting these up before it gets dark."

I lower my head and continue to cut and slice and wipe seeds to the side while she slips into boots and braves out, plunging into unshoveled snow to light her lanterns. I love that about her. She can take an empty page and color it in. Like this entire day.

After the last cut, I dry my hands on a towel.

"Come see," I hear as she bursts her way back.

I take a drink of wine and join her at the window. We look at the light that sparkles and shimmies across a fine coating of ice. The sky's indigo. The winter moon is rising. "It's nice," I say. "Really nice."

"How far'd you get?" she wants to know.

I walk her to the kitchen.

She likes what I've done and gives me more. "Cut these in half, too, and set them all around where you see gaps like this." She cuts a small tomato to show me. "Don't worry. Just cram these in, you know, anywhere you find. I'll work on the ricotta."

"This is easy."

"Whatever, Jess." She rolls her eyes.

"I love the lanterns."

She lifts her lashes. "Nice touch, right?"

As I slice, it dawns on me that I rather enjoy doing this, with her at least. It's peaceful. This would definitely be my first cooking date, and I can't help but wonder if I've been missing out all these years. She doesn't catch me watching her.

"Like this?" I ask.

She reaches around from behind and sets an onion on the cutting board, and that's when my heart sprints around the block. The voice near my ear says, "Yes, just like that." The wine's not helping matters. "You'll want to cut this one fast."

"Really—why?"

"Trust me," she says, watching as I peel flakes. "About this thick," she demonstrates, resting a hand over mine. This is so distracting, which is not good when I have a blade in my hand. That's when I realize I need another sip of wine.

It takes a bit more maneuvering to cut the onion. But I'm beginning to get the hang of this. Rings collapse on their side. This is when I slow down so I can get just the right thickness.

That is, until a sting pierces my eye and I'm immediately tearing buckets. I don't even know what's happening.

And she has no empathy. "You're crying," she says, hunched over in one of those nose-crinkling belly laughs as streams make their way down my face. "Are you okay?"

"Does it look like I'm okay?" God, it's painful.

"I told you—cut fast," she says.

"I thought I was. Stop laughing at me. Stop looking at me."

A hand touches me and then a tissue. "Here, let me wipe your eyes."

"Gee, thanks." She's so close I sense the Lambrusco in her voice.

"Look, you're almost done." As if that's any comfort. It's not. I don't want to go back to that cutting board. I don't want to go anywhere near that onion.

"I thought you could make me like cooking."

"I thought this was easy," she says sarcastically.

I scowl. But, still, I persevere, slicing the second half through blurred eyes. When it's done, I take my drink and pace around the kitchen, dabbing.

I need a minute.

Okay, make that five.

"Would you please stop smirking?" I tell her. She's mocking me. So why does that make me feel invincible? How does she do this to me, even when I'm crying?

After a while, I'm next to her again. And as much as I'd like to turn away from those eyes, that glass of wine's dropped my guard. Her lips are wet again, like they were before. Like she just licked them. I have to suck in my guilt-ridden urge to kiss the wine that lingers on them. To gaze at them. Not only that, my mind's drifting miles beyond that innocent kiss and it's doing horribly wicked things to her on this floor. I could easily end this stare down, but that's not exactly what my heart has in mind. I wonder if she might be thinking the same, and if she thinks it's wrong, too.

"All that's left—almost all," she says, "is this ricotta." And with that, the moment vanishes. It could be that she saved me from a big mistake. "Here," she shows me. "Just spoon it into each." But I'm less interested now in what I'm doing.

When she steps away, I sink into a pit of regret with a hundred pounds of disappointment strapped to my back. It's for the best. I really shouldn't be thinking these things.

I try to muster my initial enthusiasm, but I'm drained now. I beckon her back. "How much in each pepper? I mean, like this? Am I doing this right?"

She sets the bag of mozzarella on the counter, reaching around to show me how to scoop. "This is how." And she slips her finger down the bowl of the spoon to push the filling off. When it's my turn, she takes a sip of wine, peering up at me. Here come those nerves again. I watch as her gaze falls to my lips and lingers there. I grin. And she looks away.

"Will this taste as good as it looks?" I want to know because it really doesn't look that appetizing.

"It's amazing."

She pinches shredded cheese across the top—like, a lot. Which is good because I happen to love cheese more than life itself. Then she pulls a sheet of tinfoil across and slides it into the oven. "It has to cook, you know, slow and low." She slips her iPod into the dock. Then she asks, "Music?" It makes a ticking sound. "How about a blast from the past?"

"Like?"

"Kris Delmhorst? Jen Foster? Etheridge?" And then she blurts out, "No, wait—my nineties mix."

"Aren't you feeling nostalgic," I say and she gives me the cutest grin ever before hitting play and grabbing a wooden spoon. I would recognize this song anywhere, even from the first few chords. That's when we just look at each other asking. Her eyebrows want my approval. And this is the part where she starts singing to me over Sophie B. to the tune of "Damn I Wish I Was Your Lover" and I start to melt a little. Make that a lot. Are you kidding me? I crank up the volume, lean back against the wall, cross my arms, and watch the show.

Here's my soundtrack.

❖

Did I just hear Hadley say, "Let's play truth or dare"?

"Are you kidding me?"

"Come on," she whines, tucking her feet under. Then she knocks me over with those melt-me eyes.

"There's another movie to watch." Not to mention we always play the extras.

But she strings out a *please* because she knows it makes me cave. She knows.

"We haven't played that in—"

"Well, yeah, humor me. It'll be crazy fun. We always did on movie nights, didn't we?"

It'll be fun. That's what I'm worried about, especially after—how much wine between the two of us? I was having a good enough time reciting lines together.

"Yeah, I remember those…" I tell her. Truth is, she landed me in some serious hot water in days past. Stuff that makes that after-Pride bash back in 2002 look tame.

Except she's not letting up. Instead, she shuts off the television. That's when I stretch an arm across the sofa. I lean back, propping an ankle across my knee and caving. "All right. Fine." And I give her a look. "Truth or dare?"

She chooses the latter, pouring another glass of wine for each of us. And I know exactly what that dare is. That is, after a fair share of planning, plotting, scheming.

"I dare you to come by my place…every Friday night…for two months…"

I hear an echoed moan of hedonism through the glass at her lips. All right, that was distracting.

"And give me a few more lessons. You know, we'll stay on the easy track."

She looks dissatisfied. "Cooking?"

"Of course."

After some silence, I get, "Yeah, well, I'm glad you have a new goal in life."

"Did you have something else in mind," I joke.

"No, no, not at all."

I lean off the couch, wrists slack on my knees. The gaps are wider in the hardwood. Her legs are beside me twisted and bare. She raises her knee to cross the other way, her skirt rising with it. I need to get a grip.

"All right, well," she says matter-of-factly, "my turn."

"Shoot. I'm an open book."

"Are you, now?"

I look back at her. "With you I am." I like how her eyes don't really leave mine.

"We'll see about that. Truth or dare?"

I tilt my head. "Truth." Her grin curls into something sinister. I admit, that expression makes me somewhat terrified. Like I said, she can be a troublemaker. Why else would we get along so well? I take a drink myself.

Then I hear, "Did you ever wonder…How do I say this?"

"Spill," I tell her. That silence, though, is like the worst suspense flick ever. Either she can't find the words or she's intentionally stalling.

"Well, did you ever think of me, you know, as more than a friend?"

"Oh, don't go there."

"Why, babe?" Her expression's intoxicating.

"Why are you doing this?"

"Just answer." That's when a car door slams outside.

"All right, all right...yeah."

She raises an eyebrow.

"Sure I have."

"Really?" I don't get why she's befuddled.

"Yes," I admit, defeated. "Really."

"You have?"

"Yes!" I say, a decibel higher. "I have."

"When?"

"Here—and there."

"Oh, like, more than once?"

I clear my throat. "Hadley."

"What?"

I seem to have her undivided attention now, not like I want it, and she's waiting for me to finish. But I'm not sure I want to.

When I get up, and as I cross the living room, I can feel my shoulders tighten. The tension grips like a vise straight up to my neck.

In the window, I can see her reflection on the couch. "You remember when we went kayaking—all of us?"

The muscles in her calves are pronounced, and she's running her hands up and down as if applying suntan oil.

This game doesn't feel funny anymore. And the more I reflect, the more it all just comes out in a tangled mess and I'm not really making much sense.

"You took the yellow one, the two-seater. It was your first time. I was behind, paddling in that solo kayak, burning up, scorching—it was hot, like ninety, and I'm watching you guys," I say. She's still an image in mirrored glass. She's still rubbing her leg. "Your hair, it was longer then, pulled back. You were soaked. I remember. You were so ecstatic over that girl, so...Well, more than I'd ever seen," I say. "And, damn. I remember thinking, why can't that be me? And she's gone. Really gone. I'm going to lose her."

She's wearing a loose blouse casually unbuttoned that dips when she bends for her glass, which is at her feet.

"And then I'm thinking, why? Why am I so worried?"

I turn around, uneasy like maybe I'm dumping too much on her. It just feels like it's been in me so long, and it's not like I've ever told a soul—not this much. I cross the floor and sit beside her. My elbow nudges her. I think I'm trying to go back to that fun game again, or something like that. "Why am I telling you all this?"

"Why didn't you tell me then?"

"You still have that bikini?"

"Somewhere."

"It's hot."

"You think?" she asks, inviting more.

"Yeah." She's grinning, quite pleased with herself. Her pinkie rubs her bottom lip and it tugs. I'm curious, too, if she's thought of me in that way. Why would she ask this, and why tonight? But as much as I'd like to know if those feelings are mutual, I'm not ready to ask. What if the answer's no? I'd just end up making things more awkward between us. Then again, what if the answer's yes?

So I take another sip of wine. Those lanterns are starting to burn out. Soon the stillness in the room feels like a plate I just need to break. I mean, she's got the upper hand here now, doesn't she? And she's rather pleased with herself. I blurt it out. "Didn't you ever think of *me* that way?"

"Oh yeah! Of course I did."

"Okay, then."

She pauses to watch me blush. I'm grinning ear to ear. Then she asks, "Do you ever wonder now?"

My stomach just tanks. How much am I going to tell her? I shift in my seat, a little tense and clearly weak willed, in a good way. Her expression's hard to read.

"Yes," I admit. "Yes, I do."

She likes that.

"So do I," she tells me. When I see her eyes again, they're not playful anymore. They're not even combative.

Is this an invitation? I lean closer. I'm thinking, Who is this? Her lips are bare.

"Damn you." I shake my head.

"What?"

"You always get me to say these things that I don't want to say."

"I thought you were an open book."

Her eyes are trying to tell me something. And I think I'm agreeing with her. She reminds me of something I can't quite place. We're quarrelling, inaudibly, and her hand reaches my thigh and right there, right then, it's all over for me. It's over because I can taste the cherry-raspberry on her lips and her breath is thick and sultry and sticky. I'm telling her I want her. I'm saying more than that.

And a palm glides beneath her blouse where she's warm and taut. I linger there, my heart racing too soon as lace peels effortlessly under and she billows over. I'm not accustomed to nerves like this. So what's this reluctance?

Still the scent of her skin draws me in. And I'm thinking about the newness of this kiss as our knuckles overlap and she's crawling over, straddling me, that skirt now hiked above her hips. I sink back into this plush couch. She's nearly bare against my buckle, and just the thought of that...

It's clever, I think, how she tries to break and breathe when I can't. When I'm reaching. When every sense of reason's abandoned, for me at least. When I want those gravelly whimpers. When something's this unexpected. When I need her to be insatiable, because I already am with just this.

She must feel my heart heavy. She must, because she's reaching behind to unzip her skirt as I finger the crevice on each button of her blouse, pushing through fabric slits. It's painfully drawn out until her blouse parts open and she bends over me again.

I have her breathless and bared, radiant. And she's curiously torn yet insistent. I fear she's looking for some sort of promise that I just can't give her. So I'm telling her, again, as I pull her in, "I want you."

And that must be good enough because her palm's slipping between us and I love that. I love what she's doing. I love her, I think, and then I take that back if only from myself.

"Like that. Don't stop," she says.

Like that. Don't stop. Don't stop. I'm smashed against skin that's moist as I push inside and she moans into my mouth as hips push deeper. But I love you, I want to say. I'm mute. Fuck—why am I doing this?

Sunday

CHAPTER SIXTEEN: JESSIE AND HADLEY

Jessie

She had the lamp on when I woke to her cross-legged on the empty floor beside my bed. How long had she been there watching me sleep? I asked her to come back to bed. When she did, she crawled over me, braless. I pulled down her T-shirt and slid hands up bare thighs. She kissed me, sat over me, then tucked beside my bare chest until she left. I half listened, not wanting to. She brushed her teeth with cinnamon paste and pulled her plaid skirt up around her waist and zipped it. I bundled the scarf under her chin and around again and again to keep her warm.

We kissed at the door and out the door and against her car and in her car. Then I tucked her coat and shut the door reluctantly with the most exaggerated frown I could muster. She blew a kiss through the icy glass and vanished.

Drive safely. I will. I didn't want her to leave. I wanted her to stay here and keep me company. Share coffee. Talk. *Call me.*

I'm not justified in feeling this much, I'm really not. Why now has every what-if risen to a boil of unease? Like, what if her chase is over?

I stare at the last cold drip of coffee—mud is more like it. Which sits next to my phone. Which is idle. I swallow. As much as I despise the taste, it'll wake me and I need that right now.

I fold a flannel throw in fourths and put it back on the chair. I straighten pillows on the couch. Where she crossed her legs. Where I uncrossed them. It makes me smile.

What are you up to? Do you even miss me?

Maybe I should just pick up the phone and ring her. What am I doing wishing, expecting, hoping she makes the next move? A conversation that could go—which way? It could go the wrong way, and I would run.

I can't go there.

I scroll down to her number. I find her name. My hands tremble.

I'm going to call her. Like we're friends. Like we've always been and always will be.

And then the phone bings in my palm.

I read it: *hey babe.* I laugh, semi-hysterically, breathing like a sigh and all the while thinking how relieved I am that she's not here to see me like this.

hey kid, I thumb back, instinctively.

meet for coffee?

when and where, I type.

brandons beans in 45?

That's so close I could walk there. I will.

affirmative.

I'd rather arrive first so I can settle in and watch her scout me out. Nothing beats that walk, as if she's tall even though she's not. When you're first, it takes the pressure off, unless she's late, as is the case, which is putting the pressure on.

I thought I'd burn some of this nervous energy walking here. But I didn't. Along the way, I moseyed into that new florist a block down and came out with roses. Red ones. Cliché, I admit. He wrapped them up in an obvious box tied in a ribbon. I felt good tucking my billfold back in my pocket, like I did the right thing. But I'm moody as heck and that confidence blew off the second the door slammed shut on my heel.

And this iced coffee is only making me jittery. I just watch that hipster at the counter ordering. He's tucking the latest *Adbusters* under his arm. It's a typical Sunday for him, likely. Not typical for me.

And I ponder, did the architects want this to look like an ice cream parlor, a library, or a bar? They have clever drink names and rolling ladders. Free truffles at each table. Two servers break and chat with their hands, both in white aprons. I adjust the flowers in the vase. The box is at my feet out of sight.

That's when I hear my name. Not a quick *hey* or *hi there*. But my name. Nothing more. I get up right away, giving her a hug—a deprived hug, a relieved hug that she's finally here. She feels good.

How is it that this girl next door can take me someplace else, make me unsteady, by simply speaking, by showing up? I loosen up and let my hands slip low on her back to the zipper on her skirt. We don't kiss.

Instead, I drag the chair out from under the table.

"I guess you were thirsty," she teases pointing at my empty glass. Then she hangs her coat across the back of her chair. She has nothing to drink. So I ask if she wants something. She tells me no. She wants to talk. She gets more serious and detached. I don't know how to take it, so I clam up. I study the brick wall beside us.

"I wanted to tell you, you know, why I took off so early."

I nod, straight-faced, propping my elbows on the table like armor.

She's nervous. I can tell. "Well, you know how I used to have a humongous crush on you? I felt like a complete fool. I wasn't anything to you but, whatever, maybe one day. Maybe—if I stuck around." She scratches the back of her neck. "And it was okay. It's nice that you came to me. That I could go to you."

What does this mean? I have to look away because she doesn't. It's mildly uncomfortable. It hits me that maybe we should be holding hands (or I'd like to) across the table, but we're not. It's that kind of feeling. But I'm too concerned about rejection.

"Well, this is hard for me," she continues.

"Don't stop."

"All right, let's see. I think it's just our history. It can complicate things. Or not."

That urge gets stronger to get this over with.

"So, you know, I'm getting a little sidetracked. Stop looking at me like that." We turn to look at the commotion and stomps at the entry.

"You were saying?" I lean in to her. She does this thing where she smiles and then looks away. But I don't—look away, that is.

"Well, what I was trying to say is this. Every time I fell in love and out, I fell apart. I could come to you and you were there to pick me up and it gave me hope. I don't know."

"You're beautiful, you know that?"

"Oh no. Stop," she says, blushing. "Well, don't you think—we've been good? This is ridiculous. I don't even know if I should say this, but I'm going to because I told myself I would. You know a few times I thought I'd never find someone—"

She drops her head.

"You were always, in the back there, that someday girlfriend and all that." She crosses her arms across her lap, raising a hand to push her bangs aside. It's adorable.

I finally do find that hand under the table. I don't let go. She doesn't either. "And you, too. You with Ella and all that. You know? Well she's the only person you kept in touch with, right? I guess we just had something different and it was really good. I'd never lose you. I'm just so afraid of that—I'm sorry."

She drops her head to the side and looks up at me from under those lashes.

"You know when I threw that question out, that stupid truth or dare?" I don't answer. It's not actually a question. "How did I know? I didn't. We had a few drinks, that's why. I'm having a good time with you. When I took off last night, it dawned on me. We spent this entire weekend together. We don't do that, right? I was feeling way more comfortable, I guess, than I usually am because there's no Ella, there's no Alicia. It's just the two of us. Well, I didn't think what happened would actually happen. And when it did, I felt sort of…dazed by it all. I don't know what to do. All those years, you were the one I could talk to. I can't talk to anyone now—if I screw everything up. That did freak me out. I mean, whatever comes of this, I'm losing you…at least a side or part, that is." It's what I've been thinking all morning. But I don't tell her that. Then she continues, "I don't even know what to tell you now because, you know. You're. Just. Hot. And I'm blushing again, right?"

"You are. Don't stop. I like it."

"Well, let's just say, I don't know, I wasn't disappointed. That was apparent, right?" She rolls her eyes. Her smile lights up the place. "We've always been honest. Let's stay that way. For me at least, it was just so…so perfect. This."

It dawns on me that I'm breathing; I'm relieved. I wasn't sure where she wanted to take me. But I'm all right now.

"Well, now that I've said too much and—who knows—maybe

I've just made a complete ass of myself, I'm handing this over to you."
I catch a glimpse of that hipster as he ducks out the door into a gust,
magazine still tucked under a crooked arm.

Then my confessor adds, "You know, one more thing."

"What's that?"

"I left not wanting you to feel obligated in a way. We can be
friends, babe, and pretend this didn't happen. You know, chalk it up to
that storm. A rebound, whatever you want. I'm okay with that. That's
why I left. You and your space. I get that. I mean, I need space, too."

I'm thinking about how easy it is to talk with someone who gets
me right from the start. There's literally no explaining. I'm chastising
myself for taking so long to see it. And still, I don't think I could
physically get close enough to her. But I keep a distance.

"There's something else I need to set straight." Her expression falls
blank once more. "If, by chance, you wanted...Look, I don't want to
be your next ex-girlfriend. You know, it would have to be one hundred
percent. That's just how I am. And I want *you* to be one hundred percent
with me in this. Potentially eventually maybe...that it could be forever.
Possibly, you know? One day. Otherwise, I'd rather just stay the way
we were. I'm fine with that."

"Okay," I say and she pulls her hand away to sit back.

"I'm going to pass this ridiculously messy topic to you." She slips
me an innocent grin.

And sure, I'm still listening at this point. But for the past few
minutes, I've glazed over it all because, of course, she and I are in the
same place. I'm falling in love with this girl. I am in love with her. And
I'm amazed she doesn't see it all over my face. I can't peel my eyes off
her. I can't get enough. I'm giddy and I don't get this way, and it doesn't
seem plausible that I could even hide that.

I pull the hand she took away, sliding my fingers into hers until
all I see are knuckles. I trace her fingertips. Her stare's unbroken and
curious and a tad painful. "Hadley," I say, my voice dropping, "I'm one
hundred percent in this with you."

She lights up.

"And I can't believe I'm saying this—" My voice fails me, so I
force the words out. "But I think I might be falling in love with you."
Why can I say it a million times in my head, but vocalizing, that's
excruciating? I'm not regretting it.

She tries to stand, but I yank her down to my lap and she tumbles and our smiles become a kiss that feels familiar but not. Her thighs are heavy on mine. Her body is limp, and I steady her and need her and have since her voice said my name. From the moment she left my apartment. From her dance before dinner. From the night she touched my hand under those covers.

Her kiss isn't patient. It isn't shy at all. It's assertive and effortless until I find myself wanting more than that. Wanting her like I did last night and the night before. And suddenly I just want to get her out of here and alone.

I love how she feels. Then our kiss wanes as if to say good-bye. There's a lump in my throat. Is this wrong?

"You're such a tease," she says.

And it's not until I slide my foot back that it hits me—the roses.

I'm grinning.

"Hold out, hold out," I tell her. I lean and nearly drop that box. I don't think I'll ever forget the look on her face when I hand it to her. And she unties the ribbon, like she kisses me, with eagerness and skill and impatience.

❖

Hadley

It's a remarkable day, curious and seriously sublime. But I'm tangled in too much of my own drama to find any sort of peace in it. I want to, though. Happy calm is so much better than *I'm freaking out*. Plus the pavement's slick, almost slippery in parts, which isn't helping matters. It keeps me on edge. That and constant dodging of pedestrians. It feels almost too crowded, and everyone's too busy studying mannequins or display windows or talking on their phone as opposed to watching where they're going.

It's not until I reach the coffee shop that I pause. I don't walk in. I just wait, inhale, again, and then another until my lungs feel wide and tight. Then I let it go. My hands are shaking. When I glance through the glass, there she is at a table for two, waiting. She's hunched over, head in hands. It's the way you would sit if you just heard the worst news of your life. But I can only see the back of her. Maybe she's just exhausted. I don't know. It's not her usual posture, reclined or even slouched, boots up on the next chair. My heart sinks. I wonder if maybe she's nervous. But maybe it's something else. She could be thinking about…I don't know, something I don't want to know, as if my heart wasn't racing enough. I can't do this.

I don't go in. Instead, I step aside to let this man in, and then I pace the sidewalk.

How many times have I watched this without her knowing, her composure, that poise, understanding all there is behind and beneath it? She could laugh, but there was struggle. I always knew her intent, even defended and encouraged it most of the time. Now I'm worried I'm blinded to it. I won't even care. I'm too partial. But I don't want a smile on the outside if that's not what she desires on the inside.

I glance through the door once more. She's leaning back now, unbuttoning. Her coat's almost off. And she does this thing where she crosses a leg and then uncrosses. She rests back and up and over again.

So I take another breath. And with fingers trembling, I pull the handle. Here goes nothing.

❖

Jessie

After lunch, which consists of deli sandwiches (and a bag of kale chips for her), we make a spontaneous loop through the co-op to get water because we're completely dehydrated from all the salt in the processed meat we ate. It's boxed water sold in a carton like milk, so I think it's recyclable. This means less guilt, though I hate to pay money for something that drips free from the tap.

It's a yellow day. Not gray or even blue but sunny. Out front, we pass a display of new sleds, which gives me an idea. This guy's clearing snow off and restocking boxed Fatwood, which I always see people buying. A couple of wreaths draped in berries and bows and brown paper price tags are hanging from beams right above, $39.99 apiece. She goes inside ahead of me and we meet up at the juices, most of which cost more than our entire lunch. I roll up with a cart that's far too small for my sled. Between red and army brown, I choose the latter, a deluxe model. She just looks at me, like, *What's this?*

We hit the checkout line with no line and I slide my debit card in—no signature required because it's less than twenty-five dollars.

Then we hit the road chugging down our boxed water and singing to the radio. Big dudes stand on top of roofs shoveling. Some of these cars are feet under mounds that have already refrozen. Good luck with that, I think.

When we get to the schoolyard, which is tucked against a hillside, I see that a good ten cars have beat us to it. She stops around the corner, so the car is sandwiched between thick trees and brush. We can hear squeals in the distance over the aggressive blow of the car's heater.

She gets out and into her back seat and starts unzipping her backpack. I lean between these bucket seats just in time to catch a glimpse as tights slip off the last heel. Her skirt's hiked up to those boy shorts. All I can say is, "Wow." I'm so ready to get back there with her. But she gets on her back, working up a pair of Levi's, feet on the black door panel, before stripping that skirt down and stuffing it into the same bag.

I'm hardly in the mood for sledding at this point, so I sulk.

Even still, she gets the sled out of the trunk and I carry it, making our way over to the hill. In mittens and hats. Knit scarves. Coated up. I can see her huffing. I am, too. We don't say a word the whole way. I do glance over a few times with this (probably cheesy) smile I've got going on.

The snow's bottomless, but there's a winding path alongside that's pretty packed. Kids are running up beside us, screaming—sleds on heads and dragging. How do they get that kind of energy? We're out of place here, I'm thinking, with the hordes of mouthy middle-schoolers and middle-aged moms and dads. We're too old, or maybe we're too young. Probably too gay-looking. It's packed. So I lure her to the loner hill.

That's another hike.

And along the way, we're blinded by sun, which drips down trunks and bare tree limbs. It's stretching shadows over and up mounds of marshmallow terrain. At this point, I'm beginning to feel my sense of adventure return, though I'm still preoccupied by that little wardrobe switcheroo back at the car. We stomp our own path. Eventually the knoll levels out.

When I drop the sled, it tries to skid down without me. I crouch, weighing down the back, which lifts the front. My boots dig in like cleats. I tighten my thighs around her and wrap my arms across her rib cage. She leans in to me, which I'm so getting into, knees tucked up with her feet propped against the front lip. She should've worn more appropriate shoes.

"Trust me?" I ask before lifting my boots.

"No," she's shouting as we start down. But she wants to. And she shrieks the whole way. I laugh. It gets slick and steep pretty quickly, though, and we sort of lose control. Finally we hit a clearing. My boots dig in to brake, but we just lean and tip and she goes down with me. I top her, shadowing the sun from those pearly whites and squinting eyes. I hear that sled skim down the hill driverless, and it's like my heart races away with it. She's catching her breath, lifting and reaching for me. She looks absolutely radiant out here.

I tell her she's not good at steering. She says I can't brake. There's a shadow from my hair that moves across her skin.

That's when her face goes blank. I want to know what's on her mind.

"Oh, I don't know," she tells me. She rests on my forearm as the ancient pines bow down to eavesdrop.

"What don't you know, babe?"

She shrugs. I try to interpret. "Honestly?"

"No," I joke. "Lie to me."

"It's easier to lie sometimes," she tells me, "than do this."

"What do you mean?"

"I'm just afraid, you know, Jess."

"Why are you saying this?"

"Aren't you?" she asks.

"Afraid?"

She just looks at me as if to ask the same question again.

"You're cute," I say with a chuckle.

"I'm freaking out a bit. I like this—I like it a little too much. Doing this right here. I don't want this to be over."

"It won't be."

She struggles to sit. I'm telling her no. I thought we were having fun here.

"You'll bolt," she says. "I'll bore you."

So I tell her again that I'm not going to leave.

"How do you know that?"

"I don't," I say. Her eyes show fright and hurt and something else I can't quite figure out. Then she covers them. I don't like that. "And neither do you," I say. "Nobody knows. Nobody knows what'll happen tomorrow, do we?"

She can be so evasive sometimes.

"Hadley."

"Don't do this."

"Why—all of a sudden—don't you trust me?" But her response doesn't come. "Kiss me," I say leaning in.

"I don't know why—"

"Nonononono, kiss me." When she does, her thighs grip me. She can't *not* want me. The weight of her head gets heavier on my forearm. And I feel this kiss everywhere.

"You know I can't make promises," I say. "Even still you're acting like this is a new thing when I've imagined it—"

"Since last night, I know."

"No. Not last night." I'm beginning to get annoyed and short-tempered. A bird flies overhead and she follows it. I can't see but can hear it. It's a whine that repeats and repeats. And then shadows darken the glare. There must be a flock.

"A long time. Years."

"No you haven't."

"Why would I—"

"Don't make this out to be something it's not. You've been with Alicia and everybody else."

"Because you've been with Kate and everyone else. How many times did I hear about Kate? I talked to Kate today. I ran into her, wanting to know if you're supposed to be this nervous around someone. What does that mean—you ask me. Then I hear through the grapevine that you took off with her and nobody even knew where you guys went."

"I can't believe you even remember that."

It's not like I could forget.

"You weren't jealous," she says.

"Of course I was. And you can't possibly compare this to some booty call I've had. Nobody's ever measured up to you. Why do you think I never stayed with anyone?"

Her lungs must be empty. She can't fill them. I hear her say, "I love you." I can't say it back though. It's like I said too much already. So I just find my balance in this snow.

"Hey, why not try this again, don't you think? Without freaking out on me." I get to my knees and extend a hand. The sun blinds her, but with a tug, she's on her feet. Her mitten stays there—in mine—and we walk that way until we find the sled.

And it didn't actually go that far. She brushes it off and carries it over her head. But we're done after just one more run and head back to the car to thaw. I get in the back seat as soon as the lock beeps, and extend a hand. She's indecisive at first but eventually succumbs with a look that all but wonders. I take her keys, reaching into the front to crank up the heat. And when I kiss her, I get playful back though I was hoping for something more along the lines of aching. We'll get there.

Because I haven't stopped thinking about that skirt hiked around her hips back here. "Was that our first fight?" she wants to know, following my lead and stripping that wet scarf and mittens off. Her seats are leather and black. The center console's down, so I flip it up.

"I think it was." And here's where we could drive to my place. We could go even closer to hers. But that's just not my style. Because those eyes, they're smoldering. "Just look at you," I say with palms warming those pink cheeks. "You're so fucking gorgeous."

She's going for demure right now, which is why she misses this hand that's now underneath her sweater where her insufficient something-or-other is masquerading as a support bra. I'm tracing over lace and that crease between cleavage. She has to be catching on because she's tugging at her coat until I toss it in the front and away.

"What's this about not trusting me," I ask. "You do, I hope." We don't need caution or doubt or uncertainty. I want irresponsible and impulsive. But instead I get this look that says, *if only*. And this kiss is too sweet for my liking. So I'm going to change that.

Hadley has this way of accessorizing her unease with adventures. Mad adventures. She doesn't spend too much time discouraged like this. Which is why it's no surprise when I hear, "Of course not," followed by, "just shut up." And she all but flings that prudence out the door.

"Is it bad that I want you so much?" I say. "Maybe we shouldn't have waited two decades."

"In a cold car in the middle of winter?"

"It won't be cold for long, I can promise that." And I kiss her like

I did that first time. She lifts her hips in this shallow seat, unzipping and banging knees on those too far reclined front seats. I'm not complaining. I'm just reveling in this view, especially when that sweater lifts up and over and she's bare and teasing me with those ample shadows. And it's not like I can turn away, either, because here she is, raw and unblemished, ageless as ever.

Her kiss bends over me. It's not playful anymore, and we're breathing like a haze that accumulates into thick frost all around. It's already cloaking our view. She gets on her knees and straddles me, stripped to sheer, her breasts heavy, and the heater's already roaring to the point of scorching. I tuck a single finger around that slip of elastic between her thighs where it's warm and taut. And there's that sigh again, soft and needy and unrestrained. It's familiar now. It's mine, I'm thinking, and I want more. So I dip and glide, sliding and exploring until she's throbbing and braced against that car door.

I want her just like this, limp and trembling. And I'm set to flip her over and finish her off until something even better comes to mind, which involves me on my back and her over me. And I watch her not watching me, that fist over her lips as I shift her hips forward and above me and draw out another moan. And she glides over and with me until I lose her and she comes back and that's it.

CHAPTER SEVENTEEN: RYAN AND BRIE

Ryan

Surya Namaskara B.
It must be six a.m.
My alarm clock, she's up with the lark.
You're going to bend your knees, looking forward.
A year ago she said I saved her, mended her. Now I'm just painful to her. Painful to look at, painful to touch, to listen to. So I don't want to be seen or handled by her or coddled. I don't want to be so agonizing and flawed. I'll exist without her.
I'll die without her.
It's time for breakfast, another breakfast, another shower. Another Sunday. Like the last and the one before and the one before that. I'll floss. I'll shampoo. I'll dress in absolute solitude.
The same jeans (boot cut) and plain T-shirt with a V-neck, my navy sweater, ratty belt. I stare at the closet mindlessly. My thighs feel large. The cigar box is missing. So is everything, taken away. It's barren. There's dust settled in the corner where her boots were. It needs a good mop, the wood, inside and out where she sat. Right beside me. That's where she cried. Right by me, she hurt along with me but not for me. For what, then?
I'll exist without her because I don't exist to her.
I walk the hall and find that even the bathroom fan won't drown her now. She's littering my thoughts with cheap promises.
Sometimes the scent of my soap is more revitalizing than an entire

pot of coffee. Why is that? When your skin's damp, when your hair's still wet, the refrigerator can do the same.

It's cold. It's always cold, and it's not because I'm wet.

I'll make a hot breakfast, then.

I'm buttering an English muffin next to the skillet when I hear her talking. I did make enough for two, just in case.

"How do you like it?" she asks.

What, I wonder. But she's next to me running the sink water and repeating herself.

"How do you like it?"

She glides her hand down layers in the back and says, "My new morning hair."

I adore it. I want her fingers to be my own so I can run them through it.

You learn a lot from someone's search bar.

hair freja beha

mia farrow short

dementia coping

law firms portland me

Particularly when one's password is as common as *love*.

Would she even know if I read her email?

At least her presence in the next room, albeit lathered and far from threatening, offers enough distance from that temptation. So I decide to dive into her history, which is far from juicy. It's just a bunch of job sites.

When I hear my phone ring, her laptop won't power down quickly enough, quietly enough, because the shower has also stopped. It's that kind of rush you get when a fire alarm goes off and you're thinking not so much about running out of the house as you are about grabbing your stuff before it becomes toasty toast.

Why is it I'm always tempting fate like this?

The screen finally goes black when I pick up, and it's Ella telling me she won't keep me long. But I know she will, and she does. That's all right. I enjoy the company and the conversation, cleverly disguised as work. I can tell she wants gossip based on her *You sound different*s and *Is everything all right*s. Anything to get me to dish (which I don't) short of asking outright if Brie and I have split.

And in no time my girlfriend's in the room with me and she's sliding that laptop into her bag and over the opposite shoulder and her shoes are echoing away and out the door. She won't even acknowledge me.

And I'm okay with that, really I am.

❖

Brie

My window seat was taken by another with a laptop when I arrived, so I played musical chairs as soon as he left. I've decided to write every relevant law firm in the state of Maine an unsolicited letter and, if this doesn't pan out, I have a plan B. And a plan C. I click send on my fifth cover letter and sink into the warmth of my coffee (with a splash of nonfat milk). The barista actually left just enough room at the top this time.

There's a cowbell strung above the door and it makes a clank whenever it's banged by an incomer or out goer. It's a deep guttural noise that always precedes this burst of unwelcome cold. But it clanks so frequently that I've come to ignore it. Which is probably why it didn't even register when, just following that ruckus, I heard that sweet voice coming at me. "Is that who I think it is?"

Scooting in is Hadley along with plenty of shopping bags. She's with Jess, who trails just behind grinning ear to ear. (I get one of those up nods as she gets closer.)

"Wow, you look amazing," Hadley tells me. And then, "When did you do this?" She's touching my hair as she peels off her coat.

"Last night."

"You know, I didn't even recognize you—in a good way. You're made for short. I'm serious."

Then her companion chimes in, noticeably less dramatic, "I like it." It's kind of sexy the way she tells me that.

I'm still not used to short. I touch the back of my neck as if I'm looking for something I'll never quite find again. But I thank them. The hair, it's really changed me, my whole outlook, for the better.

"We knew we'd find you here," Hadley says. "More job hunting?"

"What else?"

"Take a day off."

"I can't. I need a job."

Instead of taking a seat, Jessie excuses herself to get a couple drinks for the two of them. She offers to buy me one as well, which is nice but not needed so I decline.

My girl is happy—blooming like springtime though her cheeks are ruddy from winter.

"How are things on the home front?"

I'm wishing I could talk, think, about anything else. "Home is not exactly the best word to describe it. We're talking. She's angry. It's uncomfortable. I don't even know what to say half the time. I'm either consoling her or dodging insults, and I don't know which is worse."

She comforts me with a pout. "Well, you did the right thing."

"I'm sure of it," I say.

"Then don't worry about it—or her." Her flippant attitude is just the prescription I need right now.

Jessie gets back. "I'm not interrupting anything, am I?" She winks, setting both mugs on the table. She sits with an air of confidence bordering arrogance.

Hadley starts to tell me that our (now her) weekly tae kwon do class has been bumped to Thursday due to cancellations over the weekend. I'm not sure why I didn't get this email, but she tells me she'll forward it when she gets home. Not that I need it. It's one more thing to cancel. She looks sad when she realizes I won't be there anymore.

I'll be back home by then. But I don't know if I'm ready for that conversation in front of Jessie. I didn't plan on announcing this move until after tonight's celebration. If I'm out fast enough, it won't even hurt. It's too much for even me to absorb. The last thing I want to do is turn a happy anniversary into a pity party about yours truly.

With inquiring eyes on me, though, I know I need to say something. I can't exactly lie. I suppose it wouldn't hurt to tell one more person. She can keep a secret. She may already know so much. So I spill a little.

"You know I won't be there."

To which, Jessie chimes in, "Have a hot date already?"

I pause, trying to find the best way to frame it. "I might not be in town on Thursday."

That's when eyebrows rise over a mug. I take a deep breath and then try to camouflage my announcement in an exhale.

"I'm moving back to Portland."

"Wait," she says. "You're leaving?"

"Yes," I tell Jessie and then I'm completely hush until she absorbs it.

"Why didn't you tell me this much?" she asks Hadley. I bottom my last inch of coffee in an attempt to wash down the bad news. Thinking, planning, that's one thing. Sharing this so widely is another. I'm not good at good-byes, not at all. And then the nerves and fears and jumbled emotions just take over and I feel a sting of tears but I hold it down. "My unemployment is ending, and I have a bed at my parents' place. I love it here—I love you guys so much. This is…hard. But, you know, I need to get out of her house. I don't belong there. We're making each other miserable. And it's just not realistic to think I could get a lease without a job and a paycheck. And besides—"

"Whoa," Jessie says, putting her hand on my shoulder. The gesture, I deeply appreciate. But the expression on her face tells me that she's definitely on Team Ryan and who could blame her?

"Sorry for being such a basket case."

"You're so not." She smirks.

"My truck's packed," I say. "She threw a fit. She doesn't get it. And I don't know how to explain this to her—how I'm feeling. She's so upset. And I get that. I'd be angry, too. But I'm not made of stone. This hurts me, too," I say with emphasis. "Tremendously."

They just listen. They're surprisingly attentive. "It's not her, and it wasn't deliberate. Why can't she understand and just respect that?" I'm asking Hadley, but I'm really directing this to the other party.

Jessie nods. "Look," she begins, finally contributing after likely scheming just what to say and when to say it. "Ryan's a really good friend of mine. This is how she deals. She doesn't hold back, and that can weigh heavy at times. Believe me, I get that. But I tell you she's the most loyal person I've ever known. I'd trust her with my life. Knowing her like I do, I can guarantee you she wants to make this right. Right as in, you know, what you want." Then our eyes just lock, and I'm liking it. She has amazing eyes, really. I honestly do feel something, it's pretty heartfelt, and it saddens me. It makes me want to stay. I was just getting to know this one.

Hadley doesn't break our stare down. Nobody does. Until a couple of teenage girls get right outside the glass and start admiring their reflection as if it were a mirror, fixing their hair, puckering, posing lusciously. They're oblivious to the fact that we're watching. I'm not sure which of us spills into laughter first.

"All right then," Jessie says. "It looks like we'll be taking some road trips in the near future. You know, I've been itching to see the coast. And I've never in my life been to a lighthouse. Imagine that. I've lived in New England all this time and I've never been up there."

I want this to be a joyful new chapter, not a sad farewell. I definitely don't want to lose these two. So she couldn't have responded better. I'm not quite sure if I come across as warm or patronizing, but I'm going for amusing when I say, "We have a lot more than just lighthouses, doll, but I'll show you whatever you'd like to see."

"I've always fancied myself as a sailor. I could be one. Don't you think," Jessie asks, nudging my friend.

"This from a woman who's never in her life touched a dead fish," Hadley teases.

"So tell me," I say. "What are you two up to? Shopping, I see."

I hear paper crumple at our knees as my girl pulls out a black crewneck sweater. "Would you look at this? Adorable, right? For tonight."

"I take it you're wearing a skirt with that?"

She looks at me confused as if to say, *What else would you wear with this?*

"What is wrong with you? It's barely thirty degrees."

"Skirts, though, they have their advantages," Jessie adds. Which is when I notice Hadley's eyes widen like she wants to shout, *Shut. Up.*

And this odd exchange piques my own curiosity. You could hear a pin drop as we bop around the table. And they look guilty as hell. "Wait, guys? What's going on?"

And they begin some sort of telepathic conversation across coffee mugs.

"Okay. I get it. When did this happen?"

Clearly I've hit the nail because their posture transforms in front of my eyes. Jessie props an arm up, and they just melt into one person. I must admit, I'm not that surprised. I'm glad, actually. And they look unpredictably adorable. Hadley's *Breakfast at Tiffany's* alongside, well…But it works, these two. I suppose just being around one another for eons makes you automatically look alike.

I'm glad she's finally heeded my advice, if she did, and I want to know everything, every last detail. I know I'll get the sanitized version here. Which is why I concede and will be waiting it out. I won't ask the real questions, at least not until I corner stylista, alone—this evening.

❖

Ryan

From this distance and across one and then another traffic lane, it's all unraveling. I'm wondering what she's thinking behind that plate glass, the tips of her fingers curled in the shape of an r. Her coat unbuttoned but over her shoulders—gold cufflinks snapped at her wrist. I should be wearing a trench coat and brimmed hat, and it should be raining. No, pouring. It shouldn't be sunlit like this. It should be gloomy like I feel. There should be fog and shadows to hide under. I should be dripping and driving away through headlights. From here, it almost appears that she's happy.

I'm not. It hurts. I want to walk up to that window and write on the frost, *fuck you.* Instead I duck into the nearest shop. I need to buy something to make this go away. It really is that easy.

I wonder what that girl does for her that I don't. I wonder how they'll end this time. I made her laugh.

Can I help you?

Nobody can, I think. This isn't quite my style. I slide a few more hangers and exit discreetly into another store a few paces down.

That's when I dial and press talk. Jenna answers.

"Catch me up," I say. She's too familiar. There's static on the line as I move. I'm wondering about her new kitchen. She's invited me how many times? There's always something else, something Brie. I ask about her daughter at MIT. Then I ask about the empty house.

"It's empty. But I like it. My kitchen, really, when are you coming over to see it? How've you been? I haven't heard from you in—"

That's when I interrupt her. "If you could choose between gray neutral or something bold like red for the bedroom, what would it be?"

"I'd go red. You know me."

"You don't think I'd get sick of it?"

"Red makes me happy. How could you ever get sick of that?"

That's one way of looking at it.

"Where are you?"

"Shopping. For bedding."

"That could only mean one thing."

Which is why I called her. I won't need to explain, and she won't ask.

"I met this woman," she tells me. "Guess where? The doctor's office."

"Why were you there?"

"It was routine. We went out a few times—or sort of."

I'm lugging this duvet under my arm. The clerk's listening. So I empty my arms and she takes it to the counter as I dig for sheets.

Then I ask, "How'd that go?"

"I like her. We'll see. It's not like she's the best in all areas—way too sloppy. But with a little practice and coaching..." She laughs. "I'm a good teacher, wouldn't you say?"

"If you like that sort of thing."

"She has a dog. We walk the dog."

"You don't even like dogs," I say.

She laughs. "It's just a small one. Maybe a Chihuahua. I don't know. You should see her."

"The dog?"

"No, Sarah."

"Is that her name?" I ask.

"Yes," she says. "We have a lot in common."

"Like dogs?"

"Like conversations—remember those?—the kind that go on and on. It's nice being able to talk to someone who actually thinks."

"Is it?" Maybe I'm fishing for a compliment.

"Why don't we have dinner sometime. BYOB. She wants to meet you."

"Why would she want to meet me?" I ask thumbing up my credit card.

"I've spoken highly of you."

"What exactly does she know about me?" I ask.

"You know, the usual. That you were the best sex I've ever had."
She laughs at the most inappropriate things.

"That's a great first date conversation," I say.

"It was, actually. I'm trying to show her how to do what you did.
How *did* you do that?"

I could engage in this but I refuse. I'm not enthused by the idea of
teaching her new girlfriend how to get her off.

"Everyone's different," she says.

"That they are."

Then she wants to know, "Did you get to the coast like you
wanted?"

"We did," I say. "It was nice leaving our room without covering
up—no umbrella, no sun hat," I say, undoubtedly a personal dig. "Just
toes in the sand and waves—"

"If you're into skin cancer and leather cleavage. Give it a few
years. Did it look the same, our room?"

"Listen," I say. "Are you still into Guinness?"

"Why?"

"Let's say Friday I'll bring some by."

❖

Brie

I'm about ready to hit the road when I hear, "I like it." So I glance
up more than a little startled. "Can I get you another?" That's when I
recognize her voice and everything about her, beyond elated to rest my
gaze on the best paralegal I've ever had the privilege to work with. And
then, "I'm sorry to bother you. I'll leave you here to do what you're
doing." But her smile's quite the contrary.

Which is why I get up and fall into this embrace, a detached one
that morphs into professional and finally *Boy, am I glad to see you.*
"Have a seat," I say.

"The new do—would you please stop? We've missed you." She
unpeels her coat and takes an empty seat. "How have you been?"

"Things are all right," I say. "I've missed everyone."

Then she asks, "Have you, you know—?"

"Found a job? Not quite. That would be what I'm doing now."

"They haven't replaced you," she tells me. "I don't think they will. Things, well, they just went nuts after you left." Then she leans in. "I hear his wife filed for divorce."

"Do tell," I say.

"They've moved me down a floor. A lot's been rearranged or reorganized, whatever they want to call it these days. Jill's supporting Tim now. He took all your cases. They have her covering three people—she hates it."

As she rambles, I think to myself, If only I look this edgy at fifty.

"And Megan's working twelve-hour days but getting overtime, which she likes—putting that kid through college. She came in last month before anyone else and caught them in the act." Her nose curls. "And you wonder why that woman made partner so quickly. She brought her husband by the office just the other week, paraded him past us, and we're looking at each other thinking—"

"Lovely." It's the closest thing to vindication I'll ever get. "How do you manage?"

"I need to get out. That place is toxic. Everyone knows about their little affair. I can't believe she fired you for that. Correction, I can."

"It's a blessing in disguise," I tell her. "Did Jill have her baby?"

"Yes! She just got back from leave and brought her in and"—she puts her hand across her mouth—"she's gorgeous."

"A girl!"

"A girl. She was in labor for two days. But something like seven and a half pounds. They discharged her twenty-four hours later. I swear, insurance isn't what it used to be."

"I'm so happy for her," I say with the most endearing expression I can muster. "Please send her my best. How are things with you—I mean, otherwise?"

It's not like me to get this emotional twice in one day, but I am. I don't tell her about my plans. I don't even offer a hint. For now, at least, I want to amuse myself with this illusion of how it was and pretend I still have my shit together—even though that's so far from the truth.

CHAPTER EIGHTEEN: ELLA AND SAM

Sam

What possessed us to buy this insanely complex washing machine? It's computerized. It has sensors and prewash and speed wash. But why would I want to rush a load? I can't count how many times I've opened the basement door, heard the hum, and rejoiced that I didn't have to go down and fetch it yet. This thing has way too many options when the only real thing I'm looking to do is avoid a washing board and bucket.

But we did both agree on it. A rarity.

I remember those getting-to-know-you questions back in the day. Top or bottom? Do you want kids? Have you been to Michfest? Are you vegetarian? Democrat or Green Party (please don't say Republican)? You know, the really important issues. The deal breakers. I thought I had all my bases covered only to find out that our biggest arguments would be knotted around two things: laundry detergent and sorting. Me, I'm an unscented girl. My wife prefers a springtime meadow, to the point that I sneezed lilacs every time I put on a shirt. But I did win that battle eventually. I won sorting, too, because jeans don't go with towels. They just don't. They go with darks. Towels go with towels. I won't even let her touch the laundry. (Okay, maybe that's not quite a win after all.)

And predictably I've sorted out an entire pile of greens by the time I reach the bottom of our hamper.

❖

Ella

I've made this a spa day, which means, for the past ten minutes, I've been hunched over a steaming pot of boiled water with a towel tented over my head—dressed in my cinched-at-the-waist cotton robe.

When the timer goes off, it's a mad dash to the bathroom for a splash of ice-cold water. Then I pat dry. Next comes the facial mask, the whitening strips, the deep hair conditioner.

And with one sip of detox tea, that pepper-spiced steam in and of itself soothes and calms—once again prompting me to wonder why people pay hundreds of dollars for spa excursions clear across town when they could have it all in the comfort of their own home for practically free, or at least it seems in comparison. And you never have to coat up, boot up, or trek through a blizzard, either. I personally would find it impossible to leave this snug abode on a day like today.

That said, after this prolonged three-day weekend with my better half, I'm admittedly looking forward to friends. Plenty of them. How long has it been, I wonder, since we were all at the same place at the same time—short of sharing pizza and hard cider around someone's U-Haul?

And I'm admiring myself in the mirror, my face the shade of a ripe avocado, when my phone rattles, startling me from this narcissism. My wife hollers up to see if I've heard, and of course, who wouldn't? The volume's abnormally high (with the shop and all) which is just what I'm thinking as I make a mad dash like an absolute klutz to get it, clicking talk just before it drops to voicemail on that fourth ring.

And that's when I hear that deep voice of hers. I'd know it anywhere. "Hey, Red. Happy anniversary."

"Thanks, Jess."

"Are you getting all dolled up for the night?"

Okay, she knows me too well. "You could say that."

"You know, you're painfully gorgeous already."

"Well, thanks for that." I don't know if I should feel guilty or angry. So I'm a little of both. Because she's single again. How many years will it be before I hear her neighborly voice?

"I wanted to ask you something."

I'm still suspicious, so I don't respond.

"Okay, well, let's see. I know someone. She's a friend of mine. She kind of wants to do something out of character."

I laugh.

"She never does. You know?"

"Is this, like, buy-a-new-outfit out of character or something, you know, illegal?"

"Not like that. Not at all. This person, she's sort of fallen for a girl she can't have."

"Is she straight?"

"Not exactly."

"Married?"

"No, no, not married. She's like a friend—a friend of hers."

"And this person, are you saying she's not sure how to make a move—is that it?"

"The deed is done. She doesn't know if she should, you know, pursue it."

"Why not?" I ask.

She just groans on the other end. "You're right, I don't even know what I mean."

It's awkward. I'm awkward. She's awkward. But my awkward is starting to fade. Boy, I don't miss single.

"This friend of yours—it wouldn't be Hadley, would it, that met someone new?"

I listen to, well, nothing. And then she says, "What do you think of her?"

"Who?"

"Hadley."

"We get along great. You know that. Why?"

Jessie has a hard time talking about herself, and she obviously can't articulate whatever. So I ponder ways to pull it out of her.

"Not to change the subject, but did you lose power?"

"I *lost* power, past tense, which was not fun, and then my ex came by—"

"Alicia?"

"Yes." I hear a sigh. These silences always make me uncomfortable, especially on the phone, especially with my own ex, but I let it dangle between us. It's the only way to get her to talk. "And she—she meaning Hadley—was here."

"When you lost power?"

"Her car stalled, so she crashed here and that's when the power went out and, well. No big, right? But…"

Call it intuition or whatever you'd like, but I'm starting to get a sense of what might be going on through her cryptic hypothetical.

"No, why would it be?"

"I know. It's not. She was cute, though."

"Who, Hadley?"

"She walked that whole way in that storm. She was a soaking mess by the time she got here."

"You sound smitten," I say questionably. With a teaspoon of insecurity, I think to myself.

"You had to be there."

"So are you asking what I'd think if you and Hadley"—my cheeks crease into a smile, cracking this avocado mask; I'd almost forgotten I had it on—"hooked up?"

"Well, I don't know. Sure. Hypothetically, what would you think—mistake, right?"

I am touched that she called me, trusts me, with this. How Sam in there is going to take it, I'm not sure. And why my ex wants my approval—no clue, but she seems to.

"No," I say. "No mistake." That guilt, the stuff I've harbored over the years for her, over what? She's the one who left; I'm the one who got over it.

"She's a friend."

"So?"

I don't know why but I get the sense that she's smiling on the other end of the line. Especially when I hear, "That means a lot from you." Bingo. That's when I give myself a virtual high five for translating Jessie-speak.

Then I change the subject starting with, "You coming tonight?" and ending with, "You hope so?"

"Well, yes, we are. I'm waiting to see her right now." I crack my mask again because that's so cute. "I'm nervous."

"What for," I say. "She's crazy about you."

"Thanks." She sighs. "I'm psyched to see you—both," she tells me all formal-like. And when she does, I get the sense that we've crossed a bridge. Like we've never been closer, somehow, and we've never been farther apart.

❖

Sam

It's that moment when you make a forty-five yard field goal in full high-def, a play I'm still yessing when an ad comes on, which is my cue to leave the room. So I rush to haul the laundry upstairs before flipping another load from wash to dry, and dry to fold, and fold to yet another basket.

Once I reach the second floor, I find my wife seated comfortably on the edge of the tub in matching bra and underwear, blowing painted nails and donning that god-atrocious plastic shower cap that's covered in pink flamingos. It smells like—I don't even know, something that should be sequestered under a fume hood.

And I'm setting her clothes next to two other piles that are folded on our bed and still not dealt with when I ask, "Who was that?" referring to her call earlier. Obviously it wasn't work or she'd be out the door.

"Jess," I hear.

It's not the response I expect and I'm thinking, Jessie calls and my wife doesn't tell me until I ask? Then a flush and I'm trembling. So I stop what I'm doing to ask, "Should I worry?"

"Of course not."

She calls my wife while sandwiched in between quote unquote *relationships* and I shouldn't be concerned? So I ask, "Something about Alicia?"

"No. She called, I think, to get my opinion."

While I listen, I feel unsettled again. I've never been fond of their friendship, but even more now. You could say it's been boiling up this weekend. Maybe this is where I say something.

"It was unexpected," I hear her say, and then she goes on to tell me that the most unlikely duo is now a *we*. I'm not sure what she's referring to until she elaborates. And that's when my lungs steadily drain, my shoulders droop, and my neck unravels.

"Good for them," I say.

"She's nervous. Can you believe that?"

"Nervous about what? Are we talking about the same person?"

"They're planning a day—and then over to see us. I don't know, but who didn't see that one coming?" she asks.

I'm baffled. "I didn't."

"This explains a lot."

"Like what," I ask, now crouching casually beside her on the bathroom rug. And an appreciative hand slips up her ankle as she continues to blow across painted nails, acting as if she doesn't notice but she does.

I gradually tune back in to hear my wife say, "You know, Jessie's visits to the shop after my big grand opening."

"Yes, I remember," I say with a slight grudge. Okay, more than slight.

"Did I ever tell you about that?"

"Of course you did," I snap.

"Why are you this way?"

"What way," I ask. "And please don't shake your head silent and angry like that."

But she won't respond.

"Talk to me," I say.

"There's nothing to talk about," she says.

"Of course there is. We can start with the double standard around here. Like, why is it perfectly acceptable for you to have an intimate friendship with this woman you called the love of your life."

"Then," she clarifies.

"Still," I say, "after we met."

"No."

"Yes, you were hardly over Jessie. You talked about her incessantly, usually under the guise of that shop, and you wonder why I never want to set foot in that bakery of yours. It's like half hers. How would it make you feel?" I ask. "No, wait, don't answer that because I can't even talk to anyone at work without you questioning my motives."

"You wouldn't cheat on me," she says rather sure of herself.

I just give her a look.

"I'm not interested in Jessie. And I can't believe you just used the word *intimate* in the same sentence as her. Try *platonic*. I'm in love with you."

I can't even look at her. I just have to wait for the awkward ending of this conversation to pass because she knows better than to talk when I'm angry like this. I focus on that nick in the door frame likely where the vacuum hit it. Then I catch my wife stretching her legs out, reaching behind, and her bra just falls to the rug.

"Sorry to get so heavy on you. I need to rinse," she says—removing that hideous shower cap and letting wet strands fall limp across her shoulders and down her back. Then she gets up and slides elastic down her hips and, forgive me...

She's cranking the faucet until water gushes to the drain and then diverts that pressure up to the showerhead, pointing a single toe over the edge of the bath to highlight those lean muscles up her calf. The arch of her back curves around the curtain. Then she glances back and might as well bat those eyelashes at me because she throws out, "You are welcome to join me."

It's not like she's generally this way, forward. Every so often she fawns, but lately she's preoccupied, indecisive, hoping I'll take the lead. But she has that side that can't get enough of me, sometimes. A side that clings. Her eagerness, our unacquaintedness that fell into predictability once everything became more and more complex. It's not like she's insensitive or unaffected when she's quiet or looks away. I do understand where she's coming from.

And I'm already okay again. So I step in. The water's just a fine mist from where I'm standing, and she gives me a look that's conciliatory.

I'm admiring the beads of water against her face—that lazy flow over damp lips. Her pace is unhurried and focused as each gush wraps and clings down her bicep and around her elbow, dripping to her abdomen and finally to the flesh between her legs.

And I watch her expression as she's slipping over me and around, molding against my fingers and gushing down my hand until she's drifting in and out, from frustration toward impatience. She's soaked, with hair that's clinging against white tile just beside her.

I want to hold her with every bit of mistrust and possessiveness ever felt until she's defenseless. It's that look, drenched with hair that now pours down into one continual flow. Then she nips her bottom lip as if to ask me, but she already knows. She knows how to do this to me—even still. And the way she's touching me, it makes me selfish and vengeful for no reason at all. She doesn't even want an explanation.

I just want to escape without her knowing where.

It's almost hateful how it intensifies. Her wrapping a knee around my hip and sliding against my thigh. Here's my apology, I think, as I lean in and breathe against flesh. And her sigh after sigh becomes urgent. I drown inside each, breathing against her. And my lips linger down curves to her hips until I'm kneeling under parted thighs and she's warm and throbbing—her knee lifting to the side of the tub. And I choose painfully deliberate and drawn out as I inhale deep lungsful of steam with flesh slick at my tongue. She begins to move without me.

I find where she's unguarded and quivering. Here—she moans from barely a touch at all. I linger until she's shifting and pressing against me and I'm drawing her in and done and she's arched and over me and trembling.

CHAPTER NINETEEN: JESSIE AND HADLEY

Jessie

Skirts do have their advantages, I contemplate as I check out Hadley's chiseled calves just four paces ahead of me. Maybe I should take up tae kwon do.

Then I think, why do this tonight, out in the cold and dark and surrounded by people? Couldn't we just stay in, kick it at home, like, alone?

"Hold up," I shout, sprinting to catch up. Then I grab those hips and twirl them around. "Kiss me," I say. There's a car gushing by.

She sounds like a spring breeze. "What if I don't want to?" What a tease.

I inch the hem of her skirt up and she brushes it back down. "Do you have any idea what I'd like to do to you right now?"

"Why don't you tell me?"

"I'd rather show you," I say.

That's when I finally get what I want—well, sort of. She does this thing where I can't quite reach her lips, and then I do just before she takes them away. "Mmm."

Which only invites more.

"Let's go home," I say.

She curls a finger over my waistband. Mercy. Then she starts tugging my arm down the sidewalk saying, "You know we can't disappoint our friends." As we near the entrance, there are so many words that try to find their way but they never do. I can't say much to her. I don't say anything, really. Neither does she. We reach the door too quickly, and it releases a gush of music and warmth and conversation.

I shove my way through the dense air. Admittedly it's nice to get inside. It's toasty. Unbuttoning my coat helps to cool down, especially when I pass the blazing hearth. It's a bit much.

Soon we're surrounded.

Even with four tables fitted together, they spill over. With gaiety. With rowdiness. With incredibly bulky coats that fill the empty space between chair backs.

I toss out a greeting and drag two more seats to the party, one that I set near Brie, who looks incredible as usual. She's all smiles (knowingly) for the two of us. I ask if she's getting used to it.

"I need a scarf. Like an extreme arctic chill one," she says. And then she does her best rendition of shivering.

Her ex, who is far too distracted to catch my arrival, gets the elbow. I scan the table already cluttered with colored drinks, fizzy and foam-topped, steins and stems. At the center bursts a huge blooming centerpiece.

I apologize to my hosts for being late. Then Ella and I share a glance as I stretch my legs beneath the table.

By the time our waitress dips in, I'm exchanging words with my better half. She orders her drink and motions to me. I order a beer, running two fingers up her knee and drifting into my own other realm. It takes all of my resolve to stop at her hem. But soon enough, her hand tops and redirects mine and that ruling is made for me.

The waitress walks off as I'm whispering, "We might be a little behind in the drink department." She silences me, disapproving. And then I lose this girl to another conversation.

So I turn back to Sam, who seems withdrawn. I dive in to break the ice. There are few things in life quite as stiff and clumsy as chatting it up with your ex's new wife. After we cover the usual, I try to envision our two pioneers out there without any electricity. Sam lackadaisical as ever, and Red over there flipping the whole scene out *Days of Our Lives* style.

How our conversation coils around to Hadley, I do not know. Possibly it's the safest topic, so I bite, and soon enough, we're buckled over and cracking up about who knows what. I have to admit, she's rather amusing. Stoic and indifferent, yet entertaining.

Just then, speak of the devil, Hadley pulls me into a conversation and the waitress dips in with my drink. I take a long, slow swallow. Then Red sashays her way back from the bar with a topped-off martini, which she gives her wife.

"What's she trying to do to me?" I overhear.

And Ryan jumps in with, "It is your anniversary. Drink up."

"And one for you, my dear," Ella says to Ryan, our dark cloud over there, who grips the frothy mug and raises it to the table. "To the best set of friends a girl could ever ask for. I mean it," Ella adds.

"To something like that," I say.

I clink.

Ella chimes in again with, "To electricity," followed by her wife's toast to gingers. Gag.

That's when my girl takes it up a notch pointing to the music overhead, which is fading into one of our favorite bands of all time. "Oh my God, do you hear this?" She elbows me. Her life-is-a-soundtrack outlook. "Guys."

I listen in as Queen belts out "You're My Best Friend."

"Guys. Seriously."

And I don't even know who starts singing first but they're no Freddie Mercury. I'm just glad we're not kicked out, it gets so loud.

❖

Hadley

Maybe that perfect fairy-tale romance doesn't have to be perfect, as long as it is for you. And maybe everything in life happens for a reason.

Me figuring out life, while Jess figured out hers. And draining a car battery as Jess—well, you know that story. Even dropping out of college to dodge that pile of debt for, what, some worthless degree in history. Still, I can't come up with a single reason why, in the eleventh grade, Nora Lowell landed the lead role as Elizabeth Proctor in *The Crucible*. But I digress.

This is not to say that the time I've spent waiting wasn't agonizing—waiting for a reason to show up, for that good to come of it, for my cloud nine or closure. But I do believe everything in life does happen for a reason. We just don't always know that at the time.

Which is why I'm not going to complain that the only person I've even clicked with over the past twenty-odd years (aside from the obvious) is trucking her tweed across two state lines never to talk, text, or tae kwon do with me ever again. I'm not squandering tonight wound up and wondering and worried about this next happens-for-a-reason. Maybe I can talk her into staying with me for a while now that Ryan's out of the picture. Or maybe I won't. And why I've wasted how many hours sharing this and confiding that only to be left empty-handed with not even useful relationship advice is beyond me.

Even still, why am I handing any of this over to questions, again? Nothing ever changes my outcome. What happens, happens. Or at least that's what I'm telling myself as I extend a glass across the centerpiece, clink with hers, and indulge in this dreamiest of drinks.

Then I take in the sweet sight of Jess. She must sense I'm now staring at her because she glances back as if she's hit the jackpot. It's funny how you can know a girl for ages and a day, practically all there is, each of her laughs, that cool way she moves, yet never actually know what she's like to kiss. It's not as if I haven't imagined the taste of her lips, down my hips, as I muse all by myself, or maybe together, wrapped up in my own little make-believe.

I'm reflecting on all of this as a certain song, that are-you-kidding-me kind, begins to pipe in just above. Which means I'm right back on Brie. Her chin's up, and her lashes are down. She's like a million miles away. At least until it finally registers, and she gives me this just between us grin because she's thinking the exact same thing I am. And that, yet again, makes my heart heavy.

Let's see.

Perhaps sometimes we need to pull apart so we can draw right back together, understand the why and the how and the who we are. Or perhaps I'm just rationalizing again.

CHAPTER TWENTY: RYAN AND BRIE

Brie

There's so much lovey-dovey floating around that you'd think I just set sail on the Love Boat. I'm not saying I expected much less than mush from the two celebrating. But now I've lost even Hadley to the dark side.

I'm still not sure how those two hooked up; in fact, stylista's way too hush-hush for my liking. And from their carrying on, I doubt I'll peel her off long enough to get any sort of explanation, not tonight at least. Not with Jessie's arm locked around her like that, sharing a sip of her beer. I'm not oblivious to their little game under the table, either. They've bumped me more than once.

The only two bachelorettes here are my ex and I, and I can't exactly hang out with her now, can I?

Our hosts over there are seated at a friend-like distance, not even close. But it's just giving them a better angle to eye one another. Couples can be so annoying.

So me and my Baileys Irish Cream over here are feeling more than a little third-wheelish. I'm just hoping Bailey here can pull me out of myself, if only for a few hours.

It's making me wish I could share something about the big move, but no. This is neither the time nor the place. When, though, I don't know. There never really is a right time, an appropriate time, to say au revoir. Arrivederci. The best I can do for myself, and everyone for that matter, is stop worrying about my issues and enjoy their occasion.

Which is why I'm tickled pink when that stop-worrying part is handled for me by an incoming call and my phone belting out Edith Piaf. That's my ringer. As I fish frantically through my coat, I find I'm scolding myself for not adjusting the volume earlier. I can't shut it off soon enough, but it's so loud in here nobody even notices. The table's singing into spoons, for crying out loud.

In such a haste, I accept before I can even glance at my screen. Once I do finally get to that part, my stomach flips itself the fuck out. It's an incoming call from *Chris*. If it wasn't for my race to stop Piaf, I probably would've just let it go to voicemail. But instead, I answer before I can even think clearly.

It's not like I would've wanted to turn on some sexy Lauren Bacall *hullo* or anything like that, but breaking through the marathon ribbon wasn't completely the effect I had in mind either, after literally not speaking for…how long? But that's what she got.

And what I hear on the other side of the line. It's that lazy, hazy, sexy of hers and it just hangs until it melts my phone. Like we just talked yesterday. And that makes me too giddy and too terrified all at the same time.

❖

Ryan

Nobody can give you relationship advice, I've learned.

But I've been known to listen, regardless. Listen to those telling me she's not really leaving (she's confused or she's going through stuff or she's restless) because that's what I want to hear. I welcome, encourage, all of her white lies, her excuses, her *I don't knows*, the *I'm not sures*. Brush it off when she insists that we're not right—because we *are*.

How am I supposed to know what to do, how to be? Where am I to go? I just know what I feel. They don't.

They know nothing about her *Yes! Yes!* her flushed face her back wet the feel of her leg stubbled from eleven-hour days. They don't stay up with her or wake with her, bathe with her, bend to her. They don't love her.

They just don't know.

Maybe this time will be different. Maybe she'll change her mind.

Maybe it really isn't me, isn't her, isn't over at all. Maybe there is no answer because I shouldn't be asking those questions in the first place. Or maybe she'll unpack. Turn around. Not right now. Not even tomorrow. But maybe I'll wait.

I try to look happy, but she radiates happy running to catch her phone somewhere private. She's quick about it. So quick that she left her drink half drunk. Mine's two swallows from empty. I need another. I motion to the bartender, who dips over. She doesn't judge me, though it's way too early for another, if you ask me.

I join the conversation and laugh for no reason. It amuses me to hear what other people find significant. *Did you hit that accident on the 91? It's probably your battery. If you're a pillow queen. You would say that. He seriously said that to you? Did she go—what'd I miss? It's canceled? You would love that show! Maybe you should see the doctor about that. You're probably just PMSing.*

I set my beer across from her drink and slouch until they meet—like when the eye doctor gives you that test and asks when one light is on top of the other. I compare colors. Hers opaque, mine was clear. She used to kiss me with those same creamy lips, that same lipstick that's on the rim. I can hear that *Yes! Yes!* I can taste it, so I take another drink to wash it down.

Is she the one? Sometimes she is.

Brie

I dodge a bunch of obstacles just to duck around the corner toward the ladies room and (non-operational) coin-op phone booth. My knees feel like Jell-O. I suck my lip, rub my neck. It's hard to believe, just a minute ago, I was sulking.

Our conversation is like Ping-Pong.

Hey.

Hey.

Hey.

Hey.

Hey.

Sounds pretty happening.

Just a few friends.

Thanks for writing me back.

But I haven't. That was—

I didn't think I'd hear from you. Things are going…good?

—saved as a draft. I do the only thing that I can at this point, which is play along—more than mildly mortified.

As good as can be. You?

Good, good. Things are really great, actually.

Really great, actually. I'm kind of crushed. Rub it in, why not? It's so good to hear her voice, it is, but I'm suddenly devastated and… don't come back to share how fucking wonderful life is now that we're apart. I say nothing.

I miss you.

She's a black hole. How can I not get sucked in?

I say the same back. Why is that? *I miss you.* It's such a simple statement, but it's not. And why is it that, when I say it, it doesn't sound nearly as irresistible as when she says it? It never does.

Yeah?

Yeah.

Of course she's delighted. I'm just glad she can't see the euphoria on my face. I can't be this easy, not after all I've been through.

I forgot how much I love your voice.

I'm shuffling my feet like a sixteen-year-old girl.

So what'd you do today?

A lot of thinking.

About?

Nothing…

Nothing?

I lost my job.

I'll hire you.

I bet you would.

Her laugh chops into three sputters.

So things are great?

Well, they could be better. You know how it is.

I like being on the phone with you.

Do you?

You make everything right.

Are you seeing someone?

Not since you.

I stare mindlessly at carpeting leading up a floor and those tourist flyers stacked on wire racks directly in front of me.

I miss you. So much.

It feels like we're in bed together. I miss you, too, I think, painfully. It's what I wanted. But I don't know if I'm ready. Do I even care? I must not because I say the same back.

Are you...seeing someone?

With a nervous laugh, I tell her no. But she's skeptical.

Can I see you? Can I drive down?

I can never move on. This is why. And she has my address, so I fixate on my unshaven legs, my winter-dry hands. What if she does drive down?

I could hit the highway and be there in a couple hours.

Like, now? Don't be nuts.

Why not?

Because.

Because why?

Because.

Because why?

Because...because...because you always do this to me.

I want to see you. I'm an idiot.

You're not.

I am.

I let her grapple. It's nothing new. I feel that drug-induced happy. Whole again. All I want is her. The world evaporates. It's like we never broke up at all. That's how it always is.

And before I know it, we're whispering all sweet and sappy. I'm confiding in her. I'm telling her all the outlandish things in my life, the important things and all the little in-betweens.

Have you seen Grams?

I did. At the store.

And?

She was yelling at a clerk.

As I get the whole story, I see her smile. She's squinting, even without sun.

I cut my hair.

How?

Really short.

Marry me.

I'm glad she can't see me.

I'm thinking about moving back.

When?

Soon.

I told you—destiny. Come live with me.

Don't be nuts.

I love you.

I can't come up with a single thing to say back. All I can do is count the hours, minutes, seconds until I can leave.

I love you, too.

We say our good-byes. Our long good-byes. Our you-hang-up-first good-byes, which nobody wins. And I float back to the table with a painful grin on my face.

Stylista's looking at me, wondering.

"Mom called," I holler, grabbing my Baileys and sinking euphorically into my seat.

Then I hear Sam ask, "Everything okay?" She's squatting beside me with her knees crooked, balancing on the balls of her feet.

"Of course!"

"You sure," she asks again.

"I'm fabulous."

"Okay then. If you need to talk or anything, you know where to find me." She puts a hand on my knee. It's warm. "Nice cut, by the way." She winks.

I laugh. I am absolutely giddy.

CHAPTER TWENTY-ONE: ELLA AND SAM

Sam

As much as I'd like to help out a damsel in distress, Brie's being tight-lipped. So I motion over to my wife to say, "Can you go check to see that she's okay?" And as expected she excuses herself, sliding graciously into the empty seat next to Baileys over there.

Then I peek at my own wristwatch and it's already half past six. So the host in me resolves that now is the perfect time to order. In fact, it's well overdue. Grabbing a handful of menus, I pass a stack to my left to distribute. "Starving, aren't you?" I ask, turning to Hadley. Her eyes are fixated on you know who, but Jessie's way too busy captivating the table to notice.

"You read my mind," she says, opening hers and gliding an index finger down its page.

"Jess isn't cooking for you, eh?"

"Oh, you know, she wants to."

"Cook?" I ask. "You can't be serious."

"She wants to be my chef now. So I've been teaching her a few things around the kitchen. I don't know," she says under her breath. "It's like I can never tell her no."

I can feel my brows pinch.

"I'm trying to be encouraging," she tells me.

"How's that working out?"

"Don't ask."

"She may surprise you," I say, reaching for my drink. Votives dot the length of our table, scattering in and out and around.

"By the way, congratulations," I hear. "Goodness, here I am jabbering about me. It's your night."

"This is just an excuse to get everyone together for once. You do know that, right?"

She takes a thoughtful pause. "The two of you are so lucky." She sighs.

"Five years isn't all that long. Come back to me in ten, twenty years," I say. "But you know, it's true what they say. Marriage is work. I'm warning you."

"Yeah, so much work," she says, rolling her eyes.

"And compromise," I say.

"Like which side of the bed—"

"Not just that," I tell her. "You're too giddy, just look at you." Then I tap her hand and ask, "So, how did this happen?"

"It just did. It's hard to defend. Good timing, perhaps." Then she folds her menu. "Of course I worry, though. I do, a little. I usually have lines that I don't cross—never, ever—when it comes to friends. Don't we all? It's crazy, you know, that's not how it works. I mean, with Jess—oh my God—it kept coming back. I don't even care anymore."

I'm wondering if she's going to turn and look away. But she won't. Not even as she takes a drink.

"I just don't want to screw this up," she says.

I lean in. "With Jessie?"

She nods.

I laugh. Then I take her menu and start motioning to others.

I follow her gaze across the table where, speaking of the devil, look who's making her way over.

That's when I catch Ella gazing at me. And Brie's lips are still near her ear. I'm wondering how long my wife has been chaperoning me. I raise an eyebrow.

I get such a look back.

So I wink.

She shakes her head.

CHAPTER TWENTY-TWO: RYAN AND BRIE

Brie

It requires two stout servers to carry out all our plates on those enormous round platters. I still don't know how they can balance so many things on top of something that looks more like an oversized Frisbee. I sure couldn't. But they do somehow, and they set those trays on a foldout cart in the aisle. And then, one by one, each plate descends to the table.

Fish sandwich? Side of onion rings? Hold the tomato?

Not one of us ordered a drink with dinner. I think we've had our fill. Besides, we have to drive home. I've settled into the seat next to Sam, enjoying a comfortable distance from my ex, who's paying no attention anyway, typing into her phone.

Sam and I both slide napkins to our laps. That's when I feel her shoulder bump mine and she leans in like she's trying to share some kind of secret.

"Ella and I," she says, finally. "We're going to help you pack up."

I think I heard her right. But I don't know what to say. I just shake my head. "What are you talking about?"

"Word travels."

I roll my eyes, wondering who at this table spilled. I'm partly disappointed, but at the same time, I'm also relieved it's behind me. And the fact that she knows, that I guess everyone knows, makes it seem a little more real and a little more sad.

❖

Ryan

The table's a hush by the time I finally muster enough courage to walk over to the opposite side. Still, my nerves won't settle. I slip an arm between shoulders, resting my weight on the table near Brie and bending until I'm at a comfortable closeness to her ear. "Can we talk?"

"Sure, sure," she tells me, scooting out. It's that perfume again. I wait out of courtesy and then motion her to follow. There's lint in my pockets. The noise elevates in the kitchen as we make our separate ways toward a quieter area in the rear. I'm just watching my feet on the floor the whole way. I sit on the second step of the staircase, knees high with my elbows resting on each side. Eventually she sits next to me. Her profile is striking.

I say something that sounds more like nonsense. That much isn't planned. I'm not sure what to expect in return. We've been fighting for days, so I'm timid and defensive. But she gives me a sweet, rather encouraging smile back. She blinks.

"I just wanted to, I don't know, about tonight," I say.

Her stare holds on for an eternity. Then it flits into the next room as if to deny me anything further.

"We have a couch. You can have it if you want. You know. If you want."

Her hands dip down her neck.

"I do appreciate it."

"So you want the couch?" I ask.

"Yes." She laughs uneasily. "Thanks."

Good-bye seems to be dragging its feet between us. But I feel more focused on this moment than I have for a really long time.

Then I hear, "I need to pack a truck tomorrow."

And even though I expected this, it hurts. It hurts badly. I shrink a bit before remembering—this isn't about me.

"I'm sorry, Ryan."

"What for?" I'm trying to convince her. Or myself? I don't know. But my head just falls into my hands and my hair is a mess and I mess it more and my heart's climbing up my throat and into my eyes and we sit, mute. She's gone this week. Knowing her, tomorrow. I just want to bring it back to business before I start out again like an ass. "So this is our last night, right?"

"It is, I think."

"Okay. I'm heading out after this," I say, struggling not to touch her. Not her shoulder, not her knee. And I try to smile, feebly. Then she lifts her eyes to me, but I can't look anymore or I'll kiss her or cry or do something I'm not supposed to do. So I focus on my shoelaces. "I think this shindig is just fine without me. When you get in, take the bed, okay? I'll take the couch."

"You don't have to—"

"No, really, I do. And I'll help you pack tomorrow, all right? I'll pack your truck. I'm taking a day off. I already told Ella." I catch her staring at me. "Maybe we can remain friends. Who knows."

I push myself up from the step and walk away without looking back.

"Thank you," I hear, and I think, *I love you.* I nod over my shoulder without stopping or slowing.

The music swells as I curve past the bar, swerving my way to the table just in time to catch Jess packing up. I swallow. "Wait up. You two heading out?"

"We have work tomorrow."

"I'll walk with you."

As I slip my arms through the sleeves of my coat, I thank our hosts. Jessie strolls over to Ella and she pulls her into this full body hug. Then they start whispering and I'm thinking *What are they saying?* and *Get a room.*

I zip, tuck my hands in deep pockets, and elbow Hadley. "What are you doing with that buffoon?" I ask, and she grins at me all dopey-eyed as the three of us push out.

Reading on a night like tonight is hard enough, but it's my escape. So I make an effort.

Still, everything in this universe is tugging my mind away from this page. Even my book light isn't cooperating. It's dim and flickering and either the bulb or battery will need to be replaced, but this will do for now.

It's not until I hear her key rattle at the doorknob that I just give up the charade, shut the shadowy light off, and close my paperback. I gaze out the window at the companionable moon as I listen to Brie perfectly hang her coat, perfectly close the bathroom, perfectly wash her face, and then perfectly sink into bed—which must seem rather large without me in it.

That's when I close her like a novel and place her on the bookshelf along with all those other stories I've dived into and held on to but never actually picked up and read again, felt again, loved again. I just move on into the next one instead.

I'm going to take a trip. I'm not sure where, but it's going to be far away. It's going to be remarkably foreign.

Why is it that under no circumstances have I ventured out of this state, let alone country? Let alone solo. But I'm going to.

Maybe I'll stand under the Eiffel Tower. Sink my toes into O'ahu. Better yet, tour Italy, trace my roots and see all those towns I've been told so much about.

And when I do one day decide to be with someone again, I'm going to focus not so much on finding someone I think is perfect but, instead, look for the one who thinks I am.

CHAPTER TWENTY-THREE: ELLA AND SAM

Ella

"We're last," I tell my wife, glancing across the table now speckled in spilled salt and crumpled-up napkins.

I hear a loud slurping through her straw.

"I had a good time," I say.

"I did, too."

"I could fall asleep right here and now, though."

"Me, too," she says. "We're too old to be out this late."

"No."

"I'm sure I missed a lot."

I just shrug.

"You'll catch me up, right?"

"I will."

She seems rather introspective for some reason, that piercing gaze, those nude lips. I notice the fine hair where her shirt sleeve is cuffed, nubby fingernails, the curvature of her jaw. Eyelashes barely noticeable in the candlelight.

"What are you looking at?"

"Nothing," I say. I pat her hand.

I feel the muscles in her grip around my own, and I detect a slight touch of sinister. Could she be thinking what I am?

As she rises from the table, I lift my gaze toward her outstretched arm.

"Can I have this dance?"

Okay, I'm sort of melting.

We make our way steadily to the dance floor and a single palm rests at the base of my back. Her breasts against mine. Her hips. And there's that smirk.

Her voice tickles my ear. "Happy anniversary." Her grip is secure, tighter than usual. It's that kind of epic. When I glide a hand up the nape of her neck, she stands up straight, head tilted back, looking down her nose at me, and gives me the sexiest stare I've ever seen.

Then she twirls my wedding ring.

Sometimes you don't even need words.

Chapter Twenty-four: Jessie and Hadley

Jessie

I'm pondering labels we tack on one another like *significant other* and *partner* when I come to the conclusion that they're all so self-indulgent and restrictive. *Lover* conjures images of fleshy Europeans in bikinis straddling scooters. (Maybe that's just me.) It's just an extended-stay booty call, both as companionable as dust mops. Still, the opposite, *life partner*, is terrifying.

Which lands me on the fail-safe *girlfriend*. Ryan called Brie her booty call until she became her girlfriend and then her ex. Speaking of, all that ex needs to do is reapply lipstick in that pocket mirror like that and my pal's fawning all over her again. Ryan, I'll hand that much to her. She's got a wicked smile. No, really, girls love it. I totally get her appeal. It's that Italian in her.

Our hosts over there, they call each other *wife*.

"What are you smiling about," my girl asks privately. "You doing okay?"

She breaks an hors d'oeuvre in half, rests one part on her tongue, and brings the next to mine. "I am," I say before biting in. I watch her chew into a smile. It's nice. But she pushes off too quickly, abandoning me and chitchatting her way around the table like a socialite at some gala where I'm the stalker peering until she catches me and studies me just the same.

I think I need the waiter and another shot of water. Short of taking a cold shower, that's about the only thing that's going to get me through this.

A diversion couldn't hurt, either, so I drum up an innocent game we all could use about now. "What would an anniversary be without a little sap," I announce finishing this near-empty bottle of Perrier they gave me. "Can we do this?"

And Ryan, just for a second, rests her head on her own forearms. She's had enough of me, I get that. Still, that protest of hers is moderated by a cool with it grin.

"So riddle me this," I say. "If you could describe your soul mate in just a single word, each of you, what would that be?"

I gesture to our hosts. "Guests of honor?"

And we all settle on Red, who's settled on me and giving me this look like—something. Hers isn't the answer I'm most interested in.

So I guess it's fine when her wife answers for her. "*Capable*, whatever that means." That's when Red's eyes finally leave mine and this whole exchange becomes some kind of esoteric joke among those two that I can't quite decipher—nobody can—nor do we want to. "Am I right?" Sam asks.

Fearful to linger too long on that one, I scout out my next victim, Ryan. Meanwhile I catch Red and her wife over there making out behind that hair of hers.

But Ryan raises a hand and answers, "*Trustworthy*." Her ex appears to be taking that as a personal attack and I'm thinking this maybe wasn't the best topic to bring up.

"Brie?" I ask.

"Let me see. I think…she'd be attentive and she'd be…soulful."

I lift a finger to slow her down. "Just one." Then I peek across at Ryan, who's examining the girl's answer over imaginary reading glasses.

Brie sips the last few drops and smacks her lips. Then she does this sexy little move as if to challenge me. "That, sweetheart, would have to be *soulful*." She's having a much better time than anyone else here. I'm not sure why, but it's borderline vengeful.

And I'd be full of it if I said I was calm and collected about now. I mean, it is officially Hadley's turn. She could completely sabotage me among our distinguished company. I don't think she will. Still, I'm unusually moody, which means I'm not sure how I'll take it even so. Why does this feel like our grand coming out? I fake coolness.

"One word," I tell her as I lean back in my seat. It creaks.

"Well, you really know how to put a girl on the spot. Maybe you could go first?"

"I could if you want."

"Please."

I give her this look that doesn't want to stop. "Okay, then," I say with a shrug. "I take your dare." She tips her head. I wink. She twists her napkin. And that's when I recite a short bucket list interrupted only by a few pensive pauses.

"Babe, you said one thing, didn't you?"

I hear conversations around me, but I don't see where they're coming from.

If she's going to play hardball and hold me to my own rules, well, that's fine. I shift and fix my posture. That ruckus smears into a monotony of white noise. My eyes lift to hers and plunge to those lips and I linger there for a few heartbeats.

This is nerve-racking, I think to myself as I try my damnedest to block the rest of the table and everything out. For all I know, she already knows what I'll say. Then her face lights up, and she's cupping her hand over mine, which is wandering past her skirt.

"You," I say. "If I had to describe my soul mate in just one word, it would be *you*."

About the Author

C. Spencer spent two years as an art major in college only to switch midway to English literature, which led to her unnatural obsession with Hester Prynne, Lady Brett Ashley, and Henry David Thoreau's lifestyle of resistance. After graduating, she moved to Vermont sight unseen, living in the land of maple syrup and snowboarding for ten years. During that time, she met her wife online. Soon they both relocated to Massachusetts, which is where they currently reside with their daughter. She's worked as a freelance copywriter since 2001. In 2013, she began writing fiction on the side.

Books Available From Bold Strokes Books

A Country Girl's Heart by Dena Blake. When Kat Jackson gets a second chance at love, following her heart will prove the hardest decision of all. (978-1-63555-134-1)

Dangerous Waters by Radclyffe. Life, death, and war on the home front. Two women join forces against a powerful opponent, nature itself. (978-1-63555-233-1)

Fury's Death by Brey Willows. When all we hold sacred fails, who will be there to save us? (978-1-63555-063-4)

It's Not a Date by Heather Blackmore. Kade's desire to keep things with Jen on a professional level is in Jen's best interest. Yet what's in Kade's best interest...is Jen. (978-1-63555-149-5)

Killer Winter by Kay Bigelow. Just when she thought things could get no worse, homicide Lieutenant Leah Samuels learns the woman she loves has betrayed her in devastating ways. (978-1-63555-177-8)

Score by MJ Williamz. Will an addiction to pain pills destroy Ronda's chance with the woman she loves, or will she come out on top and score a happily ever after? (978-1-62639-807-8)

Spring's Wake by Aurora Rey. When wanderer Willa Lange falls for Provincetown B&B owner Nora Calhoun, will past hurts and a fifteen-year age gap keep them from finding love? (978-1-63555-035-1)

The Northwoods by Jane Hoppen. When Evelyn Bauer, disguised as her dead husband, George, travels to a Northwoods logging camp to work, she and the camp cook Sarah Bell forge a friendship fraught with both tenderness and turmoil. (978-1-63555-143-3)

Truth or Dare by C. Spencer. For a group of six lesbian friends, life changes course after one long snow-filled weekend. (978-1-63555-148-8)

A Heart to Call Home by Jeannie Levig. When Jessie Weldon returns to her hometown after thirty years, can she and her childhood crush Dakota Scott heal the tragic past that links them? (978-1-63555-059-7)

Children of the Healer by Barbara Ann Wright. Life becomes desperate for ex-soldier Cordelia Ross when the indigenous aliens of her planet are drawn into a civil war and old enemies linger in the shadows. Book Three of the Godfall Series. (978-1-63555-031-3)

Hearts Like Hers by Melissa Brayden. Coffee shop owner Autumn Primm is ready to cut loose and live a little, but is the baggage that comes with out-of-towner Kate Carpenter too heavy for anything long term? (978-1-63555-014-6)

Love at Cooper's Creek by Missouri Vaun. Shaw Daily flees corporate life to find solace in the rural Blue Ridge Mountains, but escapism eludes her when her attentions are captured by small town beauty Kate Elkins. (978-1-62639-960-0)

Twice in a Lifetime by PJ Trebelhorn. Detective Callie Burke can't deny the growing attraction to her late friend's widow, Taylor Fletcher, who also happens to own the bar where Callie's sister works. (978-1-63555-033-7)

Undiscovered Affinity by Jane Hardee. Will a no-strings-attached affair be enough to break Olivia's control and convince Cardic that love does exist? (978-1-63555-061-0)

Between Sand and Stardust by Tina Michele. Are the lifelong bonds of love strong enough to conquer time, distance, and heartache when Haven Thorne and Willa Bennette are given another chance at forever? (978-1-62639-940-2)

Charming the Vicar by Jenny Frame. When magician and atheist Finn Kane seeks refuge in an English village after a spiritual crisis, can local vicar Bridget Claremont restore her faith in life and love? (978-1-63555-029-0)

Data Capture by Jesse J. Thoma. Lola Walker is undercover on the hunt for cybercriminals while trying not to notice the woman who might be perfectly wrong for her for all the right reasons. (978-1-62639-985-3)

Epicurean Delights by Renee Roman. Ariana Marks had no idea a leisure swim would lead to being rescued, in more ways than one, by the charismatic Hudson Frost. (978-1-63555-100-6)